MOTHER TONGUE

MOTHEЯ TONGUE

JULIE MAYHEW

CANDLEWICK PRESS

First U.S. edition 2019

First published by Hot Key Books (U.K.) 2016

Library of Congress Catalog Card Number pending
ISBN 978-1-5362-0263-2

19 20 21 22 23 24 LSC 10 9 8 7 6 5 4 3 2 1

Printed in Crawfordsville, IN, U.S.A.

This book was typeset in Berling.

Candlewick Press
99 Dover Street
Somerville, Massachusetts 02144

visit us at www.candlewick.com

For my hometown

What if we could use our first life, the one we've already lived, as a rough draft for another?
—Vershinin, *Three Sisters*, Anton Chekhov

HOME

1

THE DAY OF
KNOWLEDGE

I'm going to speak to you in Russian. If I speak in English, I
won't know enough words. In the language of home, I know
too many.

I got up early that day — neither light nor dawn. Word
had spread the night before that the Day of Knowledge
ceremony would begin one hour earlier than expected.
I took the call. Everyone knew to speak to me and not Mama.
They had forgotten that I was Nika's sister. Afterward, they
remembered. Afterward, it was an important distinction. I
became a child again then, not a mother, so what would
I know about pain?

My alarm went off, and the moment that it did, Nika was
jumping on my bed. We shared a room. In that way we *were*
like sisters. On one side: Nika's Barbie dolls, an alphabet
poster, a mug of colored pens. On my side: stacks of *Elle Girl*

and *Oops!* magazine, a basket of stubby makeup. I had my latest collection of books from Yelena across the hall, not yet explored. I was hoping for more tales of romance but could see at least one dystopia in the pile. Nika stopped jumping—dropped the whole weight of her warm body on top of me. I pulled her close, squeezed a breath from her, then let her go. *Today*, I thought, *in one small sense, is the day I can let her go.*

Nika and I had been looking forward to the first day of school all summer. For different reasons. Nika said hers out loud; mine were kept wrapped in paper. I was her protector, and that meant saving her from the ugliest of my thoughts too. *I am drowning, Nika*, my mind cried. *I am so desperate for someone to share the weight of you.* I was ready for that day, you understand. My little sister had been my responsibility for a long time. But, please, also understand that I loved her with all my heart. I loved her more than anything else in the world. More than my brothers. More than Papa. More than Mama. But when she started school, I would have some time to myself during the day. Time to work out what I was going to do with the rest of my life. The thing we did agree on, the thing that we could both say aloud, was that July and August needed to hurry up and end. Those months were there only to infuriate us and keep September out of reach.

Nika was giggling, chattering, full of energy. She kept saying that she had woken up "bigger."

"I am older today," she said, as if someone had cast a spell overnight. Or removed one, perhaps. I knew that this could happen, because it had happened already. To me. When

4

newborn Nika came home from the hospital but Mama stayed—abracadabra! A fizz and a poof!—I became older.

But there was no change in Nika that I could see: long black hair, a buttery scent to her skin, a tilt to her head that meant one of her beautiful eyes was always ready to pin you down and make you do what she asked. Still a baby girl, though. She had Zaychik in her hand as she bounced around on my mattress that morning. That little bunny had come home with her from the hospital in lieu of Mama. It had been there from the start. Patches of its fur were worn away with love.

We went barefoot into the kitchen, Nika and I, across the cool, powder-dry tiles of the hall onto the sticky blisters of the kitchen linoleum. One of Nika's fingers was casually linked with one of mine. I'm glad I have memorized things like that, those physical sensations. Papa was standing by the stove in the kitchen, a stout gray brick in his work shirt and trousers. The smell of the *zharkoye* that I had made the night before still hung in the air—musky garlic, sharp celery. Papa was scraping a large, gloopy helping of the leftovers into a tin box to take to the factory. The beef always tasted better after a night of wallowing. I hoped he had left enough to put on the tray for Mama at lunchtime. Enough for me too. Papa turned as we came in and lurched toward us, making a grab for Nika's waist.

I would read a whole book today, I thought, my first day of small freedom. Three hundred pages without interruption.

Papa swung Nika around while I tipped kasha into a pan. He was saying, "Who is this grown-up girl in my kitchen? Who can this be?" Nika was laughing and laughing—a glass bubble of noise. He spun her around and around, up high in the air, then low, low down.

I wouldn't care if it was a dystopia or a romance; I would disappear into it and start thinking about the future only after finishing that last page.

Then Nika's toe caught the top of Papa's lunch tin and sent it crashing onto the floor.

KLATZ!

We all stopped what we were doing. Froze.

The lid of the tin was shut tight; we weren't worried about it spilling. We were only scared of waking the house spirit, our very own Kikimora. We listened for movement above the weary shudders of our fridge, something distinct from the cotton-batting voices that throbbed through the walls from neighboring apartments. Papa stroked the black wire of his mustache, and we watched his fingers do their work, waiting for his nod to say that all was safe. As soon as he was sure, he sprang back, playing the fool again, covering Nika's face with noisy kisses. He hoisted her high up into the air. Nika lifted her knees. Papa plopped her down onto one of the red padded chairs, with their cracks and splits and runaway stuffing. I twirled over to the stove and clanged down the kasha pan, then twirled away again to place a spoon in front of Nika. A little comedy routine. Everything would be all right!

But then Papa picked up his dropped tin and moved toward the door. I stopped spinning.

"You're not coming?"

"I have to be at the factory." He shrugged.

Nika hummed a tune, made her spoon dance.

It was going to be just me. Papa had taken the morning off for my first day. He had done it for Boris. And Igor. But Nika . . .

"Tell me about it tonight." He slipped out of the kitchen with a hushed "See you later." I looked at the spot where he'd stood spooning out his serving of stew. He'd left splatters on the yellow flowers of the wall tiles.

No one ever said it out loud—*mistake*—but you could see the word buzzing around her crib. I was only eleven years old when Nika arrived, but still I understood. I made it my job to swat that word away. When Papa's brother Misha visited from Balakovo not long after Nika was born, when Mama had just finished her long stretch in the hospital, he and Papa looked down at Nika sleeping in a basket, and Papa said, "I thought that moving here had solved all our problems. . . ."

Misha shook his shaggy hair and tut-tutted at fate.

"But she is beautiful," I announced. "Don't you think, Dyadya Misha?"

I said this for Mama too, who was in the armchair, stunned. She had come home from the hospital with something terrifyingly missing, or else something had joined her, a dark thing that kept her in silent conversation. She took to her bed after that.

"She really is beautiful," I said, over and over. This was how mothers talked about their babies, wasn't it? Or would I only be attracting the evil eye? I didn't know for sure, but I kept going, kept saying it, until someone agreed out loud.

There would be no Papa at Nika's Ceremony of the First Bell. So I made a decision: I would wake the spirit. I had tried to do this before. On my twelfth birthday—the first after

Nika was born. Mama would rise, like a miracle—this is what I had believed. She would tug on my ears and ask what dreams I'd had the night before, the ones that would tell my fortune. But that time, Papa pulled me away from her door, told me to leave her be. He sang the birthday song from the crocodile cartoon, something that Mama always did better, and guided me back to the kitchen table, where a present was waiting.

And I'll play on my accordion, in sight of all passing near.
How unlucky that a birthday only comes once a year!

The present was a doll that I was too old for. The song had never sounded so sad.

Nika's Day of Knowledge would be the thing to rouse Mama from her bed, I was sure. I had a vivid memory of her from Igor's first day, Papa's arm around her as they sang along to the old songs, the tail of her bright head scarf dancing in the wind. If a spell could be lifted from Nika overnight, why not from her too? We could all be set free. I left Nika eating kasha.

I paused by the closed door of the living room, where the boys were still asleep on their camp beds. They hadn't heard about the start of school being moved forward an hour. They'd been out on their bikes when the call came. But I didn't knock to wake them. Something stopped me. I find myself going back to that moment in my head quite often. Me, standing there at that door, not knocking, just listening, the sound of Nika gabbling in the kitchen, the same two lines of a poem she was going to say later at the Ceremony of the First Bell.

Goodbye to play and summer days,
We welcome in our future, bright and new.

Boris had turned sixteen that year and shed his soft, boyish
skin in a monstrous transformation. He had grown wide and
solid like Papa, but already he was taller. His eyebrows had
thickened; his top lip was spiky. To distract us all from this
new unsightliness, or perhaps to complement it, he had begun
to play the fool. I think we were supposed to find it amusing,
the dim-wittedness. I wanted the old Boris back. The sweet
one I had mothered a little, even though he was only two years
younger. He was a man now, Papa kept telling him, and the
idea scared both Boris and me. I retreated, left Boris to his
manly things, whatever they were. Igor, meanwhile, at just
fourteen, was still smooth-faced, trophy-eared, and lean — but
he looked to Boris for how to behave. He always had, ever
since he was first able to walk. If Boris crashed his toy car into
the sofa leg, Igor crashed his too. If Boris spent the evening
out by the back of the apartments, chain-smoking Winstons,
then so did my littlest brother. The boys relied on each other.
They grunted as one.

I didn't want them to come. That's why I didn't knock. The
morning's ceremony was going to be special, but even more
special without Boris and Igor acting like fools. So I let them
sleep in, having no sense then of the consequences.

I moved on to the next door, rapped gently, pushed it open.
I could see a thin shape under the blankets. She had her back
to me, but I could tell that her eyes were open. Don't ask me

9

how I knew this for sure. The tune of the crocodile song was running through my head all of a sudden. She would leap up and sing it, pull my ears extra hard to make up for all those birthdays missed.

"It's Nika's first day," I whispered.

Any moment, any moment she would move. . . .

"Are you going to come?"

She was awake; I knew that she was awake. Papa getting up would have made her stir. There was a shaft of sunlight coming through the blinds, zigzagging over the floor and across the blankets. We were idiots, all three of us, if we believed that the crashing tin hadn't woken her up.

"Mama?"

There was the sound of her conscious breath, but still she did not move.

"Mama?"

Later she would accuse me of not waking her.

"Mama?"

Later, she said that if *she* had been there instead of me, it would have turned out differently. Maybe this is true. I had only been guessing at what it took to be a mother. She was the one with experience. She was supposed to pass it all on to me so I would know what to do for my own children one day. But we had skipped that part.

I gave up. I closed the door. I didn't want Nika to come down the hall and see me asking and getting no answer. We finished our breakfast, Nika talking the whole time through milky mouthfuls about what kind of balloons she wanted;

me batting back her high hopes, saying we'd have to wait and see what they had at the store, that you can't always get what you want. I got up to wash my bowl, and when I'd finished, I clapped my hands together twice, really loud. A hurry-up sound. Nika jumped. She turned in her chair, that tilt of her head accusing now, eyes afraid.

"What?" I said. "What? Soap yourself! Move your behind!" She leaped up, leaving her bowl on the table. That bowl remained in the same position for more than two weeks, an abandoned boat on a sea of blue-marbled melamine.

I wore a summer dress with small pink flowers and an apron front and a cross of fabric at the back that left my shoulder blades bare. The heat from August was still lingering. We had sweated and turned pink in the harsh sun last May for my Ceremony of the Last Bell. One girl had fainted. Only four months ago, I had been a schoolgirl too. What was I now? If anyone asked, I couldn't say. So instead I concentrated on making myself look good. A brilliant distraction. I had to be better, more attractive, than Nadya and Olya, Galka, and Sonja. The four of them were going to university. They would get to move away, not far, but far enough for them to not be here. They might live together. They might talk their way through the nights, play music loud, fall in love. I knew what they were thinking: *But you were so much better than us at all that grammar and symbolism, Dasha! Yet here you are, staying put! So not fair!* I hadn't passed my exams. I had missed some of them. I was looking after Nika and couldn't always get to school. I read all the time, though—the books Yelena got from her teacher friend but rarely read herself. Stories sometimes, novels, plays— all those different roles for you to be. But it had not been enough.

Nika wore her beautiful new uniform: a blue pinafore dress with an embroidered white collar. This was a new thing. There were no uniforms when I started school. On my Day of Knowledge, Mama put me in a red dress she had made herself. I stood out like a prick of blood in the gray. I felt like a *prinsessa*. We had recently moved to the area so Papa could take the job at the factory. They chose me to sit on the shoulders of one of the oldest boys and ring the first bell, an honor to welcome me to town. But as I was hoisted up, my skirts arranged by Mama, I overheard one mother ask, "Why her?" There were plenty of local girls who could have done it, girls who deserved it more. Those words sliced into me and stayed there. They changed the way I grew.

Nika's uniform had been hanging on the back of our bedroom door, wrapped in clear plastic, for weeks. Every so often, we would lift its protective cover and touch the fabric, chattering out our excitement about September 1st. I had sewn white flowers onto black ponytail bands, and that morning I made Nika sit in front of the mirror so I could brush her hair into two neat bunches. As I did, I watched her mouth repeat the same pattern over and over, those two lines of a poem. Such concentration in her eyes.

Goodbye to play and summer days,
We welcome in our future, bright and new.

I took a pair of scissors and cut a small tuft of her hair to put in my locket. My hands were shaking with anticipation, and I lopped off a little more than I'd planned. I looked at her crooked bangs in the mirror and wanted to cry, but Nika burst into the most infectious laugh.

"I only did it so that I'd be with you all day," I said, snapping the locket shut, sealing in the memory of her laugh along with the strands of hair.

"So I'll be with *you*," she said, correcting me.

Our apartment overlooked the school. We lived on the fourth floor and you could see the playground and the roof of the gym from our kitchen balcony. We left early, just after 8:15 a.m., because we needed to make a detour to the shop. Other children and their relatives were there already, lining up to use the canister of helium. Filled balloons bounced against the ceiling, tethered to little wrists. There were girls with lace collars, boys in bow ties and waistcoats, grandmothers in church best. Nika had said at breakfast that she wanted a heart-shaped balloon, and I was surprised to find they had them — left over from Valentine's or Women's Day, I supposed. Now it seems too painful a coincidence that they had exactly what she wanted. As a final gift, was a balloon enough? In the crocodile song, a magician in a helicopter flies down with free movies and five hundred ice-cream cones. And that's only for a birthday, something that comes along every year.

Nika chose four round blue balloons and one pink heart. Papa had given me enough money to cover the cost, and also to buy flowers for the teacher. We had not accounted for chocolates, which the other mothers in the line had under their arms. I took out the housekeeping money I had salvaged for train fare to the city. I thought I might go there during the week while Nika was at school and see about secretarial exams. I could picture myself behind a desk in a good blouse, my hair tied back and my lipstick neat. I'd have a small glass pot with sharpened pencils and a nail file. I'd spend the money I earned on new books with uncracked spines, dresses bought from the more expensive section of the catalog. My boots would have heels. I'd eat dinner with the other office girls, and they'd tell me about the boys they might marry, and we would sigh wearily if we ever mentioned girls who still studied, because they did not understand what life was about at all.

I chose a tray of Babaevsky pralines for Nika's teacher so my little sister would be the same as all the others. I could save that money again, I told myself. I had only one chance to make Nika fit in with the crowd.

When we got to the school, we went to her classroom to prepare for the procession. The room smelled of fresh paint. Of promise. I chatted with some of the mothers I knew from our apartment building and whose husbands worked with my father. Nadya and Olya were in the corner, fussing around a small boy with an accordion who must have been a nephew or a cousin. They had not dressed up at all. Instead they wore cutoff jeans and tank tops. I pretended to be too engrossed in a conversation with Yelena from across the hall to notice them. She was there with her daughter Polin'ka, a good friend of Nika's already.

"My girl is so excited."

"Yes, Nika too."

One woman who didn't know our family stepped into our exchange.

"Has your daughter learned her lines?" she asked me.

"Oh, no, she's not my little one. She's my sister."

I had been proud of my dress when I left the house, but now I saw that it made me look old. I had dressed like all the other mothers, done my hair and makeup wrong. To think that was the thing on my mind in that moment. It didn't matter, yet it mattered so much.

We were called into the hallway, and the headmistress organized the line of children in the correct order. I hung back to straighten Nika's pigtails. She was nervous now, trying to smile but chewing her top lip, her gappy bottom teeth on display. When it was time for me to leave her, I cupped her face in my hands, looked her in the eyes, and said, "I love you." You couldn't ask for better, could you? I wanted her to know that she had never been a mistake, not really. That for all the trouble she had caused, she was the best thing to have happened to me. I wanted her to think so, even if it was a lie. But how do you put it into words for a seven-year-old? Instead I told her I was proud of her and that this was a big day. A happy day.

No. Those weren't my last words.

After "I love you" I wiped my pink lipstick kiss from her cheek and took Zaychik out of her hands. I told her, "You're all grown up now. You can't carry your little bunny with you down the stairs." And she nodded in a way that was so grave and so adult that I laughed. I patted her hair one last time. I walked out into the sunshine.

The bells rang three times, and the older children took their positions. I looked for Boris and Igor even though I knew they wouldn't be there. It felt odd not to be standing in my place in the yard as I had done in May. But I had no place now. I couldn't see Nadya and Olya, but even if I had spotted them, I would not have gone over to be with them. I stayed by the boiler house, surrounded by parents, and I waited for the ceremony to begin.

When the new children paraded down the stairs, Nika was in the middle of the line. She stepped out and closed her eyes briefly to adjust to the brightness. When I think of it now, that closing of her eyes, I see it in slow motion. Of course, it couldn't have been. I tucked Zaychik under my arm and clapped along to the loud music, the PA system growling. I whooped along with the others but could barely hear my own voice.

Then there was a bang.

Balloons popping? Nika and the other children jolted. We all did. The women around me put hands to their chests, then laughed at themselves for being startled. The men returned to taking photos, recording videos. It did cross my mind that it was gunfire, that someone had decided to mark the Day of Knowledge with a gun salute, as if it were a wedding. We looked around to see who could be so audacious with their celebrations. And that was when I saw the men in masks. Running toward us. They were angry with the sky, firing at the heavens. I looked back at Nika. My heart lurched forward, as if it could grasp hold of her. She hadn't seen how the day had turned.

"Nika, no, look at me, look!" I yelled it first in my childhood Russian, the language that gasps to the surface when there is too much passion or too much pain. But Nika wasn't listening. I changed to Ossetian, the language of her childhood. I screamed. But she wasn't looking. She was watching her heart-shaped balloon disappear into the sky.

2

HE WHO SAVES
ONE MAN

I watched as my little sister was scooped up by the flow of people. The sudden, spiraling tide pressed me back against the wall of the boiler house. I could only keep watch on Nika in the crowd, attempt to follow the flowers in her hair—a scene straight from a nightmare. The schoolyard was a sea of dark heads and dancing flowers. In our effort to make our loved ones look special for their first day, we had made them all look exactly the same.

My own voice was lost to the screams of mothers, to the shouted orders of the masked men—"Go! Move! MOVE!" And the masked women, just as ferocious, their mouths pulled back to bare teeth. I remained pinned against brick, watching the butts of weapons forced into spines, heels of hands driven into flesh, fingers tearing at the skin of bare arms. The tide dragged people toward the school, and the crowd spilled into the gym, taking Nika with them.

My last glimpse: she was looking for me over her shoulder as she stumbled up a pile of sand left behind from that summer's renovation. As she climbed through that open window, her expression seemed to say, *Is this right? Is this what I am supposed to do?* But she couldn't find my face in the crowd to get her answer. She disappeared from view. Gone.

That was when the pressure against me released and I took advantage. I could not fight a path out of the yard—they had steered us like cattle. All exits were blocked. Gunshots whistled and snapped from all directions, shrinking our necks. So I pulled open the door of the boiler house, and I staggered inside. Others followed, pushing from behind. Our breath was loud; we stank of fear. I grazed my elbows on the wall. We couldn't see where we were going. After the bright sunshine, we had blundered into blackness.

"This way, this way," a voice wheezed from over my shoulder and he shoved past, taking my wrist and dragging me. My arm collided with steel—a door being yanked open by this wheezing man. He pulled me forward and my brow connected with the door edge, serrated like a saw. Something warm and wet dripped into my eye, but it was too dark to see if it was blood. I didn't cry out.

"Shut the door! Close it!" urged the man we couldn't see. There were ten or so of us in there. Some children too. I could feel bodies all around, heartbeats, the warm, clammy fabric of other people's clothes. We crouched down. It's your instinct to go toward the floor, make yourself small. *He who saves one man saves humanity.* I learned this later. But does saving yourself count?

19

"Now, keep quiet. We must. We must."

We listened to him, the wheezing man. We listened to the hiss and whistle of the water pipes above us, carrying on as if nothing had happened. I crouched in the dark and thought about my mistakes, every small moment where the path split and I could have done something differently to ensure Nika had stayed with me. I wanted to run from that boiler house, climb in through the window of the gym, find Nika, and pull her close. I wanted to touch her, hold her. But I couldn't decide if doing that would be another mistake. So I stayed still, as if that was no decision at all.

Then there were noises. People. On the other side of the steel door in the main part of the boiler house. We became stiller. Did not breathe. We listened to feet scuffing, some whimpers, a word said over and over—"No." Then there was a woman's voice. She was trying to throw out a blanket of calm, but her words were charged, so terrified, and they did not work. A yelled instruction cut her down, spoken in Russian, twisted by an accent. Movement. People were being forced out of the building, out of their hiding places. They would come for us next. Silence. Silence. And just when we thought we might breathe again, the crack of gunshot spitting against brick. We jolted as one fearful creature in the dark.

"Shhh," warned the wheezing man, and we swallowed our gasps.

The angry voice grew distant. We waited to be found too, but the world went quiet. I tried to picture Nika in the gym, sitting with friends, being comforted by a teacher, but my mind refused. It played me a video of her being tortured, a rifle butt whipping her across the face.

We did our time—three hours, maybe four. The wheezing man came upon a vent at the back of the locker room, pushed it open, and signaled for help, and the security forces outside pulled us free. The sun was high in the sky, burning everything to white, as we made our escape. We went from a darkness to a blindness. We ran until we could see, calling out, "What's happening? What's happening?" the replies coming back level and hollow.

They are in there.

The children.

They are being held hostage.

I searched desperately for Papa in the faces in the streets and saw lines and lines of women wringing handkerchiefs and beads, men squatting on their haunches, quietly plotting, or up on their feet, sweating and stamping like tethered horses. The children who had escaped clung to their parents' legs as if they would never let go.

When I found Papa, I vomited on his shoes. He tried to hold me up.

"Let's get your gun," I said to him.

That was the solution. Simple. We must fight.

Papa gestured behind me. Boris was standing in the dry grass, already clutching Papa's gun. Igor was next to him. Both of them puny. Eyes wide. My boisterous brothers, embarrassed by a rifle. I turned back to Papa, wanting him to tell us what to do next. But he only took hold of my chin, twisting my head this way, then that. I had not realized that my face was a mask of blood. There was a deep gash above my left eye. I put my hand to it, felt the stickiness. The pain had not yet begun to register.

"It's nothing," I remember saying.

Then Papa was looking at my hands. Zaychik. I still had hold of Zaychik.

"Dead?" he said, voicing the word before I could wound him with it.

I shook my head. "No, she's in there."

Papa started to sob. I had never seen him cry before, not when the old Saratov factory closed, not when Mama was in the hospital, not when his own mother died.

I barked at him to shush. "There's no need for this!" We needed to fight. To fight! But he kept crying, pinching at the bridge of his nose, his back shaking.

"Stop it," I said. "Stop it. Please."

If Papa was broken, what hope did we have? What hope was left at all?

We kept our vigil, captivated by the school, that hideous magnet. I told myself that the nightmare would end soon. We would go back to normal. Someone would laugh, poke a finger at the air, and say, "Tricked you!" I don't know what gave me permission to imagine a happy ending. I ignored the teenager in the tracksuit lying facedown in the grass by the school gates, didn't let myself understand what his stillness meant.

We waited.

Mothers quivered in the cooling air, touching one another's shoulders, anointing themselves with hope. The silent men sat in the gutters, reconciling themselves to the toughest fate. Every gunshot from within the school made us howl and double over, as if we were taking the bullet ourselves.

We waited.

A nurse came along the line in the evening, a light strapped to her head, and she pulled me to one side. Gently she washed my face clean of blood. "This may hurt," she said, applying alcohol. Then she glued the edges of skin back together. I did not feel a thing.

Police officers, Special Forces, anyone in a uniform or a serious-looking suit — we edged closer to them, trying to hear what they said into their cell phones. We passed every little piece of gossip along the street.

You know the police only have blanks in their rifles.

Has anyone seen my Sasha? He is missing.

They sent out a woman with demands — did you hear?

They'll answer them — you'll see. Then they'll be saved.

They'll ignore them — they'll have to. This won't end well.

We waited.

On the first night, when rain soaked us to the skin, a neighbor turned to me. Anzhela. She lived on the first floor of our apartment building. She had grandchildren who went to the school.

"Who is behind this?" she said to me. "WHO?"

"How would I know?" I backed away from her, but she forced her face into mine. I heard that voice again, the one on the other side of the steel door, yelling its instruction, mangled by an accent. I tried desperately to place it.

"You're Russian — you must know!" Anzhela screamed at

me, her voice competing with the thunder. I looked to Papa for support, but he was no longer there. And anyway, Anzhela was done now. She spat in the mud, then crumpled down onto her knees. Her daughter Gulia went down too, wrapping her body around her mother, a shell against the world.

"Ignore her," Gulia whispered. She stroked her mother's back. "My sister and her kids are in there. She is attacking everyone. She is going crazy."

"Chechens," I said, grasping at someone, anyone, to blame. "You could tell they were Chechen." Though I couldn't say anything of the sort for sure.

Only then did I understand what we might be heading toward. Until that moment, I had not let myself think of Moscow theaters filled with gas, hospitals held hostage, or the bombs in the marketplace close to home. These were things that happened to others. Our town was small, and so was I. My focus was only ever on Nika, on my own diminishing options, or else I was lost in a book, trying to escape.

I needed Papa. I scanned the crowds for him. No sign. Boris and Igor were sitting, hunched over on the grass behind me, sharing a cigarette, cupping its burning end from the rain. Boris realized what I was looking for and jerked his head toward the garages. Papa was there, talking to a young woman whom I didn't recognize. His hands gripped the tops of her arms. The woman was nodding and crying as Papa spoke, and I felt an admiration for him, consoling this distraught stranger. They both leaned forward, and for a brief moment their foreheads touched. The contact sent a bolt of something through me, as if I had felt it myself. When Papa returned, sitting with my brothers, draping an arm across Boris's shoulders, gripping and rubbing vigor back into him, I asked, "Who was that woman?"

Papa replied, "What woman?"

The adrenaline was making everything too close, too sharp, as if through a microscope. It was only a madness.

We waited.

We put Nika's name on a list. Then another list would come around, and we would put her name on that one too. Then another. On some lists, I think we must have written her name twice, three times.

A car exploded in the street, and we all shrieked as if our hearts had been shut in a vise. No one knew who had done it. Was it us? Was it them? Either way, the smell of gasoline hung in the air like a warning.

We waited.

Some mothers with tiny babies were released, and we all set upon them, needing information. Needing it desperately.

Did you see my son?

My daughter?

My sister?

Was she alive?

Was he OK?

Are their spirits holding?

Some of the mothers gave us comforting answers; others let sentence after sentence spill from their mouths in torrents. *There is no water in there*, they said. *They are dying, slowly dying.* The journalists gathered like sparrows, waiting for crumbs. We took our seats in the Palace of Culture in the early hours of the third morning to hear a doctor tell us not to worry—our loved ones could live without water for days yet. *Days.* We muttered the word to one another. *Days!* Our own hearts could not hold out. We wandered into a new sunrise cloyed by fog.

We waited.

We waited.

We waited.

And then, on that third day.

BA-BAKH!

On the third day, my whole world exploded.

3

BE CAREFUL WHAT
YOU WISH FOR

I do not like the English word *BANG*.

Where is the crack down the middle? *BA-BAKH*.

Where is the fracture that separates then from everything afterward?

The sound wrenched wails from us all. We had pleaded to God for a change, but not this. Not this. The force of the explosion sent the wind in a different direction, as if the Earth had stopped on its axis and decided to turn the opposite way. We looked at one another. The strangest silence. Where had the blast come from? Who had the blast come from? The only answer we received was an eerie twist of smoke drifting from the roof of the gym, quickly growing into thick coughs of gray. There was no time for questions anymore. A second blast followed, a third. Snakes of men in green uniforms slithered past. No more waiting, no more standing still. We lurched toward the building to salvage what we could from the fire. From every direction came the spit-spat of gunshot. But we ignored it. We had to. The windows of the gym were glowing a furious red, the heat smacking against our faces. The peppery tang of fireworks seized the air. Men shouldered their rifles, ready to fight back.

Then, one by one, small pink bodies started to flit from the building. The fire—thank the skies!—did not have all the children in its grasp. They darted across the playground; tiny limbs, feet too big and hands too large for what they had so swiftly become—skin and bones. They wore just their undershirts and underpants, flowers still in their hair, stripped down to cope with the heat.

These little bodies of hope ran and ran, onto the streets, away from the flames. Their wild eyes were buried deep into sockets. Their faces had become old. We chased these aged children, grasping them by an arm to bring them to a stop. We pawed at them, pushed back their bangs and peered in, looking for the person we loved behind the soot. If they weren't ours, we gave them water and sent them running, spinning, wheeling again.

Then I saw her.

There was gunfire and screaming. There were people and cars, children and dogs, tanks and falling fences. There were ambulances honking and snorting, rude and insistent, through the crowded streets. There were *babushki* running to fetch white sheets to cover the dead while photographers snapped. Yet still I saw her—a solitary woman cutting a slow path through panic. She walked into the road outside our apartment building.

Everyone on the street was up on their toes, ready to move in whatever direction they were bid, scanning the crowd for the next laden stretcher, the next man in uniform with a child in his arms. Desperately we searched for a someone who could be our someone. But this woman, she was not fired up with a sickening adrenaline like everyone else. She was still, pale, barefoot, wearing her nightgown.

The explosion had woken Mama up. There she was—our house spirit. A ghost foretelling the disaster but arriving too late.

The people surged this way and that, sheep being herded by too many dogs, but no one collided with my mother. They worked around her. I picked my way through the frantic swarm to grasp her hands. Her fingers were white and clean; mine were black, shaking. I tried to pull her with me, into the throng, but she wouldn't move.

"What have you done with her?" This is what Mama said to me.

I could barely hear. Bullets sang flat notes in the air. I leaned in, my breath rasping. I needed to move, find Nika, yet I stopped still for Mama. She was back! Mama was back! Pull my ears, Mama! Sing the crocodile song seven times over! I put my hand to her forehead as if checking her temperature, just as she had done when I was small.

"What have you done with my daughter?" Mama did not raise her voice to compete; she expected the battle to hush. *My daughter.* I thought she meant me, that I appeared changed to her, or that she had forgotten what I looked like. We hadn't been back to the apartment for three days straight. I kept my hand on her forehead. *Too hot? Too cold? Just right?* When

Mama did this to me, she never revealed her answers. Maybe you don't get one.

"I'm here, Mama," I told her. "I'm safe." I melted forward, put my arms around her. She stayed frozen.

"What have you done with her?" she repeated. "Where's Nika?"

This made no sense, Mama calling Nika her daughter. But I buried my confusion. She was surfacing from the longest sleep; it would all become clear to her soon.

"Nika's inside." I nodded toward the school as if it stood as it always had, as if we weren't choking on the sour smell of a thousand prayers being turned to ash. All my focus went into comforting my mother. "She'll be coming out any minute," I said. "Just wait." I was promising sweets to a child in return for her patience. You see, I had wished for so long that Mama would wake up, and there she was. In the middle of all the dread, I felt as if I had been given a gift. But there is this saying: *Be careful what you wish for.* Not because you might get what you want, but because you might not get the chance to make a wish like that ever again. Did I have any wishes left to save Nika?

Then, there she was.

Sprinting, her hair loose, ragged in the wind. She had stripped down to her small pink underpants. Her body was smudged but intact. She was running like I had never seen her run before, away from the school, a fleet-footed fawn. She was covering her head with her hands, and her face was gripped tight as if ready for another blast. In that moment, I thought, *Here it is, my second gift! I am saved! I am saved!* Because that is what it felt like, as if a hand had reached down from the heavens and plucked me from the fires of hell.

30

I flew toward her as she headed in the direction of the railroad tracks. I skidded and tripped over myself. My heart was exploding with such colossal gratitude that I found it hard to breathe. I called her name: "Nika! Nika!" But she kept running, and I kept chasing. She only stopped when she came by a public faucet that was gushing water onto the street. She fell to her knees and, pushing her face into the flow, slurped like a farm animal, letting her hair and legs get drenched. Her body rejected the first mouthfuls of drink and she vomited into the drain, but she went straight back, shoving her hands into the water, scooping it into her mouth.

I knelt beside her. I was very much aware that Mama had remained where she stood in the middle of the street.

"Nika," I said. I placed my hand gently on her back, on the warm knots of her spine. After wanting to hold her for so long, I was now scared to touch her. After all she had experienced, I was frightened that I would cause her damage. "Nika," I said again, but it was hard to snap her from her worship of the water.

"Nika."

This time she turned to look at me. She jerked away from my contact. I might as well have been the dragon ready to pull her back into the fire. She was terrified of me. This girl. Not Nika.

It wasn't her. It wasn't Nika.

I pulled myself up straight. I nodded. The bewildered girl nodded back. There was a curious understanding between us. I walked away.

I am not sure to this day if the child said it out loud or if I said it to myself, but this is what I heard: *Nika is dead.* I shook the idea away, even though the future hung before me as ominous as a gray cloud. If she died, it would be a punishment. I didn't deserve Nika's love. There had always been a part of me, a very small part of me, that had resented the responsibility Nika brought with her. I would shut myself in our room sometimes, tell her I had important grown-up business to deal with and she shouldn't come in, when all I was doing was lying on my back, staring at the ceiling, doing nothing, being nothing, running along imaginary airport corridors with Leonardo DiCaprio, thinking about Kolya Galkin, who had come back from university that summer somehow transformed. At the most, I would be practicing drawing a line across my eyelid without a wobble, without my little sister there nudging my elbow, insisting I draw on her eyelids too.

And because of that I would be punished, I would be forsaken. I knew it. I had not been plucked from the fires of hell. Nika would not be returned to me. I would not be saved.

4

WHAT FOLLOWS
AFTER TEA?

Families kept their hope alive for days, weeks, months. They curved their hands around the sputtering flame and protected it from harsh winds. They convinced themselves that their child had been flown to a hospital in one of the many European cities that were helping with casualties. They told themselves that their loved one had escaped and fled, shell-shocked, to some hiding place. People told stories of dazed children running feral on the scrubland on the outskirts of town, as happy as deer. Others distracted themselves with fury, with plans for revenge against our bordering republics, against the government, against anyone who was good for the fight. Papa and I engrossed ourselves in the search. We visited the hospitals and morgues every day. We moved ourselves from here to there. We played the roles of two people anticipating good news, and we expected no applause.

Mama held court in the living room, a seated statue of grief. The neighbors came and went, bringing sympathy. But also they visited to observe this woman in the center of our sofa, resurrected, now flesh and bone — though she'd become more bone than flesh. Her face, exposed to the light again, was etched with downward creases so precise and clean they might have been made with a knife. We did not know what to do with this person — not Boris, Igor, Papa, nor I — or how to act around her. It was hard not to see Mama as some kind of replacement, a consolation prize, to make up for Nika being missing. And it was hard not to feel sick with guilt, wishing that your own mother had been sacrificed rather than that school.

It became my task to set up the folding table in the living room, making sure it was always filled with tea for our guests. Papa got out the bottles that he brought home from the factory and made hopeful toasts with every visitor, always remembering to touch glasses. They were not, after all, drinking to someone dead.

Like the neighbors, I observed Mama, her eyes never meeting mine, her gaze fixed on the precise point in the near distance where sadness lies. I would wait. She was an animal in quarantine who would display its true nature in time. Soon I would be able to pet her. Soon she might love me back.

The neighbors' first question to Mama was always: *So, Anna Mikhailovna, what is your news?* News bred news, you see. *If you find yours, I might find mine* — this is what they were thinking. Or rather, the opposite way around. *If you find yours, there is less chance that I will find mine, so please say yours is still missing.* Somebody's children, after all, had to make up the dead.

I took each visitor's gift and placed it on the kitchen table, piling them up next to Nika's breakfast bowl, until it troubled me to see that tower of goodwill threatening to spill onto the one solid thing that suggested Nika was still with us. At the same time, I felt the urge to swipe at the present pile, send it crashing down. I too wanted someone to fight, someone to blame, because for now the only person I held accountable was myself. I put all the gifts away in a kitchen cupboard, except for those brought specifically for Nika. Those I placed on her bed, next to the sooty fur of Zaychik, ready for her mythical return.

Sometimes, I would close our bedroom door behind me and cry, secretly, sure that she was gone, my jaw locked open in a soundless howl. I pictured her last moment, tried to imagine the terror I could not protect her from. It wasn't true, I decided, that there would be no more of her, that she should simply stop. It wasn't allowed. I would protest, bargain with fate. Send me back in time, and I'd never shut the door on her again. I'd draw lines on her eyelids, flowers on her cheeks. I'd spend every moment with her, every single one, because I knew now how much each one was worth. I took the tuft of her hair from my locket and rubbed it between my finger and thumb, as if it were magic and it held the power to bring her back.

The visitors gone, I was expected to play nurse. But I wasn't willing to place my hand on Mama's forehead again. I was frightened to. I knew that she would feel cold. I answered her housekeeping demands instead, which came mumbled and occasional in the first day, then built in frequency, gaining in critical tone. All the things I had not done while she had been in bed . . .

"Find doilies," she said into the quiet one afternoon as the dust settled from a parting guest and we waited for the bell to signal the next.

"What, Mama?"

Still her eyes did not meet mine. They settled on the middle distance, somewhere in front of the row of framed pictures on the mantelpiece. Boris, Igor, me; various portraits, up to the point when Mama left our lives. I never got older than eleven.

"There are doilies in the bottom of the dresser," she said, her voice sounding so clear against the vagueness of everything else.

I fetched them and I placed them over the back of the sofa as she directed so that our visitors would not see the dark patches where Papa's and the boys' oily heads had stained the fabric over time. Slowly, slowly, Mama restored our missing pride.

Papa and I were more concerned with lists. The list on the morgue wall, the list on the wall of the Palace of Culture . . . We elbowed our way through the crowds to scan whatever new list was available. Ten times over we read those names, just to be sure. I felt like I was back at school: that awful trepidation. Who had been chosen for a part in the play? Who had passed the test? Papa and I perfected a certain solid way of standing—feet wide, arms braced by a wall—so we could keep our place during any pushing and shoving long enough to take in the whole list. Papa would whisper the names as he read, a superstitious prayer to keep our own name at bay.

"See if there is a name that looks similar to yours," an official yelled. "We may have written it down wrong. The dying do not speak clearly."

A part of me wanted to see it written there: *Ivanova Veronika Pavlovna*. An end to it. Something to grieve. Then we could concentrate on vengeance. What good is a maybe, made of fresh air and false hope? You can't get hold of it. Every time I saw a girl listed with the patronym *Ivanovna*, daughter of Ivan, I felt a sickening rush, thinking for a moment it was our family surname. *It's her, it's her*, I'd think, with the most twisted excitement.

Back home, we kept the television switched on with the sound down. Soap opera actors silently circled one another, women made faces at stains on white clothing, beautiful girls threw back their heads to glug fizzy drinks—and then with the familiar opening sequence of the local news, we dived toward the set to turn up the volume. We listened to the roll call of people who were lying unclaimed in the hospital, as if it were a poem—a happy verse made up of the living. *Seven-year-old, intensive care, identity unknown*. Good news waiting to happen.

The remaining time, Papa paced, wandering back and forth from kitchen to living room, his eyes on his shoes, squeezing his bottom lip between thumb and finger. If he paused, I would look up, expecting him to announce a grand plan to save us all. But he had nothing for me. I began to doubt him, doubt that he was the solid brick I'd believed him to be.

Sometimes, in the evening, he'd grab his jacket all of a sudden and leave the apartment, announcing that he must go to the factory to "check on security" or "follow up on a complaint." This was nothing new. He had done it before, in our old life, often, and my brothers and I had thought not a

37

thing of it back then. With Papa out and Nika in bed, we had been free to choose what to watch on TV, or at least to fight it out among the three of us, arm wrestling for the remote control, a tickle in the armpit being my winning tactic. But now we exchanged wary looks, my brothers and I, as Papa left. His excuses were lies, we suddenly realized; no issue at the factory could be more important than our missing sister, than our broken family. But no one was willing to say it out loud. Mama instead gave Papa her liturgy of fretful questions. *But who is at the factory? Will it be dangerous? The army are the ones to call on, surely. Stay at home, my Pasha, please, these are dangerous times.* And as he scolded our mother for worrying, calling her *my Anya, my sweet Anechka*, he fastened his buttons in a rush — his best jacket, not the one he usually wore to work.

My brothers and I longed for our own excuse to throw on a jacket and escape the apartment. The boys kicked around in the kitchen now that our mother had commandeered the living room — their bedroom — insisting that they pack their camp beds away every morning. I was asked to buy a can of air freshener so we might remove the smell of them too. The boys told stupid jokes, murmuring and snorting at each other as they tipped back on the kitchen chairs, a hand on the counter behind them for balance. If Papa or Mama was near, they'd drop the chairs' legs, drop their heads too, at least ashamed of their own smirking.

"Get out from under my feet," I would scold as I came in to put on an apron and start cooking. But only as something to say, something to bat at them, hoping they'd bat it back. These

rallies were the warp and weft of us. I didn't want to lose that.
I knew they could not bear to be alone. It would be too quiet.
Reality would speak to them:

Hey, Boris, how many of your friends are still alive?

Which ones are you hoping are wiped out, Igor?

*And by the way, if you have an opinion on that, it should have
been you who perished, you little shit.*

Reality spoke to me too:

*I wonder if Nadya and Olya will be heading off to university
after all.*

Maybe they each caught a bullet.

Wouldn't that teach them a lesson for being so smug!

I kept moving, kept busy, to hold the voices back.

One afternoon, when Aslan, the apartment caretaker, and
his wife, Diana, came to visit from their downstairs apartment,
Mama made a great show of testing the boys. She called them
into the living room and instructed them to get Papa's gun.

"Go on, Boris Pavlovich, Igor Pavlovich, go! Go across the
border with the other boys, the strong ones," she spat. "You
show those people how it feels to have their young ripped from
their breast."

Boris and Igor didn't answer, not knowing if she was serious,
naming them like grown men, or if this was just a show for our
guests. Behind closed doors, Mama had spoken dismissively
of the local gangs who gathered on the streets in the evenings,
putting together crude armies, making reckless plans for attack.
Which way were the boys supposed to turn? They fidgeted
in the corner of the room, toothless, humiliated, not allowed
to make use of their standard cocky comebacks. They were

nearly-men turned back into little boys, forced to watch their mother cry.

"No, Anna Mikhailovna, do not worry yourself this way," Diana said in her warm, throaty voice, consoling my mother. "The morning is wiser than the evening." She repeated this phrase over and over as Mama recounted her version of events. *Do not worry yourself this way — the morning is wiser than the evening.*

But Mama's response was "If I had been there, Diana Petrovna, I would not have let this happen. Everything would have been different."

"Do not worry yourself this way," Diana chanted. "The morning is wiser than the evening."

What else could she say? Nothing would make any difference.

I passed Mama a clean handkerchief, pleased that someone else was there to stroke her hand. I couldn't even bring myself to sit beside her, because it had begun to edge in — something was cutting a path through my shock. Anger. *Ripped from her breast,* she said. But *I* had fed Nika. From the bottle. Me.

Aslan and Diana soon made their excuses. They, like everyone else, did not know Mama well. I was surprised they had visited at all. They must have been bothered by guilt, having not lost anyone themselves.

"We have a journalist staying with us," Aslan said to explain their leaving. "So we must . . ."

They were everywhere — the journalists — blocking our paths to the lists, taking photos as we picked through bodies in the yard outside the morgue. *Can I ask you some questions?* they'd say in mock sorrow, coming too close, tape recorders tucked tight to their thighs, a weapon concealed. Some people used the journalists as doctors for their failing hearts and gave them all their sadness. Some made them their allies in the fight with the government over the handling of the siege, a different way to bloodlet their pain. Others chose the journalists as an enemy themselves. They were spirited opponents, after all, willing to lock horns. Others, meanwhile, were seduced by their glamour.

"He's from New York," said Diana, her eyes shining. "He works for a very important newspaper."

"So we must . . ." said Aslan again.

I wondered what you must do for a New York journalist, but they did not say.

I showed them to the door, and in the hallway Diana took a moment to examine the gash above my eye.

"Such a very pretty girl," she said, shaking her head. "What a shame."

And then they left.

In those days of limbo, I made a lot of tea. I did it in a deliberate way, concentrating on each step of the process. I let the leaves fall like black snow into the kettle to make the *zavarka*. I warmed the separate pot for water, feeling the heat of the stainless steel, getting it just right. I put everything on the tray. Everything. Lemon slices, sugar, milk, honey, jam. The arranging of these things calmed me. Something to control. But I also did it because I did not know how Mama took her tea. I knew how the woman who had lain in her bedroom all day liked to drink it — weak with just lemon. But this woman who sat on our sofa in a tidy black dress? She might decide any minute that she liked it strong, with a good heap of jam to make it sweet.

We developed a ritual. I would put the tray down on the low glass table in the middle of the living room. The boys would slink in from the kitchen, then Papa would stop his pacing in the hallway and come to do the pouring. Each time, I hoped that Papa would tell his usual teatime joke — a glimpse over a shoulder at our lives before.

"What follows after tea?" is what Papa would ask. Then — *shlop!* — Boris, Igor, and I would smack down a hand on the table, saying the answer with him: "The resurrection of the dead!"

Then we would laugh, even though we didn't really understand why it was so funny in the first place. Papa never told that joke again.

It was on the sixth day, when we still had no news of Nika, when our nerves were like a damaged rope relying on threads, that Mama said, "Pour it strong for me today."

Papa paused, looking at Mama, only noticing in that moment that she had woken up as someone entirely different. I stared at her too, as if this change in the way she drank her tea might signal something more. Had she woken with an oracle's gift? Would she now reveal Nika's whereabouts?

But, like Papa, she had nothing for me.

He poured her tea. I spooned the jam.

5

LEARN HOW
TO HOWL

On the seventh day, I started smoking. As if I'd not had enough of burning. I did it to be closer to my brothers. What I really wanted was to sleep beside them in the living room at night, but I was too scared to say that. I didn't want to be rejected. I didn't want to be mocked. In the dark, I cried, alone, looking across at Nika's bed, loaded with its weight of gifts that she might never see, watched by the sad, stitched eyes of Zaychik. Smoking was the best bond I could hope for. What else could we do? Play Chapayev checkers on Papa's broken board, make Battleship grids in the back of our old schoolbooks, ride bikes to the scrubland? This wasn't a time for games. But I needed to be with them—needed to be with someone, doing what they were doing. If Nadya and Olya had escaped like me, they would be comforting each other now, sharing their fears. Even in disaster they triumphed.

Boris and Igor had taken to smoking their cigarettes on the landing outside our front door instead of hiding downstairs by Aslan's shed at the back of the building. Smoking had become too small a thing to ignite Mama and Papa's anger. I went out into the concrete lobby and found my brothers leaning against the wall next to two coffin lids and a handmade wooden cross. They belonged to our left-side neighbors, the Chagaevy—who had their bodies and their answers. I asked Boris for my first cigarette, and the boys made no comment. No teasing, no threats to tell.

I was a born smoker. My lungs did not kick back, and smoking soothed me like nothing had since the siege, rounding off sharp edges, giving me a flat line of emotion that was easier to cope with than adrenaline jolts. If I was very lucky, I inhaled and got a swooping arc that mimicked pleasure.

I leaned against the wall that day, next to the coffin lids and my bare-chested brothers, and I blew smoke toward Yelena's open front door opposite.

Everyone in our building had taken to leaving their doors open. The foul, cloying stench coming from the burned-down gym filled the apartments; you couldn't keep it out by shutting a door. More important, an open doorway meant you heard what was being said in the corridors. If there was any news, it reached you. This is how we learned that they were parking freight cars on the railroad tracks. Soon they would be asking us, one of the families left with a question mark instead of a child, to go inside and look. If you walked to the end of the landing on our floor, you could see out through the bars toward the tracks. We were waiting for a movement of people in that direction; then we would think about following.

Through Yelena's open door we had a line of sight into her bathroom, where she was washing clean her eldest child, Grigoriy. He had recently been found, blackened and bewildered, at the hospital in the capital. He was thirteen years old, but by the way Yelena washed him, he might as well have been an infant. She was still waiting for news to reach her of Polin'ka—Nika's classmate, her sometime play friend. She had not been returned. And though I did not say this to Yelena, it offered me comfort to think they were lost together. Nika and Polin'ka—on an adventure of their own decision. I even dared to think that they were with the deer, skipping, merry.

Grigoriy was standing in the bath while Yelena wiped away the mask of filth from his face, revealing her baby Grishka beneath. She savored every moment, each small section of his body: the earlobes, the webs of skin between his fingers, the cleft in his neck, the furrows around the bones of his knees. She washed him back to being her precious child, not someone who got under her feet, who played too loud, and stretched her shopping budget so taut that there was no room for anything nice. Grigoriy saw us watching him but did not flinch. Boris and Igor snickered at their friend, at his exposed penis, at his mother treating him like a tiny infant. Still Grigoriy did not flinch. He looked back at his mother, trying to grasp who she was now, who he was to her.

The boys continued to snicker. My fingernails wanted to claw at my forehead where the hard scab was tightening.

"Stop that!" Mama would snap every time I scratched, slapping my hand away from my face, as if I were tearing at her skin, not mine. "You'll only make it worse."

The boys' snickers grew, so that Boris's deep *hur-hur-hur* must have traveled into Yelena's apartment. I thought for a moment of joining in. To live among wolves, you must learn how to howl, and in addition to quarreling, snickering was something we used to do well together when we were younger. I was out of practice. I had lost my sense of humor. But perhaps it would bring us closer if I laughed along. They would see me as their sister again, the kid they used to play with on the scrubland, not this stand-in mother without a child. But I had been a mother. And that meant I did not get the joke.

"What's so funny?" I said, quietly at first.

They didn't answer. The siege had slit my brothers' vocal cords. It had cut off their balls. Why would they not fight with me? I wanted us to lock horns, if only to stop us from falling apart.

"Why are you laughing?" I asked again.

Nothing. Boris looked sideways at Igor. I saw the roll of his eyes.

"Why are you laughing?" I screamed it this time. I howled, and I gave them no chance to answer. "Shut up!" I hissed. "Just shut up!" And I punched Boris very hard in the face. His nose exploded shockingly, satisfyingly, with blood. My littlest brother I kicked in the shin.

Then I went inside.

On the eighth day, I went alone onto the landing to smoke and found a man there I did not know. He was admiring the coffin lids. That is how it seemed—stroking a hand down their sawed

46

edges, assessing their smoothness, as if considering a purchase. I moved silently out our front door and crouched by the wall. I had brought with me a play from the recent pile of books from Yelena. A hopeful gesture. Since the siege, I could not get the words to lift off the page, and neither could I fall into them. I was stuck in the first act. Smoking was the easier habit.

"*Ah, hi, hello*, hello!" said the stranger at the strike of my lighter. He spoke in English first, then Russian, his voice too jolly for a town like this, his smile too unfailing, his skin too rich. He was an outsider, and I felt small and threatened, even though he was friendly. I nodded him a greeting and my goodbye.

"Are you reading that for school?" he asked, pointing to the book by my feet, the word *school* heavy with a meaning it had never had before.

He was tall and lean, this man, with waves of blond hair. His shirt was pink and creased, but deliberately so. If he was an American, I knew he must be a journalist, but he did not look like one, or behave like one. He looked more like a movie star. I considered the possibility that he was a spy.

I picked up my book and stood. I didn't want him towering over me. I pulled myself up straighter so that he could see that I was an adult, not someone who read books for school. There had been a conversation in the play—the battery commander is due in town, and one sister asks, "Is he old?" "Not particularly," is the reply. "Forty or forty-five at the most." Which had not made sense, because forty is old, yet this man was around that age and did not seem ancient at all. His eyes were animal-bright.

In the play, another sister falls for the battery commander, charmed by him from the start.

"Jonathan Bruck," he announced, stepping forward and striking a hand out toward me. I looked at it, floating awkwardly in the air — at the neat fingernails. I realized too late that I was supposed to shake this hand; I had never done that kind of thing before. "Sorry, sorry," he said, taking the hand away again, wiping its unwantedness away on the back pocket of his trousers, amused by me at the same time. I looked over toward Yelena's apartment, embarrassed. I knew her doorframe so well I could draw a picture of it from memory — every dent and scratch. The familiarity of the damage was somehow reassuring.

"I've seen that play," he said. "In English. My Russian isn't that great, as you can tell!"

He chuckled, an absurd sound. I thought about how my brothers' laughter had upset me, yet Jonathan's laughter was captivating — warm, genuine, and easy. He seemed captivated by me too, or interested at least. I could not remember the last time anyone had looked at me with such a level of fascination. I realized then that I was used to being invisible.

"Did you want a cigarette?" I asked, feeling my face burn with the attention, thinking perhaps that was why he had approached me in the first place, to steal a smoke.

"No, no, I . . ." He twisted to point at the coffin lids behind him. "I was just wondering . . . Are these . . . ?"

"Mine?" I asked.

He nodded. I shook my head. Then, from nowhere, tears

came, rolling down my cheeks before I could do anything about them. My chin was shuddering. I expected Jonathan to laugh again. How ridiculous to be upset that a coffin lid did not belong to me! How absurd! But his eyes were wet too, not with tears, exactly, but certainly with compassion. His face took on the shape of all that I was feeling. I had been wanting to be with someone, doing the same thing they were doing, so perhaps this counted.

"Darya Pavlovna," I said, using my formal name to be safe. I wiped away tears.

"Pleased to meet you." He nodded, keeping his hand behind his back.

"My sister is still missing." The words fell from my mouth, like coins rejected from a machine. "But we will find her soon."

A precipice of ash hung from my fingers. My hand was trembling. Jonathan gave me a smile of pity that I thought might break my heart.

"I have to go," I said, giving up on the cigarette and letting it drop. I would need to fetch a broom later, I told myself, as a way to think about something else.

When they opened up the freight cars, Papa and I walked to the railroad track together. Mama stayed at home—a *tsaritsa* ruling from the sofa. She had taken a pillow from Nika's bed and liked to hug it to her middle, leaning in every so often to inhale its smell. I didn't understand how this could mean anything to her if she had never hugged the real Nika, never experienced that buttery scent on her smooth skin and in her thick hair. All Mama was doing was tainting the pillow, draining it of any solace it might have offered me, replacing Nika with her own bitter perfume.

Still, I would have chosen the tart smell of Mama over the stench coming from those freight cars. It hit us long before we reached the steps leading to their terrifying insides. A woman gave me her handkerchief as she left. She had daubed it in lavender oil to place inside her protective mask. Even now, I cannot smell that flower and not think of that day.

"Anything?" I asked her. I offered my hand as she made her way down. She shook her head. I couldn't tell if she was happy about this or not. I'm not sure if she knew herself.

I did not want to go up those steps. I had been so desperate for an answer, but now I could be happy with a maybe. Until we found her dead, she was still alive. She was hand in hand with Polin'ka, disappearing over the horizon on an exciting adventure. She was running on the scrubland, transformed into a deer. I would come across her one day and know her by her missing tuft of hair. I'd release her with a spell, a sprinkle of healing water that could cure even the fatal. Papa saw that I was hanging back. He gave me a dark look that said, *We have to know.* He took my hand. We climbed those steps together, with Papa leading the way.

This was not the first time we had examined the dead. We had picked our way along the rows laid out in the yard in the city. We had peered very closely at those bodies — some of them not even recognizable as bodies. We had searched for clues among the flesh and cinders; something to tell us for sure: *No, this isn't her. Move on to the next.* But as I worked along this new line of corpses, looking for traces of Nika, I realized I was incapable of seeing. Everything was just passing through me now, causing no sensation. I had seen every possible distortion of the human body, every kind of degradation—and this was nothing. I backed away from the rows of people laid out before me, and I started to gag. Papa held me up.

"Nika?"

I shook my head. I couldn't find the words to explain to him why I was choking. I did not want Papa to be as disgusted with me as I was with myself. I had developed a sick appetite for bodies, to see more of them, all of them, just to make sure that they were not her, my beloved girl. Nothing could move me. Nothing. I would never feel anything again —this is what I believed in that moment in the belly of that revolting freight car—I would never again feel love, or regret, or real physical pain. The best I could hope for was a cigarette's swooping arc that mimicked pleasure. I had seen the worst that life could deliver and I had become immune.

So when we did find her that day, identifying her by her flower necklace and by the moon-shaped splodge of her birthmark, it came as the most predictable defeat. Numbness. Emptiness. I opened my locket, took out the tuft of hair, and held it against the place where I had clumsily cut. I remembered the way she had laughed. A perfect match. The shoe fit. I put the curl back, snapped the locket shut.

It wasn't her. Not really. A person is not what remains, their body, but how they moved in this world. How they turned their head to pin you down with one of their beautiful eyes. How they casually linked a finger with you as they walked into the kitchen. How they pressed the whole weight of themselves onto you in the morning. The buttery scent of their hair, their skin. How they tried to smile but bit their lip with gappy teeth.

How they watched, mesmerized, as a heart-shaped balloon disappeared into the sky.

6

WILD DANCES

The town started a new cemetery—a dank expanse of earth beneath a sallow sky. Too many mounds of mud. Marble hurriedly chopped. Stripped wood markers at awkward angles like lollipop sticks in the dust. Cars lined up to enter, sounding their horns, bringing with them morsels of color—wreaths, teddy bears, and flower petals pressed beneath their tires.

I played no part in the preparation of Nika's grave. Papa, Boris, and Igor split the earth. I was to stay at home and be silent, prepare food, hold Mama upright as we staggered to the cemetery. I was to moan and cry as Nika's coffin was lowered. Her closed coffin. Even though she was too damaged to be seen, still we put her in a white dress and belt, laid her comfortably on a stuffed pillow. I was to curse the skies and call for revenge, but not so much that I would upstage Mama. She played her part very well. Afterward, we threw away our handkerchiefs. We went home.

It was not enough.

They had not let me dig her grave; I needed to dig my own. I wanted to work down into the mud, feel it beneath my nails, break a sweat. I wanted to stand, filthy, above a great hole of my own making, then drop myself into it, test its depth, know that it fit me better than it did my little sister.

I put on a pair of Boris's too-big army boots, and I rang the bell for Aslan's apartment.

He took in the sight of me, and his face sagged. I was not myself, or at least not what had gone before — neatly dressed, good. I stamped out my cigarette and stepped across the threshold, following Aslan through to the kitchen, where Ruslana was gyrating on the portable TV set, singing about being *wild* and wanting to be *loved* — English words I knew because they were in every song.

"You're smoking now," Aslan said, walking to the other side of the kitchen counter, putting it between us.

"Yes," I told him. "I think it's only right."

He nodded. Perfect sense. Being good now was a hopeless quest. My destiny lay downhill.

"So what can I do for you, Darya Pavlovna?" He started to heat some water.

"Oh, no need for tea. I only need a shovel."

We moved back to the front door, where he collected a large bunch of keys from a hook on the wall. The applause for Ruslana was dying away, and I could hear another voice, separate from the up-down chatter of the TV host.

English words, being spoken in Aslan's apartment.

The New York journalist.

I'm embarrassed to admit that, despite everything, I felt a spike of excitement. Perhaps it was the possibility of something new. The chance to be wild. The chance to be loved. As Aslan fumbled with the zip of his jacket, I leaned back to peer into the living room. There he was—the journalist with feathers different from those who flocked at the morgues and cemeteries. This one had not asked me who I thought should suffer for all that had happened. He had not asked the question that was at once obvious yet impossible to answer—*How do you feel?* A journalist in a creased pink shirt. My battery commander from the landing. Jonathan. He was in the armchair, hunched over a laptop, a cell phone to his ear.

"*Yes, yes,*" he was saying, raking stress from his blond hair, then, "*Fuck, fuck.*" Another English word I knew somehow.

Jonathan turned, sensing my gaze upon him, and smiled at me in recognition. I could only stare back, not knowing the right reaction. What do you do when handed the gift of attention? What must you do for a New York journalist? I had no idea. I think I wanted to call out to him, across that hallway and living room, *We did find her, but she's dead.* That way I could have felt the warm blanket of his compassion again. But I didn't call out, because he knew that she was gone. He knew it before me.

"We can go now," said Aslan.

I didn't have the energy to feel embarrassed for peering in on his guest.

"So how is your New York journalist?" I asked as we headed out across the apartment lobby, hoping for some trinket of information to take away with me.

"Still here," said Aslan. "How is your mother?"

I sighed. "The same."

We made our way down the side of the building, to where the smell of piss lingered on the weeds. Aslan walked ahead, his khaki trousers bunched up around his backside and gathered beneath his belt. He had been a bigger man once; in the years we had lived there, I had not noticed him shrink. Aslan still had not asked me why I needed the shovel and as he worked at the bolt of the shed, his usually slick gray hair arching forward over the concentration on his forehead, I willed him to say something.

"Here we are."

He swung open the doors, and we stared into the gloom, listening to the scattering of rats. He bent down and pulled a small blue-handled trowel from a bucket by the entrance, holding it out to me. I shook my head and pointed. What I needed was hanging on the back wall alongside a rolled-up hose and a mangled rake. He dropped the trowel with a sigh and pushed past piled-up crates, empty water canisters, and drunken ladders. He reached up, his jacket climbing, his white undershirt riding free from his trousers. He returned to the entrance, clutching the shovel to his belly, the question creasing his brow before he opened his mouth: "So, Darya Pavlovna, why do you need this shovel?"

At last. I thought that if I told him, he would give me a face of compassion too. But I could see that he was weary. He and Diana had lost no one, yet still his soul was leaching. I could have replied, *I need that shovel to kill a man*, and I'm sure that Aslan would not have balked. I wanted to speak the truth—*I need that shovel to bury my sister*—but instead I looked Aslan in the eye, held his tired gaze for a moment too long, before saying, "For digging." I could not bring myself to burden him. And Aslan replied, "Of course." The shovel was mine.

I walked out of town, past the stinking whale carcass of the gym. Security Force tanks sat at its edges like discarded toys. Still a few people—women—picked through the fetid rubble. They should have been at the city market, rummaging for bargains, but instead—this. Every post, every billboard, every piece of wire fence was covered with photocopied pictures of children. Under each face, a phone number. From a distance, they might have been flyers asking for the return of lost pets. I was grasped by an urge to draw mustaches on these children, to scrawl *Give up, stop pretending* across their foreheads. *Let us go and find the bastards who did this instead!* My soul was leaching too. I was becoming my mother—my mind turning to the idea of crossing the border to kill, indiscriminately, if only as a balm for my wounds. All I wanted was honesty of feeling. A way to know it. No more papering over, no more making good. I walked on. The lost children's faces riffled in the wind.

On the scrubland, burrs skipped across the ground, catching my bare legs. Autumn had arrived and was putting up no resistance to winter. The trees looked like lungs stripped of their flesh. Snow was settling on the mountaintops. This was where I played with my brothers when I was a child, spending hours in the dust. Later I would bring Nika to the same spot. We had a make-believe house. Just a cattle herder's shed, a place once used to watch for danger. There was no glass at the windows and only the broken bones of a roof, but there was a green front door with a loose and spinning latch. There were stone partitions, so you could imagine rooms.

I went inside to smoke a cigarette, propping the shovel against the wall beside me. All was quiet. Children were being held close at home. I traced the ghost of a climbing plant with my finger, its journey up the inside wall from floor to ceiling in search of light, only to be dried to a husk by the cold. There were faded ice-cream wrappers and crushed drink cartons in the corner of what used to be our imaginary living room, a reminder of the summer gone.

I took Zaychik out of my pocket, stroked its long, greasy ears, and looked into its stitched black eyes. Mama wanted it left at the cemetery, next to Nika's framed photograph (we had one now, too late), next to the flower arrangements we couldn't afford, the bottles of water to quench the siege's thirst (too late, too late), next to the tea lights and candlesticks. But I had hidden it from her—pushed Zaychik's soft body into the gap between two pallets of pickled tomatoes on the kitchen balcony, our stockpile for winter. No one went out on that balcony anymore, except to collect a jar. The view beneath . . . In the days after the siege, men had been left slumped against the walls as if only dozing in the sun.

Mama had staggered through the apartment before the burial, wrenching open drawers and spilling the contents of cupboards, cursing me for losing the toy.

"I'm sorry, Mama," I said, meaning it but also not meaning it, her not believing me.

"What else will you lose?" she wailed, rapt by her anguish. "There is nothing left for you to lose." And I tried not to think of how she was right.

I pulled Zaychik close to my face to inhale the last traces of Nika. We had found a hare's nest out there one spring, my sister and I. A little bunny, all wide-eyed and ready for the world, was lying dead in its furrow. The soft bedding its mother had prepared, bitten from her own matted fur, was scattering, useless. Nika had crouched, knees high, to stroke a finger down the unlucky baby, nose to tail.

"Still warm, Dasha," she'd said.

I had also been thinking of warm hare—baked—wondering if a leveret would come to much in the pot.

"Poor *zaychik*," she'd said, immediately cutting down any thoughts of dinner. Instead of carrying it home by its big back feet, we'd covered it in rocks to mark its untimely death and given it a prayer.

I remember the sensations of that walk home so clearly—the wind warm, the sun a hot blister about to pop behind the black mountains. She'd asked me to tell her the story of the little brave hare, one I'd read at bedtime so often that I did not need the book in front of me.

There once was a little hare who was scared of everything—the wails of the wind, the coming of the night, the long grass, the short grass, and the murmuration of the birds. Though the bigger hares were scared too, they were still able to play, forgetting their worries in the light of the moon.

"Come and dance, Little Hare," they would cry, thumping the earth to the rhythm of their hearts. But Little Hare would always refuse.

"What if the wolf should come by?" she'd say to them, cowering in her nest.

"Well, then we'd run," they'd sing as they twirled and bounced. "But only then. Only then would we run."

I put Zaychik in the pocket of my dress, stubbed out my cigarette, and went into the yard of my make-believe house.

I started to dig.

It was as satisfying as true love. I began in the early afternoon, and by the time the light was fading, I still had not finished. I did not really know what finished would mean. The ground was dry despite the rainfall that week, but became sticky underneath, with large stones peppering each shovelful. They grated against the metal—a noise I felt in my teeth. But it was so gratifying. Lifting and throwing, lifting and throwing, lifting and throwing. It filled me up. I sweated hard. I did not drink. I did not eat. I did not pause to smoke. I only stopped when the fingernail moon pressed through the cloud.

I had dug down so far that I was able to stand in the hole with the lip of the small grave at my elbow. It was getting hard to lift out the soil, and I feared the sides might collapse in on me. Though I didn't fear it as much as I should have. My work slowed. I was shaking from the exertion and from my wet skin meeting the bitter air. I kicked a toe of my boot into the wall, dug my fingers into the muddy edge of the grave and heaved myself out onto my belly, my body convulsing now.

So, perhaps I imagined the red deer standing a few feet from the edge of the grave, skittering at the sight of me emerging from the ground. It froze for a moment, watching, snorting its steaming breath into the night. Then it kicked its heels and ran—a white tail bouncing away into the murk. Before I lost sight of it completely, I noticed that there were other white tails, so many of them, dancing, joyous, moving in circles.

I lost some time. It oozed through my fingers like wet soil. I know I put Zaychik in the ground and, using my arms like snowplows, pushed the earth back on top. I wanted a place I could return to—that's what I had thought—anywhere but that new cemetery with its identical graves repeating like echoes. I could not mourn one little girl there, could not see what she had meant beyond her small role in a cosmic tragedy. Perhaps I made a marker from sticks and stones. I don't remember.

I got myself home—I know that. At the apartment, Papa waved his arms and bellowed phrases that were only sounds. Boris was ordered to run a bath. Mama drifted through the hall, saying something about catching a chill, leaving behind a vapor trail of disapproval. I went into the bathroom and watched water thunder into the tub. From behind the half-closed door, Papa barked instructions to undress. I passed him my clothes, and Igor was told to put them in the rubbish chute, but I had wit enough left to protest. I had so little else to wear.

I got clean. I put on a nightgown and was ushered into bed. Time became sludge again. I could not keep hold of it. I was hot and cold, sleeping and not dreaming, waking eventually to a short, high, delighted note in the hallway outside my room — a chirp from an unfamiliar bird. I pulled myself to a sitting position, leaving a dried crust on the pillow from the cut on my face. The locket snagged at my neck. I swung my feet to the floor, tested my weight. I had the confusion you feel after an accidental nap, not knowing what you're waking up to, knowing only that you can't expect the usual routine of the morning. I opened my bedroom door onto an afternoon. Life had shifted forward. Igor was standing in the hall, watching Mama through the kitchen doorway. When I stepped out, he turned to look at me, scared.

"What's going on?" I said.

He gestured that I should come and see. Mama was a specimen of wildlife we must not spook by talking. I crossed the hall to stand beside him. At first my attention was not on Mama but on the kitchen table beyond her — a clear blue sea, missing its boat. Nika's breakfast bowl had been cleared away. By Mama, I supposed, because she would not have known its significance. I imagined her huffing at the congealed milk, the grains growing spores. I felt a desperate urge to rewind time, if only to put that moldy bowl, not Nika, back in its rightful place.

Then my eyes were on Mama — laying cautious hands on the smooth white sides of an absurdly tall fridge. It was twice the height of our old, fat, squat one. She seemed to be embracing it, gently checking for its pulse. Perhaps she was making sure it wasn't a trap, that the thing wouldn't blow up in her face. She pulled away the last remnants of its cardboard and cellophane packing. Then she stepped back to admire it. The corners of her mouth hinted at a smile.

"We have a new fridge, Dasha," Igor said with quiet horror. "Everyone who lost a child," he explained, "has been given a fridge."

7

SHALL I BE MOTHER?

In the days following the funeral, my family dusted off their hands. We had a new fridge; now we could carry on. That was how it seemed. Only I was stuck in a boundless limbo.

Papa went back to the factory. The boys left the apartment too. Mama's words had seeped into their souls, so they began patrolling our apartment building, a finger on the trigger of Papa's rifle, ready to protect us from our unknown enemy, should they dare to return. Mama made an occupation of Nika's grave. So many years she spent hiding in her bed and, as soon as my sister dies, Mama discovers her sense of duty. I could not fathom it. *Too late!* I wanted to scream into her face. *It's all too late!* And I wasn't thinking only of Nika. Where had Mama been when I needed her? She was living on a volcano, fit to erupt; that's why she went to the cemetery so often. To keep away from me.

I found myself remembering the time, before Nika, when I craved time alone with Mama. I liked being home sick from school, a secret passenger in the apartment, watching her go about her housework, observing her quiet industriousness. When all of the family had been there, Mama did her everyday tasks with exaggeration, puffing and bustling, putting on a performance and looking for cheers. On the rare days I got her to myself, she glided. I stayed mute so as not to spoil it. Only Mama broke the silence, asking if I could manage a small something for lunch. She'd light the gas, pour oil, crack an egg on the edge of the pan and discard the shell in one deft movement. That conscientious face, her hair pulled back under a head scarf. I would find it hard to eat, because I was too busy savoring this hidden version of my mother, magnificent and solid.

To outsiders, Mama was solid now. She tidied Nika's grave, went to church again, and attended meetings organized by the other mothers, joining in the campaign for answers about the handling of the siege. She took the minutes of those meetings sometimes, and this filled her with a pride she could not conceal, because she thought it made her better than the others, more educated. Though with teachers in that group, I couldn't see how that was possible. They had given her the role out of sympathy, I decided. And anyway, these activities were only a way for Mama to build a hard shell around something soft and difficult. I understood her guilt. I could have cracked *her* with one deft movement.

Alone in the apartment, I thought of the train fare that I had saved, spent on a tray of Babaevsky pralines never to be tasted, the secretarial exams I had not asked about, the pile of books I had given up on, stuck in the first act of a play I might never finish. I thought about the New York journalist in the apartment on the first floor, his compassionate eyes. My charming battery commander. I smoked on the landing often, hoping he would return.

One evening that week, Mama set six places at the table. It could have been forgetfulness, that cruel hangover, if she had ever done this task while Nika was alive. If she had ever eaten with us at the table before the siege. It was a grand gesture to the dead, I decided, and I would not acknowledge it, just as I would not comment on the new dress she was wearing—a striking deep blue with purple flowers and a belt that tied around her expanding middle. Mama's figure was filling out now that she was eating properly. Where there were bones, there'd be meat again.

But Mama had not made a mistake with the knives and forks. As I mixed together a salad Olivier, I heard Papa greeting an unexpected visitor in the hallway. There was hearty laughter that made me stop stirring, my spoon poised in the air.

"Dima! My Dima! Come in, come in!" Papa boomed, and I kept my spoon raised as Dmitriy Vasiliev entered the kitchen. I knew him from school—he was two years ahead of me, a wiry boy with an unfortunate lump on the bridge of his very long nose. He worked at Papa's factory. He had no reason to be at our home.

"Come in, Dima, come in," said Mama, parroting my father, showily smoothing the skirts of her dress, as if she truly wanted the evil eye upon her.

Dmitriy moved toward me, Mama nodding her encouragement, and he offered a gift—a packet of sweets tied up with a ribbon. I looked down as his present, at his obscenely long fingers wrapped around the plastic.

"For you, Dasha." His voice wobbled.

"Put them on the counter, Dmitriy Dmitrievich," I replied, using his full and formal name to show that I was above all of this; no *Dima* would pass my lips. "My hands are greasy from preparing dinner."

Mama leaped in to cough away my stiffness, ushering him into a seat. Papa placed a bottle of Fat Man beer in front of the boy, clapping him on the back, congratulating him for the mere act of wearing a clean white shirt, well tucked in.

"We should set up a table in the living room, Mama," I said loudly, putting the last skewer of mutton *shashlik* on a serving plate, "since we have a guest."

"Oh, Dima doesn't mind!" said my father. "We can treat him exactly like family!" The merriment in his voice was unbearable. "I have recently promoted Dima to supervisor on the bottling line," my father went on. Dmitriy grinned at the boasting done on his behalf. "Did I tell you that, my Dashen'ka?"

I stared. "No, you didn't, Papa." *And why would you ever?* They wanted rid of me, their strange daughter who disappeared and returned all covered in mud. They had no use for me now that Nika was gone. I opened a bottle of beer and drank down its sourness. The spaces set for my brothers stayed empty and unmentioned — the boys rarely came back for dinner since starting their army. No matter, when we had a third potential son right there! Fate was dropping its hints about what kind of adult I was going to be — or offering its warnings. In a year or so, the weddings would start happening again.

I clung to the picture of myself behind that desk in a good blouse, with a small pot of sharpened pencils and a group of worldly-wise workmates. But the whole scene was set behind glass. Nothing would happen until the 40th Day at least, when mourning was officially over. But even then, was my ambition enough? How would being a secretary ever lift me up and free me from who I was, from where I was?

I had no answers. Instead, I drilled my focus into the day-to-day workings of the apartment. I tidied messy corners I had previously ignored. I cleaned things, not so they were serviceable or presentable but until they sang. I moved with precision, carrying out each chore as if marking my territory. I had to lay claim to something. I fired out threats to those around me with each swirl of the mop. I did this as a show of strength against my brothers, who had become distant and frightening since taking on the role of our protectors. I did it to keep my mother at bay. But more important, I did it to prove to my father that I was worthy. I was his one true ally in the house, and he should not give up on me yet.

That week also heralded the second unexpected invasion: people who wanted to help.

The fridge had been just the tip of a large and cumbersome iceberg. We were given paintings, flowers, furniture, clothes, toiletries. . . . Our child was dead; our pickings were great.

Money was handed out according to suffering — a hand placed against our troubled brows with the answer coming in rubles. Some gave us nothing: our family did not need to make a long journey for an expensive operation; we did not have a disfigured face to rebuild, lost eyesight to restore; our breadwinner had not been taken away. Others priced us high, seeing how a missing child made a family unstable. They pushed cash into the gaps to make us steadier, not understanding the shame we felt—everyone knowing of our windfall, everyone knowing it wasn't enough to make any real difference, everyone knowing we had more than them, less than them. Envy grew in this polluted soil.

We were given food parcels—cans and packages decorated with alien words. These items led to unexpected dinners. Sometimes inedible dinners. We were sent photographs and letters—one addressed personally to Nika from a school overseas congratulating her on surviving. The Russian was so clumsy that it might have, in other circumstances, given us a good laugh. *So brave you are to have been such a terrible disorder.*

We were given invitations to thank God, though for what, they never said.

And I was given Zlata.

When she rang our doorbell, I was continuing my campaign of domestic terror in the baking of a pie—something that would emerge from the oven large and impressive, so complicated and decorated that every member of my family would know exactly what metal I was made of. I had covered the yeast dough to let it rise and prepped enough meat, vegetables, rice, and eggs for a huge *kulebyaka*. I always cooked as if expecting the boys for dinner, just in case they grew tired of their project. Boris had recruited underlings—younger boys and one particularly bold girl named Alana from Igor's class at school—and they were tasked to bring food to him at his lookout post at the entrance to our block.

I hesitated in the hallway before answering the door, cleaning my hands on my apron. They were covered in flour. I don't have the cold, dry fingers you need for good pastry. We no longer kept our door open—we had all the news we needed—and the chime of the doorbell had become a thing of dread. Someone would eventually find the courage to complain about Boris and Igor, their new system of government, and we would not welcome their concerns. The boys were acting nobly as far as Mama, Papa, and I were concerned. We were happy in that denial.

I put an ear to the latch to get an idea of how many people were waiting on the other side, the glass in our peephole being cracked and useless.

Only the day before, a weeping woman had come, asking us to dig up Nika's body. A younger woman was with her, silent and expressionless, clutching her friend's arm as if her survival depended upon this physical contact, as if they were sharing one depleted blood supply. The weeping woman spoke for the silent one, who had not yet found her daughter. Could we be sure that the body we'd placed in the ground was definitely Nika? There were other dead children, the same size, on cold slabs at the hospital, but they had the wrong DNA. What if we had buried this woman's daughter by mistake? Wouldn't we rather know?

Mama wailed. Papa got angry. I gave the weeping woman

a handkerchief to dam the snot and tears that poured down her face, but I was more terrified by the stillness of the other woman. If we had not found Nika, would we have become like this, drowned but still breathing? I should have led them to Nika's grave and handed them a shovel; I understood the desire to dig. But Papa stepped in, a voice of authority. He explained how we had seen the flower necklace still there around Nika's neck and her moon-shaped birthmark intact. I told her of the tuft of hair in my locket, thrusting the silver battered shape of it forward on its chain as proof. The weeping woman nodded firmly, helped her friend from the chair, and left, on to the next family on their terrible list.

I put my hand on the latch, ready to open the door, prepared again for the worst. The day before the weeping woman came, Yelena from across the hall had rung the bell. She had something for me — I could tell — not books. She was bursting with the joyous burden of it. I stepped onto the landing.

"We have found Polin'ka!" she cried.

"Alive?" My throat was in a vise.

Yelena nodded, tears spilling. "In Germany," she said with a gasp. "She's in a hospital. They took her there. She's being all fixed up."

I felt sick. If Polin'ka was in Germany, then she wasn't with Nika, and if Polin'ka wasn't with Nika, then Nika was alone, all alone on the other side.

"Oh, that's wonderful, Lena," I managed, but I'd left a horrible pause. She moved forward and hugged me, stroking my hair and the skin above my eye where the scar was red and flaking. "I'm sorry," she said. "I'm so, so sorry." The touch was good, but there was something between us now. She had found hers; I had not found mine.

"Look at me, clumsy," she said, soft and playful, as she stepped away from our embrace. "I'm standing on your toes." And she offered me her foot so I could tread on it back, saving us from quarrels in the future.

I took a deep breath, ready to turn the latch.

Just before supper at the beginning of the week, the doorbell had rung, and a woman was standing there—pretty, with long, limp hair parted in the middle. She was older than me but still young. She had a thumb smudge of blue eye shadow marking out each eyelid. Her perfume leaked across the threshold.

"Is Pasha here?" she asked. *Pasha?* My father did not know any young women well enough for them to be calling him *Pasha*. I studied her for a moment, her strange familiarity. I was filled with a sudden anger at her rudeness, jealous of the intimacy she was claiming.

"My father, you mean? Pavel Stanislavovich?"

She looked along the landing as if checking she had not been followed, as if marking out a route to escape.

"Pasha," she said again, looking at her shoes.

Mama wandered into the corridor then, glasses teetering on the end of her nose, her hands full of mothers' meeting papers.

"Who is there, Dasha? Is it someone for me?"

And that made the woman run, make use of that escape route, grasping her handbag to her side. It was the woman from the night of the siege. It came to me as soon as she had gone.

It was the woman my father had comforted, come now to our apartment, all dressed up.

I could have let the doorbell go unanswered. Nothing good came from opening up. But perhaps I had some hope left. Perhaps I thought Jonathan would be there, bright eyes, kind smile, the red prince on his horse, come to rescue me somehow. I turned the latch.

And there was Zlata, with her good teeth and ponytail, with her clipboard and yellow anorak. Zlata, who, like so many of our new invaders, seemed to think there was nothing odd in grinning endlessly at total strangers. I sighed, disappointed, and ushered her into the kitchen, brushing flour off one of the red chairs with a cloth. I began to make tea before offering any kind of greeting. I knew how these visits played out. There had been many — only the color of the anoraks changed. I let the person say their piece, their words in the script, then, if they wanted to give us things, physical objects, I would say yes, bypass all uncomfortable discussion, get the transaction done. If it was an offer to talk, I would say very little, hoping that was an answer in itself. Zlata came offering something new.

She took her time sitting down, turning her head this way and that, her gaze pausing on the new fridge, the old yellow flower tiles, the pie dough sweating under plastic wrap. Zlata was younger than the other ones who had come with their clothes bundles and counseling schemes, their food boxes and group activities. She was older than me, but not by much, and she resembled a loris — one of those surprised-eyed monkeys you see on nature programs. Papa and I had fallen into watching wildlife documentaries in the evenings—when he was here—something safe, nothing that could remind us.

I arranged *sushki* on a plate, and Zlata competed with the boiling kettle to deliver her speech. She had a peculiar way of talking. The grammar was right, but she spoke too fast when it should be slow, too slow when it should be fast. I didn't listen to the words as such, just their funny rhythm. It belonged to no accent I knew.

I slid the tea tray onto the table and sat down.

"Shall I be mother?" said Zlata.

I stared. Her smile got bigger, even dopier.

"Just a cute English phrase I picked up." She raised an eyebrow as if we were in on some naughty secret, and made a grab for the pot, pouring for us both. Her nails were each painted a different color of the rainbow. She put milk and a spoonful of sugar into her cup, and bit into a *sushka* without dipping it first, without invitation. "How do you take yours, sweetie?"

"The same."

"Tea twins!" she exclaimed. There was a true bounce to her voice, not affected, not like the hosts on TV who sound happy for no reason. Still, I waited for her to change tone, express the expected sorrow for our family's loss.

"This is the best bit about house calls," she told me, staying sunny and light, holding up her half-eaten *sushka* as evidence. "Did you bake these yourself?"

I nodded.

"Then I simply must get the recipe from you, darling." She beamed, mushed-up *sushka* lining her teeth. "So, what do you think of our proposal? What will your boys think about going to Moscow?" She swiped crumbs off the table, making a mess of the linoleum instead.

"Sorry?" I'd not paid attention to her earlier words, only their mesmerizing pattern. "To Moscow?"

"Yes! To Moscow!" Her biggest smile yet.

"Leave?" Until I had put the word in my own mouth, the thought had never occurred to me. That a person could leave this place, all this sorrow. Go. To Moscow. That my brothers could leave. That I could leave . . .

I took a good gulp of tea.

Zlata pulled paperwork from her satchel. "There would be absolutely no cost to you, Anna Mikhailovna. No cost at all. The places at the school are covered by our sponsors."

Fate had delivered its sign — like in that English story I'd read, where a miserly man is sent three ghosts to show him the way. The desk, the blouse, the glass pot, and the worldly friends could all be mine, and they would not seem too small an ambition if they were in Moscow.

"Wait," I said. "Anna Mikhailovna? I am not Anna Mikhailovna."

"Oh . . . " Zlata pulled her clipboard from beneath the stash of leaflets and application forms. "But it says here Apartment 4C, Ivanovy. Pavel Stanislavovich and Anna Mikhailovna."

"Yes, that's right. But I am Darya Pavlovna, the daughter . . ."

"But it says here that the daughter is —"

"The other one," I cut in.

Zlata shut her mouth, let her fluttering rainbow fingers come to rest on the table.

"Anna Mikhailovna is my mother," I told her, offended. *Do I look like an old woman?*

I got up from my seat. It was time to roll the pastry flat. "But you can speak to me while Anna Mikhailovna isn't here." I whipped the plastic from the bowl and smacked the warm weight of dough onto the table, scattering flour. "Tell me again about going to Moscow. . . ."

8

WET HENS

I had heard that children were leaving, taking up school places in other parts of the country. But I thought it was only the hostages, those scarred deep and in need of fresh scenery. The gentle animals—not Boris, whose response to the violence of the tragedy was to meet it with violence of his own. And if my eldest brother was to stay, then Igor must too; one did not exist without the other. But Zlata claimed Boris and Igor were just as troubled as the boys who clung to their mothers' skirts. Instead of hiding from their monsters, they were fighting them.

"You will not convince them to go," I told her. I knew my brothers, their stubbornness. I had fought them for everything—the remote control, second helpings, the last word. They had refused to go to their new school in town; why would they ever say yes to this?

"We have our methods," Zlata explained. "We talk to them in their own language."

"Russian?"

"That's not what I meant."

So I told her. I explained the checks that Boris and Igor carried out on our apartment every morning in the belief they were saving us from further attacks. How it had gone too far, edged into lunacy. I only wanted to dent her clarity, warn her of the consequences.

"They flip our mattresses," I said, "thinking they're going to find something. They empty all the cabinets, unscrew every lightbulb. I come home some days to darkness. I have to grasp around for the bulbs they've left spinning on the tabletops."

Zlata nodded, taking it in; not surprised, not impressed.

"And have you seen the holes in our walls?" The plasterboard was shredded where the kitchen cabinets ended. "That's where Boris has punched his way through so he can poke a flashlight into the gap. He pulls out any suspicious wiring that might lead to a bomb. Half of our sockets are useless now."

More nodding. Still she could not see. So I told her how I had been pinned down on the floor that week because I'd made a joke about hiding things in my room and Boris had taken it as truth. The pain of his forearm heavy across my collarbone was nothing compared with the shock. This was no playful wrestle; I could barely breathe. Igor had stood and watched as I beat my legs against the floor, as Boris spat insults into my face. "Go on, try and punch me now, Dashka!" he'd said. "Go on! Give me your best shot!"

A terrible shame engulfed me then, for saying all this to Zlata. What kind of person condemns their own family to a total stranger?

"It's our own fault." I tried to make it good again. "I broke his nose and . . ." Worse! I was making it worse! I shut my mouth — or else I would start telling her how ugly my mother had looked as she'd goaded her sons to get guns and cross into Ingushetia, how my father was never there.

All quiet. Until Zlata said, "I know exactly what I'm dealing with, Darya. I went through 'Security' to get up here."

I thought of her differently then. If she had passed through Boris and Igor's border control in the downstairs lobby all alone and not been scared, then she was no wet hen. Everyone who entered the building had to answer Boris's questions and open their bags. Even Aslan tiptoed around them, finding so many other maintenance tasks more pressing than restoring order to the apartment block he supposedly managed.

Zlata put her jaw into the *sushka* again. Nothing hampered this girl's appetite. Nothing could amaze her. I could tell her anything, I thought, ask her anything.

When Zlata came back the next day to explain to Mama and Papa her proposal for the boys, I decided to follow her when she left. Her charity would be based in a makeshift office in some hall or back room somewhere — a mishmash of tables and chairs, piles of leaflets, boxes of supplies. These kinds of setups were all over town. I would find it, put my question to her, and cool, bold Zlata would not be fazed.

The meeting with my parents did not go well.

Mama was in favor of the scheme, echoing back Zlata's phrases as if they were her own personal insights: "It is clear we must consider where the boys' needs will be best met."

79

She wanted her hostile children as far away as possible — that was the subtext. She had a newfound standing in town to preserve. I wondered if she had thought of asking for me to be sent away too. *Go on, wish for it,* I thought as we sat around that table, *because you will only be helping me out.*

It was Papa who was unhappy. Wounded, I suspect. The boys' behavior was his fault — that's how he heard Zlata's words. So he told her that he would cure them. He would channel their fight into sports, into a regular job.

"*I* will find them something," he decreed. "At the factory. Something that requires a sweat and a focus." Papa thumped his fist on the table to emphasize each point. Sweat — *batz!* Focus — *batz!* It rattled the teacups. Zlata did not flinch. She put on one of her stupid smiles, but a smile that seemed to say this time, *I know more about this than you, Pavel Stanislavovich.* Then she proceeded to shred every one of his theories.

I put on a denim skirt and a bright pink top that morning, ready to follow Zlata once she left our apartment. All I needed to do was take off my head scarf and apron, put on a little lipstick and a jacket, then run. I hadn't worn that skirt and top for a while, and they were shorter and clingier than I remembered. *Or you have woken up bigger,* came Nika's voice as I examined myself in the mirror on our wardrobe door. Each time I thought that the pool of my grief had begun to calm, life would throw in a stone. The smallest, most unexpected things made the memory of her ripple and swell.

I left Mama and Papa sulking with each other in the kitchen. I slipped out of the apartment and headed down the stairs, listening to Zlata's sneakers scuffing just ahead of me. I paused, giving her a chance to get past "Security"; giving me a chance to toughen myself, ready to face Boris and Igor too. I zipped up my jacket, changed my mind, unzipped it again, my fumbling signaling my arrival. They all turned to watch as I stepped into the concrete lobby.

My brothers' border control consisted of two plastic chairs and a picnic table, taken from who knows where. It might have looked like a friendly information desk if not for Papa's gun laid ceremoniously on the tabletop, if not for the gang of boys missing all their manners. They sat on the disgusting floor, leaning back on their hands, reaching forward occasionally to flick ash at their shoes. Even Alana, the only girl in the gang, was sitting cross-legged on the floor. She counted out small somethings from one pot to another.

Boris lifted his feet off the desk at the sight of me, and pulled the black roll-neck sweater away from his mouth. One boy wolf-whistled, and the whole army cackled.

"Where are you off to, Dashka?" said my eldest brother.

"None of your business," I replied quietly, firmly. I thought of calling him Bor'ka in return but did not push my luck. I zipped up my jacket again and made for the doors of the apartment building. Boris's hand moved to the butt of his rifle. I walked faster, stepping over the sprawled-out legs of the army boys. Sleeping crocodiles. I had my eyes on the door, the flash of yellow anorak beyond, so I was on my hands and knees before I saw the boy lift a foot to trip me. I fell, my short-skirted backside in the air. The lobby exploded with laughter—

children's laughter—Boris's booming *hur-hur-hur* providing the bass. I scrambled to standing, and as I did, a kid much younger than Igor slapped the bare skin of my thigh.

I looked to Alana, hot tears in my eyes. I needed a friend. Really needed one. She paused from her counting, holding one of the small somethings between her fingertips. I could see what it was now: a bullet. She wasn't laughing. If it hadn't been me, could it have been her? Boris's gaze went in the same direction as mine, and Alana found some laughter quick enough then. They say a wolf won't eat a wolf, but it's best to be sure.

Suddenly, a new voice: "Darya Pavlovna!"

The laughter fell to a spatter. I turned with the whole army to see the man on the bottom stair. My New York journalist. My battery commander.

"Jonathan!" I said, throwing out a rope. "Good afternoon."

The army turned their heads from me to him and back again: a game of mesmerizing tennis. Their smiles went out, their mouths fell open. They were boys—all of them—and here was a man. I experienced a small buzz of power and understood, just for a moment, what Boris might get from behaving like he did.

"Good afternoon!" he replied, tension in his voice—and for very good reason. He knew what was going on here. He buffed his nose with the back of his hand—a considered gesture to make himself seem relaxed. "Just the person I wanted to see! Shall we?" He nodded toward the doors. The sea of sprawled-out legs shifted to let him through. What must you do for a New York journalist? Exactly this.

"See you later, Boris," I said. "Igor." Jonathan's hand went to my back, warm against my spine, guiding me past. I think I must have braced myself to feel a bullet in the neck, believing Boris just might do it, but not believing it either.

Instead came my brother's voice, low and threatening. "She charges twenty dollars per blow job, mate. I'll be after my cut later."

Jonathan winced. The army's laughter followed, a sound track added to a sitcom in an effort to make it funnier.

9

WASH MY BONES

Jonathan rolled up his sleeves to reveal tanned forearms feathered with blond hair. He drew on the whiteboard with a red pen — a brand-new board, a gift to the town, no doubt. It was nothing like the ones we'd had at school, stained with the murmurs of lessons before.

"*A house,*" Jonathan said in English, so exotic to our ears.

"*A house,*" we said back, feeling exotic in return.

He'd put up posters — FREE LESSONS! NO CHARGE! He pointed them out on our journey. I was not convinced. Who would believe they needed this in the circumstances? And also, that word: *free.* Does anything come without a price?

Three women were already there, waiting, sitting at desks. Women just like me. Older, much older, but still women with handfuls of time, I guessed, now that their loved ones were gone. I sat down and felt the charge of something unexpected. An opportunity regained. I had always wanted to learn, always enjoyed school—the lessons if not the playground. It was only caring for Nika that had kept me away.

Or perhaps what I felt as I took my seat in the Palace of Culture was fear. This was a reckless act, being lured by the glamour of a New York journalist, the firm set of his jaw, all those thoughts and experiences locked within. I was opening myself up to something, not knowing what would happen. Papa would see it as betrayal, joining in with this outsider. But Mama loomed larger in my mind. There is nothing left for me to lose, she'd said. And she was right.

"*A house,*" Jonathan declared with an upward inflection. The hand he'd been using to point at the picture was closed tight into a fist now and held to his solid, shirted chest. With a downward inflection, a greater significance, he said: "*My home.*"

We repeated those sounds and all they meant.

Jonathan and I had almost run from the apartment lobby after the encounter with Boris and Igor, Jonathan muttering, "Do you know those thugs?"

"Yes," I told him. "They're my brothers."

"Oh. I'm sorry. I didn't mean . . ."

"There's no need." We crossed the road, heading north. This was not the right direction to catch Zlata. I would have to get dressed up another day, follow her all over again.

"Well, you're very brave," Jonathan told me as we slowed our pace.

I wasn't brave—I knew that. There was nothing bold about cleaning a house to a threatening shine. Nothing tough about silence. *I am the hare that is scared of everything*, I told myself, and remembering the story only made me think of Nika. I reached out my fingers as if she might be there beside me and I could touch the crown of her head. What I wouldn't have given to work my fingers into her hair, rub the skin at her nape, one last time.

We passed the café not yet reopened, the iron-barred shop fronts and the muraled walls faded by the summer, washed light by the rain. Nadya and Olya were sitting on one of those walls, chewing gum. The sight of them was startling. They were alive, just as they had always been, their eyes following me as we passed. Until then, I had not known for sure that they were OK; I had never once asked. Yet all I could think of, seeing them again that first time, was how pleased I was for them to witness me striding through the town with this handsome outsider. The siege had changed everything and nothing at all.

"I should like to talk to you properly, Darya Pavlovna." Jonathan spoke louder once we were some distance from the apartment building. There seemed to be no air in my lungs; excitement had stolen it. I loved the way he said my name, used formal pronouns when we spoke. I think perhaps he was the first person not to make me small. "I would like to know more about your family," he said.

I shook my head. All those awful things I had said to Zlata about Boris and Igor. If I were to talk to anyone about my family again, I would make it up. Another fairy tale I knew by heart. *There once lived a beautiful girl named Vasilisa whose mother died when she was very young, leaving her a living doll to care for.* Take this doll with you everywhere, *said the mother,* and she will bring you solace . . .

"Perhaps I could make you a deal," he said. "Perhaps you'd let me write about you in my newspaper if I gave you something in return."

I didn't want anything from him. All the gifts we'd been given only filled me with guilt. So much stuff, and still I did not feel better.

"What do you say you give me some of your words"—he turned to me as he brokered this bargain, the skin creasing at his eyes, his smile genuine—"and I'll give you some words right back."

So I took my seat with those other women, and I tried to remember the English for *window* and *ceiling,* words I'd learned long ago at school but never used and had quickly forgotten. I didn't want Jonathan to be like all the other journalists, only after our stories. I wanted him to want me. I felt it sharp and sudden. I felt it as a pain. I wanted him to want me, story or not. So I took those lessons, I entered into our deal, but only because I was hoping for a different outcome. What do you do for a New York journalist? You fall for his charm from the start.

Beside the house, on the board, Jonathan drew a large square and divided it into smaller squares—a floor plan. In one of the rooms he drew a sofa and a television.

"*Living room,*" he said. The music of his American voice was engaging, so unapologetically positive.

"*Living room,*" we echoed.

87

Then he invited each of us up in turn to put objects in one of the squares.

A woman named Marina, with a split lip and a bruised neck—badges to say she'd been part of the siege—drew an oven and a saucepan in her square.

"*Kitchen*," we learned.

Another woman, Olga, intact but pale, came to the front and drew a bath and a shower.

"*Bathroom*," we said.

Luiza, though her good arm was in a cast, managed to draw a toilet, and she let herself, despite the seriousness of the lesson, giggle at its crookedness. "*Restroom*," we said. Then we couldn't help it either. We joined in with Luiza's laughter—a release of steam from a lidded pot. We were able to look one another in the eye after that.

My turn came when all the easy options, the safe options, were gone. I wrenched down my skirt as I stood. I had dressed to impress Zlata, the foreigner, not to be with the women of my town. They'd wash my bones after this. *Did you see how Anna Mikhailovna's daughter was dressed today? What does she think she's up to?* I went to the front and took the pen from Jonathan. I suppose I could have drawn objects to signify hallway. But what? My stick-figure father putting on his coat to escape? My mother fretting? My brother pinning me down on the floor?

I would not do *bedroom*. Two beds, one forever empty, piled up with gifts that would never be received. Marina, Olga, and Luiza shifted in their seats. We all had an empty bed, or an empty space in the bed next to us, where once there had been radiating heat. No one needed reminding. So I marked out a long, thin rectangle and filled it with wavy lines. I carried on — drawing a figure in the waves, her hair in two neat bunches. I see what I was doing now, giving all that water to one little girl. Jonathan looked confused as I handed back the pen. He stared at the board for a long and awkward moment.

"*Swimming pool?*" he offered eventually.

I mimed the front crawl. He watched, steady eyes on me. *Everything I do delights him,* I thought. I was the ballerina in my jewelry box, turning to a song.

He nodded. "*Yes, swimming pool.*"

I'd seen houses like this on television. Perhaps I would live in one just like it when I got myself to Moscow.

"*Swimming pool,*" I repeated proudly in English.

We allowed ourselves one more small giggle, because I'd saved us. From reality. From the cold and empty sheets.

At Zlata's next visit, it would happen — she would tell the boys that they were going to Moscow. No one had asked the question, *How will we get them to sit around the table?* Not me, not Mama, not Papa. We didn't have the spirit, and we certainly didn't have an answer. Still, Papa said he would take the morning off from the factory to be there for the summit.

"No, Pasha," said Mama. "You go." Not playing the martyr at all, though it was the perfect opportunity to do so. "They won't act so proud with you not here." But really we needed someone to return to the apartment afterward, unscathed, to report on what they found in the wreckage.

I put on the pink top and the denim skirt again, ready to follow Zlata when she left. I covered myself with an apron before leaving my room, convincing myself—fooling myself—that Mama could not see what I was wearing, that she would not get the back view at any time, my length of uncovered thigh, the slap mark still there from my fall in the lobby. Mama put on her new blue-flowered dress, and for an instant I feared Dmitriy Vasiliev would be joining us too, ready to flex his nonexistent muscles when the conversation got heated.

The doorbell rang, and Mama ushered me down the hall to answer it while she scuttled into the kitchen to heat water and to rearrange the chairs one last time. Zlata appeared as scheduled, with her clipboard, ponytail, and smile—and behind her was Igor, and behind him, Boris. I stood aside as they trailed down the hall and into our kitchen, this firebird in a yellow anorak, luring the young men of the village with a promise of riches. I followed after them, sharing a baffled look with Mama before we sat down to drink our tea. A moment of fleeting solidarity.

And the boys did exactly as Zlata predicted. It was astonishing. Mama and I had prepared ourselves to step up to the gallows—and here was our humiliating reprieve.

"OK," they said after Zlata laid out her offer. Boris first, of course, then Igor right after: "I'm in." They put down their weapons, just like that, just like Zlata had said they would. When she explained how the minibus would come for them the week after next to take them to the airport, they showed no resistance. Their shoulders noticeably dropped—soldiers released from a war they had never supported in the first place. And at the same time, I was free—free to follow Zlata when she left, no "Security" to pass through on my exit. Such lightness. Such a strange disappointment.

"Where's Igor?" asked Alana, loitering in the downstairs lobby, her pot of bullets hugged tight to her JUST YOU WAIT! T-shirt.

"Watching TV," I said, and the army of boys who had busied themselves with a boxing match in their leaders' absence, stopped squeaking their sneakers on the concrete. They watched me leave, dirty fists hanging by their sides.

10

IF I WERE A BIRD

I followed her to a block of apartments in the south, then sat smoking on a bench in an empty playground, hidden from the main door by a thorny bush, waiting for her to resurface. If Nika had been with me, she would have insisted I push her on the swing. I closed my eyes and let the swooping arc of the nicotine take over. I pictured Nika diving through the air, hands on the chains, hair in the wind.

When she emerged, Zlata walked a loop to one of the town's other schools. I went too, finding a wall to perch on outside, discovering then that I was not the only sleuth in town. As I waited, Alana sidled past in her too-long boy jeans and that JUST YOU WAIT! T-shirt, with its pipe-smoking wolf grinning at a hare.

"Whatcha doing?" she asked me, trying to sound casual, failing embarrassingly. She had ditched the bullets and was carrying a stick, using it to rake out soil from the cracks in the sidewalk.

"What are *you* doing, Lana?" I asked back. "You don't live at this end of town."

"Neither do you."

A standoff.

I jumped down, put my hands on her shoulders, and turned her around. Her ponytail had been bothering me ever since I'd seen her that day in the lobby. It was always lopsided, always spilling hair. I pulled the elastic free, making her yelp.

"Hold still!"

I took a comb from my handbag and worked through the knots. Her hair was greasy and gritty and in need of a wash, but I pulled the sides smooth with the edge of my palm.

"Doesn't your mother do this?"

Alana shook her head.

"Hold still, will you? How can I do it if you wriggle?"

I fastened her sandy hair back into its elastic, then held out my compact mirror so she could see the improvement.

"Pretty," I said, snatching it back. I needed to press more powder on top of my scar before Zlata saw me. Diana's words were forever there. *Such a very pretty girl. What a shame.*

"So, are we friends now?" Alana asked, twirling the stick—a clumsy drum majorette.

"It isn't like that," I told her, "when you're an adult."

"When who's an adult?"

"Me! I'm eighteen, you know."

"Oh, right." She poked the stick under a loose edge of rubber at the front of her sneaker. "How is it, then?"

"Oh, just get out of here, Lana, will you? I'm busy!"

She sighed, sidled away again.

93

* * *

I followed Zlata past the train station, beyond the shops, and through the gates of the white church, along the path beneath the beech trees. When I found her office, I would knock on the door and enter, confident and impressive with my suggestion of what her charity could do for me. So when she stopped dead beneath the trees and called out, "Darya Pavlovna, are you following me?" I was gripped by the desire to run.

I stood my ground. "No!" I called back. I shot a look over my shoulder and saw Alana and her stick skid into a side street.

"It's OK, sweetie," Zlata said. Her loris eyes were smiling. "I'm not angry."

I couldn't see why not. I was angry with Alana.

"Come in for a Coke." Zlata started for the back of the church. "You may as well, now that you're here."

They'd taken over one of the church's small stone side rooms. Icons looked down from the walls, their fingers raised in the air as if wanting to object to the tables piled with cardboard boxes.

"This is Vitaliy."

Zlata leaned over a broad-shouldered boy with white-blond hair, slouched in a chair. He was eating a packet of peanuts and reading a magazine, his yellow anorak tossed on the table in front of him. She kissed his cheek, and, as she did, she stole a handful of nuts. In return, Vitaliy kicked her on the backside.

"Fuck off, Zlats," he snapped, and Zlata let go of a peal of laughter, stuffing all of the peanuts into her chipmunk cheeks. I watched this whole exchange, mesmerized. They moved and spoke as easy as oil.

"Hey!" She toed Vitaliy's boots. "Offer Darya some nuts, you bozo."

Vitaliy put the packet under my nose, looked me up and down, his eyes settling on my thighs, the point where the skirt stopped and flesh started. I prodded at the powder on my scar, convinced it had caked off in one disgusting lump. I took a nut and chewed, waiting for it to release its special powers, making me as carefree as they were.

"Sit down, my petal!" Zlata shifted boxes off a chair and pulled a can of Coke from a huge flat pack, shoving it into my hand. Above me, the Virgin Mary looked with sorrow at the child on her lap—a child painted in the proportions of a doll-size human. In front of me, Zlata hummed the Fabrika song we'd been hearing all summer—the one about being a bird and flying to the regions to find a prince—shaking her hips in Vitaliy's direction.

"Bet you can't wait to get out of here," I said, laying my foundations.

Zlata ripped open the Velcro fastening of her bag, pulling out folders and forms.

"Oh, no. I'm really pleased to be here."

Vitaliy snorted.

"What? Oh, shut up!" she shot back. "I didn't say anything funny." Her expression was as guilty as when she'd mistaken me for my mother. "I'm not saying I'm pleased that this has happened here or anything. I'm not saying that."

"Oh, no, of course not," I said, to show that I wasn't offended, that I was on her side, but it was Vitaliy she needed to satisfy. He shook his head, smirked into his magazine.

"I mean," she said, "I'm pleased to be able to help. I mean, this is what I want to be doing. With my life. Helping people."

I nodded my support, sipped my Coke. It tasted too dark and sticky, different from the cans of the same drink in our own shops.

"Nearly all of the kids I've spoken to here want to be doctors or nurses or soldiers or firefighters now. They all want to be lifesavers. You've found that, haven't you, Vitalik, sweetie?"

Vitaliy did not reply. He continued chewing his peanuts. She sighed, turned back to me.

"Do you feel that way, Darya? Do you want to help others? Is that what you want to do with your life?"

"Umm . . ."

"Not that you have to feel that way, darling! It's OK not to feel that way!"

She started to riffle through papers, pretending to have moved on, saving me, or possibly herself. Her eyes darted to Vitaliy to see how she was doing in his opinion, a nervous skater waiting for her scores. He still wasn't interested.

"Actually," I said, "shall I tell you what I really want to do now, since the . . . ?" I never knew what to call it out loud: the siege, the disaster, the tragedy, the end.

"Sure, darling, why don't you go ahead?"

"I want to go to Moscow. With my brothers. Do you think you could get me there?"

She had said no. The scheme was for schoolchildren only. "You're too old, sweetie, too grown-up." But she'd spoken to me like I was a seven-year-old, someone who hadn't yet grasped that the world isn't flat.

"I don't want to go to *school* in Moscow," I explained. "I want to go there to work." The good blouse was clearer in my head, real. It had a bow at the neck, and those crystal buttons that hang from their threads like charms. I'd added a neat pencil skirt to the picture and a pair of glasses I did not need. I would remove them at the end of each day in a startling transformation.

"Aren't there lots more jobs here in the regions?" Zlata countered.

I shrugged. Maybe the world was flat after all. What did I know?

"Well, here's a job for you!" And she dropped a stack of brown envelopes into my lap. "Stuff these."

One leaflet showed the tree-lined forecourt of a college and well-dressed students walking purposefully. Another had a bundle of laughing children crowding the camera. As we worked, Zlata talked about herself—told me that, like Jonathan, she was an American. "Well, dual passport, actually." She said this proudly, looking to Vitaliy, a pure Russian, for a reaction but getting none. Zlata's father was from Volgograd. "So I grew up speaking Russian and English. I can see the world in both languages." And she had spent the last few years working for the charity in their UK offices. "Speaking an entirely different version of English altogether!" But for the most part, she had lived with her mother, an American, in Westport, Connecticut.

"They're not together, your mama and papa?"

Zlata made a face and jerked back her neck, as if the idea was ridiculous. "Of course not!" And the thought flitted through my mind—of course it did—that Mama and Papa might be better off without each other.

We headed home in the dark, Zlata locking their church office with a key so large it belonged in a fable.

"So why did you think, before, that I was Boris and Igor's mother?" Somehow in the moonlight it seemed safe to ask. I did need to know. Was the Earth flat or was it round? Was I destined to become a factory girl and marry Dmitriy Vasiliev after all? At least that would please my father. Perhaps he would be around more if Dmitriy was there.

Even in the dusk, I saw Zlata's cheeks bloom red. "I'm sorry I upset you, sweetheart." She started to jabber, more than usual. I had to concentrate. "I mustn't have looked at my notes properly, seen their ages, or I would have known that you couldn't possibly have been . . . Because today you look . . ." She waved a hand up and down the length of me, not finishing her sentence. Her thoughts on my outfit were the same as those of Marina, Olga, and Luiza, I suddenly saw, and I was doused with shame. "I'm not from here, you know that, so how would I understand if . . . I mean, girls as young as fourteen have babies in some places!"

Would Dmitriy and I have babies? They root you to a place, I think. Stop you from floating away, as I seemed to be.

"And, I dunno, when I was at your apartment, you just looked like you ran that ship."

I nodded. I was the captain. But still I wanted to jump overboard, if only to make the whole crew sorry.

* * *

When I got home, Dmitriy Vasiliev was in our kitchen. Fate had read my thoughts and was pulling me by the nose. He was drinking beer and eating a large plate of cold meat and black bread, made just for him. His skin was almost green under the fluorescent light. Mama sat across from him, supervising Dmitriy's every bite, checking for pleasure.

"Look who is here, Dashen'ka!" she cried as I came in, using the voice we put on for visitors, the one that suggested we were happy, a rich tapestry of shared jokes behind us. "Our Dima has come, hoping you would be here!"

"Good evening, Dmitriy Dimitrievich," I said. I would not call him *Dima*. I would not give in.

He stood as I entered—my possible future—wiping a stripe of crumby butter from his dimpled chin.

"Where is Papa?" I asked, filling a glass at the sink to wash the Coke from my teeth.

Mama ignored my question. "Our Dima has been lifting ten-by-ten racks of bottles all day." She almost squealed it. "Can you imagine, Dashen'ka? Without any assistance at all!"

Dmitriy looked down at his beer, then at me, his eyes as hopeful as a puppy's, his Adam's apple bobbing.

"Wow," I said, leaning against the kitchen cabinets. This was who Papa thought was good enough for his eldest daughter. His only daughter. I thought of the way Zlata gazed at Vitaliy, the longing. My eyes only went to that lump on Dmitriy's nose, imagining a lifetime striving to fall in love with an ugly piece of bone. Who had I ever loved the way Zlata loved Vitaliy? No one. Not even Kolya Galkin, from a distance, when he came back from university transformed. But then I thought of Jonathan. He was fascinated by me. I was fascinated by him. The thought of it made me swell so hot I was sure Dmitriy and my mama could see.

"I have been working too," I announced, startled into speaking. "For a charity."

Mama looked up, eyes narrowed. Dmitriy tried to empty his too-full mouth to ask a question. "And like you," I said, before he had a chance to swallow, "I am exhausted, so I must go to bed."

I headed out of the kitchen with my glass of water and my thoughts of Jonathan, and as I passed behind Dmitriy, I leaned over and stole a pickle from his plate.

11

A FISHERMAN KNOWS
A FISHERMAN

There was less than a week until my brothers left for Moscow. Less than a week to find a way to be with them on that flight. I kept a steady pressure on Zlata by taking lunch to them in their church office.

"You can't live on peanuts," I said, and Vitaliy in particular seemed grateful, gobbling up whatever I brought, leaving only the smallest scrap to show that he was satisfied. I tidied their mishmash of tables and boxes. I swept the floor and emptied the bins.

"Maybe I do want to help people now," I told Zlata.

"Hmm," she said, watching me work. "Maybe . . ."

She asked me to join her on house calls, the ones where she persuaded families to send their boys away. The ones where fathers rattled teacups.

"They might listen to a local person more than a foreigner," she said.

"You're half Russian," I reminded her.

"I could be all Russian and I still wouldn't be Ossetian."

"Then we're not so different, you and I."

I didn't want to go, have my bones washed all over again. *Anna Mikhailovna's daughter thinks she knows everything, telling us what to do with our children!* But I wanted Moscow more. I would not stay here, be the hare that was scared of everything for the rest of my life. I would corner Zlata with my helpfulness until she had no choice but to be my ticket out.

For one house call, we drove to a dacha beyond the edge of town in the charity's borrowed car. The temperature had dropped that day, and Zlata kept mentioning it, then apologizing, saying it was the way the English talked and that she had fallen into the habit. "Always about the weather, never about anything true."

"If I lived in Moscow," I told her, "I wouldn't care about the weather."

"I can't get you to Moscow, Dasha," she said, not taking her eyes from the road. "That's the end of the story."

The woman we were visiting had lost her nine-year-old son in the siege. Her eleven-year-old had survived, but his behavior had changed. He would disappear from the house for days, come home covered in bruises and cuts. The mother assumed he was fighting. She'd questioned him and they'd had an argument, the boy burning down the family's shed in fury. Its remains sat by the vegetable rows like sooty toothpicks. Yet still she was not convinced he should go.

"I have already lost one son," she told Zlata. "I will not lose another."

This would happen to me, I realized as she talked. I had lost my sister, and now I would lose my brothers. We had started watching TV together again since Zlata had given them permission to stop manning that front desk. We sat shoulder to shoulder on the sofa, passing our witty judgments on every person who crossed the screen. By persuading them to leave, I had gotten them back, but soon I would have to let them go.

"Why don't you explain the positive effects the decision has had on your family, Dasha?"

I sipped my tea, weak and yellow, and felt like a fraud. I didn't want my brothers to go — not if I wasn't able to go with them. But I played my part, tried to persuade the woman as she gave me her unblinking gaze.

"Oh, it's all right for you!" she said, erupting with anger when she could listen no more. I shrank back. "You only lost a sister. You have no idea what it feels like to lose a child! Your own child!"

I did not go with Zlata on any more house visits after that.

When I wasn't helping the charity, I was with Jonathan. I did not miss one of his daily morning lessons. He added a Thursday evening class, and I made that part of my routine too. I sat at the back, a little separate from the other women, who, when he was out of the room, had begun to whisper about how handsome he was. I was different from them. The words he gave us — those bright, shiny stones — they were just a new means for Jonathan and me to pass our fascination back and forth. He threw out a word; I would catch it, turn it over, examine it, feel the weight of it in my mouth — *sister; mother;*

How are you?; Where do you live?; Can you help?; I am lost — then throw it back in my own voice. His gaze was always on me, over the heads of the other women. It could have been just us, alone in that room, teaching each other about ourselves. That is how it felt.

Jonathan brought sheets of paper printed with line-drawn faces to one lesson — smiles and frowns, slanted eyebrows, and zigzag foreheads. One had a thermometer in its mouth and cheeks full of spots. He tacked them to the no-longer-pristine whiteboard, a measure of how far we'd come in a short space of time.

"*I am sad,*" he said, beginning with the frowning image, pulling his own mouth downward to match.

"*I am sad,*" we parroted back, slow and cautious. Was he mocking us?

"*I am angry,*" he said with a growl. We might have giggled, Marina, Olga, Luiza, and I, seeing Jonathan and a cartoon face with their eyebrows at exactly the same angle. But this was anger we were talking about, so we just copied the phrase. Zlata was right. You do see the world differently, feel it differently, when you speak in a different tongue. When we had said, all together, "*I am angry,*" the walls had feared us. We turned to look at one another, astonished at what had come from our mouths — from our guts.

Then came the face with a smile.

"*I am happy,*" said Jonathan, wearing one of his own stupid grins.

A pause. Again we thought he might be mocking us, and again I thought of Zlata, how she'd learned to talk about the weather while living in the UK. We'd learned it too, there in that room. *Today it is cloudy. Tomorrow it will be sunny. Maybe it will rain. Maybe it will snow.* A way to avoid talking about what you really felt. But there would be no more hiding. This was a promise I wanted to make.

"*I am happy,*" we said, only making the shapes with our lips. But inside of me, I could sense it — guiltily, secretly — the possibility that I could make it true. Or that at least Zlata could. Or Jonathan.

If he was going to stay in town, maybe I would stay too.

But I learned the true cost of Jonathan's "free" lessons soon enough. I sniffed out his motives. After all, a fisherman knows a fisherman from a mile off. He had always said he wanted a story from me, so of course he had asked for something from the other women as well.

I came back from Zlata and Vitaliy's church office one evening that week to see Luiza leaving our apartment building. Jonathan was there, seeing her out. I watched him put his hand on her good arm, heard him thank her twice, tenderly, as I approached the yellow flickering light of the doorway. He was incredibly handsome — the women were right — but now that fact made me feel sick. Something more than a story had passed between Jonathan and Luiza, I was sure of it.

"Darya Pavlovna!" Jonathan cheered as Luiza disappeared into the dark, no shame at being seen. He was playing with my name now, not showing me respect.

I watched Luiza go. She was definitely the prettiest of the four of us, and she had done her hair very special that night, curled at the sides. Luiza's arm may have been broken, but her face was clear—no scars like Marina or me, no sagging grief like Olga. She was dressed up in a way that wasn't necessary if she had come only to share her story. The person she had lost in the siege: her husband.

"What have you been up to this lovely warm evening?" Jonathan asked.

I could not look at him. I looked at the windows of Diana and Aslan's apartment instead, the lights off in the kitchen. Were they out visiting that evening? Had he been silently deciding which one of us he would invite over while his hosts were away? And if so, why had he not chosen me?

I replied in English, to show how hard I had been working on my side of our bargain. I wanted to break his heart in return.

"Yes, isn't the weather lovely and warm?" I said, spiky, the negative to express a positive. A question that doesn't need an answer.

"Well done," he replied, English first, then in Russian: "Well done."

He held the door open, and I kept my head down as I made for the stairwell so he would not see me cry. This was not a sadness that could be helped with his compassion. *Tomorrow,* I thought in the melodic English he had taught us, as my feet beat deadened steps on the concrete. *Tomorrow, there will be a storm.*

The following day at lunch, as Zlata, Vitaliy, and I blew on the *borsch* I'd made, divided into three bowls, I said, "Shall I tell you truly what the siege has made me want to do with my life?"

"I think I know the answer to this one, Dasha," Zlata said. Vitaliy grinned. They had been talking about me when I wasn't there. Laughing, probably. Silly local girl.

"You want to go to Moscow!" they said in unison.

"Very funny." I let their cackling settle, swallowed my frustration with my soup. "Let me tell you what I don't want, then."

"Go on." Zlata stabbed her fork into a cold cut from the platter on the table, rolling the pork to a cigar in her fingers.

"I don't want Papa to make me marry that idiot Dmitriy Vasiliev from his factory."

The fury in my voice was for my family and for them, but most of all it was for Jonathan, who I had thought was different, who I had thought was enthralled with me but was just the same as the others. I was invisible all over again. Completely invisible.

They both went quiet.

"You don't like him?" Zlata asked—the voice of an elderly aunt from out of town. "This Dmitriy? What? Not even for just a while?"

I made that face she made—neck jerked back.

"But you have to kiss a few frogs," Zlata went on, "before you find your prince."

I shook my head and set them straight. "No. I am the frog. The first one to kiss me turns me into a *prinsessa*." That was the way the fairy tale went. I wasn't sure what version Zlata had made up for herself.

"So, then what?" Zlata asked. She shared a look with Vitaliy, one she thought I could not read. "Do you live 'happily ever after'?"

Zlata didn't understand the shape of the world at all, round or flat. She had no grasp of how it managed to turn.

"No," I told her. "He kisses me. Then I am forever in his debt."

This was how it was played. There were two teams. Zlata chose. Young versus old. The little ones—boys mostly, with some stowaway girls—lined up with their backs against the wall by the parking area in front of the Palace of Culture, shielding their eyes from the last of the September sun. The older kids, the "bulldogs," arranged themselves in front. I joined in, Alana beside me, skipping from foot to foot like a goalkeeper preparing for a penalty shoot-out. Then there was Igor, bouncing off Alana's shoulder, and beside him Boris. This game, these group activities, they were all preparation for the trip to Moscow. Nonnegotiable. Boris made sure to demonstrate his irritation, though I knew that as soon as the game got going, my eldest brother would set his sights on a win.

"The aim of the game," Zlata bellowed, taking off her anorak and tying it around her waist, readying herself for action, "is for the little ones to make a dash for safety to the wall opposite. The bulldogs have to catch them, and absorb them into our team. Last kid standing wins. Got it?"

"Yeah!" we hollered back, our voices echoing off the smooth walls. I exchanged glances with my brothers—looks that said we were in this to be victors. A flash of happiness whipped past, so fast I almost missed it. Nika with a length of ribbon, pretending to be a gymnast.

"Right," said Zlata. "Go!"

The little ones were off, squealing, weaving around the

raised beds and the gullies, arms as propellers. Igor weaved with them, small and light, while Boris stood his ground and made himself into a wider boulder to pass. I watched Alana, up on her toes, snatching children left and right. Me—I could not move. I froze, my mind pitched back to another chase: small pink bodies, smoke in my throat, the warm knots of a bare spine, a girl at a gushing tap, the wrong girl, panic, horrible hope, sirens in my brain, my heart beating out of my neck—*tuc-tuc-tuc.* I reclaimed my limbs and I ran away, down the side of the building. Lost in the thrill of the game, no one noticed me go.

I collapsed on a ledge and lit a cigarette, smoked two or three, until my heart was racing for a real, solid reason, not because of ghosts. I listened to the screams of the game, tense and electric, unable to separate them from memories of something else. I stayed there until the voices thinned out and scattered. I thought I was alone. But then I heard Zlata, the up-down, fast-slow rhythm of her voice as she came around the corner with a dark-haired boy, their hands interlaced. A boy with a different colored anorak. Not Vitaliy. I was very still. Sparrows came to my feet to check that my ash wasn't better pickings.

"Oh, sweetie," I heard her say. "Oh, sweetie." And when the boy started to laugh at her soft words, she put her mouth on his and they stayed locked like that, working their jaws. Her hands were on his shoulders, his hands in her back jean pockets. When they finally parted, I saw the way she looked at him. Not like she looked at Vitaliy. This boy was a frog.

* * *

Boris and Igor left town days later to a round of stiff hugs from Mama and Papa and plenty of *you-be-good*s. We all sat down together in the living room for luck as you should before someone leaves, trying not to eye the camp beds, rolled up for the long term. Tears spilled down my cheeks in the silence, hot and fat. I was crying for them, and for Nika gone, and for Jonathan, who did not long for me the way I longed for him, but mostly I was crying for myself. This was supposed to be my way out too, but I had failed. I felt stupid for believing that I could have had anything more than this. People like me did not get that kind of luck.

"You can have my bike," said Igor. "If you want." He was scared by the way my back shook and my hands quivered. His thinking that the gift would make everything OK, the sweetness of the gesture, made me cry all the more.

We headed down to meet the minibus that would take them to the airport. Other boys were already fogging the windows when it pulled up at the curb, including some members of my brothers' platoon. Igor was jittery with excitement about flying for the first time. Boris was too — inside, not letting himself show it.

Alana came to wave them goodbye, pulling all the time at the pockets of her grubby jeans and at the tangled ends of her ponytail, which was lopsided and messy again. She wore her false casualness as best she could, pretending my brothers' departure was of no interest at all. Boris singled her out from the other ex-soldiers for a manly gang handshake that involved a slap of palms, a squeeze, and some pointing of fingers. For that alone, I believed my eldest brother would grow up to be all right, no matter what. The boys boarded the bus, and Alana stepped back, folding her arms behind her back, clutching at her elbows. When the engine started, she put her chin to her chest and tugged hair over her eyes. I wanted to give her a hug, if only because I needed one too. But I knew that she would have shaken me off because my brothers were watching, and she must always seem tough to them.

Mama wept, true tears, I think, into Papa's neck, until he took her by the shoulders and guided her back inside. Alana kicked her way home. She had a better chance of finding the right path now that the army had been disbanded. Or possibly she was at even more of a loss. No one was offering the girls a chance to escape. The surviving boys were heroes; the girls were just girls.

I was left on the pavement with Dmitriy Vasiliev, who had taken Mama and Papa's words to heart and started behaving like a member of the family, joining us for my brothers' farewell without invitation.

"Are you very sad, Dasha?" He approached me slowly, as if I were a feral cat who might not welcome his petting. But I knew I wasn't going to run. I took in the sight of his bobbing throat, his gangly limbs, that lumpy nose. Then his dark eyes, the neat mole that drew your attention to his lips.

"I am sad," I said in Russian first. Then, to see how it felt in English, I said it again: "*I am sad.*"

"Huh?" he said. "What did you say?"

"Nothing, Dmitriy Dmitrievich. Why don't you come with

me?" I took his hand and interlaced our fingers — the look on his face! — and I walked him around the side of the apartment building.

"I wish you would call me Dima," he bleated as we went, staring all the while at the impossibility of our hands.

"You're lucky I don't call you Ivan the Fool."

"Huh?" he said again. "Huh? Dasha, what did you say?"

"Oh, sweetie," I purred, once we were in the shadow of Aslan's shed. I closed my eyes and tried out Zlata's words again: "Oh, sweetie." Then I put my lips on his. There was his tongue, in my mouth, minty and not completely awful.

12

LYUBOV

My brothers gone, the house was quiet. I had no ticket out. This was my lot.

One evening as I did the dishes, while Mama was in the living room stitching her part in a memorial quilt, I asked Papa, "So, what now?" He was all I had left, and I needed an answer.

He did not put down his paper or remove his glasses so that he might see me clearer.

"What are we supposed to do, Papa?" I said, and the desperation in my voice forced him to answer.

"About what?" was his reply.

I turned to look at him shifting the paper closer to his face, then farther away, helping his glasses to do their work, not really listening to me at all. There was a chasm between us now, so deep and black it made me breathless every time I caught sight of it.

"About what?" he asked again, looking up this time.

About what? That he had to ask. . . . He was back at the start, the world not shifted at all. We had buried my sister and solved my brothers' problems. Mama was cured and my husband was chosen. Papa could throw on his jacket in the evenings and disappear to wherever he went, believing he had life all figured out.

"Nothing, Papa," I said. "Nothing." And ten minutes later, he was putting on that jacket and going, satisfied, into the night.

Cooking was my distraction. I no longer used it as a threat. It was a desperate act of love. The last child standing, but still I did not have my parents' attention. I worked harder. What else could I do? The mornings I spent dismembering skinny chickens, arranging the pieces in marinades of celery, onion, and garlic, leaving them for hours in the fridge. I'd set cheap cuts of beef to stew on the stove with coriander and walnuts and tomatoes. I fried up batches of *bitochki* with cabbage, ready to warm in the oven later.

Mama would come in and fuss before she headed out to one of her mothers' groups. She would scold me for spilled flour or suggest better methods for slicing. This wasn't the attention I was seeking; I met it with silence. Though if she tried to sweep my carrot ends and herb stalks into the garbage, I'd bark at her to stop: "There's stock to be had from them yet!"

She would sigh in return. "Oh, it's all so heavy," she'd say, "these things you cook!" as she knotted her head scarf and tied the belt of her coat around her expanding middle. Then as she trailed away, she'd tell me that she had inherited her grandmother's European stomach so I should only make a peck for her.

One morning, as bread rose in the oven, I stood on our

balcony to smoke. I did it as a test. I could be that brave hare. I could change. I would have to if my parents insisted on staying the same. Still, I tilted my face to the sun, away from the burned-out gym below. I listened to the birds, the way they called to one another in the trees — sharing knowledge, arguing their differences, making a date. I looked back through the glass and caught Mama bending over the stove, lifting the lid on the beef *kharcho* that was bubbling down. She dipped in her spoon and took a taste, closing her eyes in a kind of bliss.

"Good, isn't it?" I called through the open door. She dropped the spoon with a clatter and clutched at her breast. I laughed as loud as a slap to the back. She would never have thought I would dare to do this — go out on that balcony. I felt very powerful. Yet she edged out to join me, proving herself in return, keeping her eyes fixed on our stores of food, not on any possible horrors beyond. She wore a face that said she was too old, too sad, to find anything funny anymore, and that I should be ashamed for laughing.

"This needs to last us all winter," she said, poking a toe at the jars.

"I know."

I had eked them out the seven winters before, stood sweating in the kitchen with Papa that long weekend in the summer, turning all the fruit to jam.

"We can't be handing it out to whoever comes knocking." This meant Zlata and Vitaliy. She knew that I cooked lunch for them and we ate what remained for tea. Eat breakfast alone, dinner with friends and supper with the enemy.

"Well, you'd better have a word with Dmitriy Dmitrievich,

then," I told her, heading back inside to check on the bread. "Get him on to that gymnast's diet."

Mama did not know about any kissing. I did not consider it real or meaningful myself. The days after my brothers left, I drifted toward Dmitriy, meeting him when his shifts at the factory were over, but only on the days when he finished after dark. I was torn between letting my father see (to make him happy, to bring him back) and hiding Dmitriy away, not wanting to make Papa's hopes lift. Dmitriy was still a frog. Zlata would not get me to Moscow, so I would regain my strength, then get that desk in the capital, that blouse, those exotic friends pulled from the shows on television. I would not be a wife just because someone told me to. But for the time being, Dmitriy and I walked, and I let him boast.

I plan to rise through the ranks, Dasha. I'm the hardest worker at the factory by far.

We have the most boys of all the families in the town. My sister has four sons already!

Mama always manages to keep our apartment special, no matter how little we have.

What, compared to our pigsty, Dmitriy Dimitrievich?

That's not what I said, Dashen'ka. Why won't you let me say anything nice?

One evening, we went to the playground I'd hidden in when chasing Zlata, and Dmitriy pushed me on a swing. I felt happy, I think, at the real swooping arc, at the solid contact of his hands on my back. Alana slipped past, taking us by surprise in the dark.

"Whatcha doing?"

I leaped from the swing, embarrassed for behaving like a child. I was an adult, or so I had lectured her.

"Grown-ups' stuff," said Dmitriy with a grin, and he pulled me to him and tipped me backward, kissing me like they do in the old films, sending Alana running, yelling "Yuck" and "Gross" into the night air. The whole scene—the slickness of Dmitriy's response, Alana's repulsion—made me laugh so hysterically, I couldn't catch my breath.

"What's so funny?" Dmitriy kept asking. "Stand up straight, Dasha! Your face is turning blue."

We huddled on a bench for hours after that, and I drank up his touch like a cup of something warm. That was all it was. Touch. Anybody's touch. I was so horribly lonely.

"You are beautiful, my Dashutka, I cannot take my eyes off you." He covered my face with pecks, squeezing me close to him.

"Be quiet," I said. "I have a terrible scar. So that's nonsense."

He took my head in his hands and stroked a thumb over the damage above my left eye.

"Well, I've had this terrible nose all my life, so I'm not sure what you have to complain about!" He snorted and grinned, expected me to as well, but I buried my guilty face into his shoulder. He had taken away all my weapons. If I couldn't think of him as ugly without his knowing, how could he be a true frog?

"I know why you always want to meet in the dark, Darya Pavlovna," he went on, teasing me. "This is a difficult face to love."

I still took food to Zlata and Vitaliy. While I'd been busy scheming, they had become my friends. The day after Dmitriy stroked my scar and made me care, as we chewed chicken off the bone, Vitaliy asked, "So? You fucked him yet?"

I almost choked.

"Excuse me, Vitaliy Ivanovich!" Zlata cried, placing her drumstick down very deliberately, very delicately, on the plate in her lap. But Vitaliy wasn't talking to me. This was all for Zlata.

"Ah, don't give me that, *prinsessa*! If you like the ride, you've got to carry the sled." Vitaliy continued chewing, mouth open on purpose, acting like a barbarian.

"What!"

"You must have shown him your 'dual passport' by now, Zlatka. Volodya isn't one to hang around."

"What's it to you?" Zlata said, her voice level. This wasn't wit. Vitaliy stopped eating, and their eyes locked. I thought he might toss his chicken bone across the room, grab Zlata, and throw her over his shoulder. I held my breath.

You see, when I was younger, I had imagined my wedding, not obsessively, not with any strong desire, just with an understanding that it was my fate. Now that the idea was becoming more real, it was somehow more unfathomable. I only knew the actions, the dances. I'd learned those when we came to town. I'd practiced a Lezginka with my friends in those easy, playful days before Nika was born, perfecting the movement of my feet so it looked as though they weren't moving at all. I gave my palms to the sky, twisted my wrists, lifted my chin, cast my eyes down, so everyone knew I was untouchable. We would take it in turns, my friends and I, to be the man—the eagle—jumping, high-kicking, landing hard on our knees to impress our bride. But what of emotion? What part did the heart play? No one had taught me that. The magazines said you must be in love, but that was no help. Because what did love look like? What did it feel like?

Like this, I decided—the fire about to ignite between Zlata and Vitaliy.

He broke the spell, taking his paper plate and chewed-up bones and dropping them into the trash. He grabbed his anorak and stomped away to an important something he hadn't mentioned before. Zlata looked down at the remainder of her food with a small, victorious smile.

"And how are you and Dmitriy Vasiliev getting on?" she asked. "I saw you two kissing in the park."

I flushed with heat. "Oh, that! That's just . . ."

"Practice?" she said, raising her eyebrow the way she had that first day we'd met, as if we were sharing a secret over the tea.

I nodded. It wasn't real love with Dmitriy, because it wasn't like her and Vitaliy. "So," Zlata asked, picking up her bone, "when shall we move on to the real thing?"

He had had his hair cut, short on top. His neck was shaved, the skin neat and oiled. Walking into class, I considered putting a hand to it, stroking the downward growth. How brave would I have to become before I would dare to do that?

"*Good morning, Jonathan,*" I said in clear, precise English. A call to arms. I got that steady gaze of his, the thoughtful jaw. I took a seat very close to Luiza.

This was the class when we were given workbooks—lovely thick, heavy things with geometric patterns on the cover.

Jonathan burst them free of their cellophane wrappers, and we cooed as we each took one to sniff and stroke.

"Write your names inside," he said.

"You mean they're ours? To keep?"

He laughed at my excitement, and I felt it again, there for me to reclaim—my ability to be delightful.

Of all the gifts that had been dropped on us since the siege, the workbook was the best. I felt a whip-snap of happiness as I held it in my hands, fresh and untouched—that gymnast's ribbon again, bright against the gloom. I was used to getting books with their spines cracked and margins already filled with other people's notes, random offerings that were only sometimes wonderful—stories of romance, rescue, and hareskin coats. When Yelena got back from Germany, I couldn't wait to show her what I had been given. I thanked Jonathan more than Luiza did, to show that I was the one who appreciated this most—appreciated him most. I watched Luiza caress her hair to draw his attention back, and I saw how it failed.

We'd gone beyond the basics, Jonathan explained: we needed help. *He* needed help. We turned to a chapter that explained the verb *to have*—an astonishing idea. In English you are able, at least with the strength of your words, to own something outright. It isn't just *with* you or *at* you, only for a while. There were things I wanted so very badly, and English would give them to me. They'd be mine. Only mine.

"Isn't it greedy to say it this way?" asked Marina, tutting and sighing.

"Probably." Jonathan laughed. "But that's us Americans for you!"

The exercise in the book asked us to talk about our families. *Do you have a husband? Have you got a sister?* We all took a deep breath, Jonathan gently offering us the past tense whenever it was needed. *I had a husband. I had a son.* A haunting confessional.

When it came to my turn, Jonathan stopped me midphrase: "Remember that *you* are the subject of the sentence, Darya Pavlovna, not your sister."

The lesson over, Jonathan came to my desk, smiling. Though we had been forced to take stock of our families, the class had taken a lighter turn when we moved on to owning animals. The phrase "Have you ever had a dog?" made us squeal with horror. Such a rude suggestion!—if translated directly in the wrong tone of voice.

I flicked my hair from my shoulders and raised my chin, ready for whatever he had to say, ready to delight him if he gave me the chance.

"I hear congratulations are in order!" he said.

"Sorry?"

"*You have a fiancé!*" He said it in English. The smile, I could see now, was not reaching his eyes. There was a question mark to his voice. I took this new, bright stone from the end of Jonathan's sentence and turned it around and around, over and up.

"*Fiancé?*"

"The other ladies tell me you are engaged to be married." He furrowed his brow. "Is that right?"

I looked at my three classmates out the window, walking away from the Palace, new books clutched to their chests. I cursed Luiza for the game she was playing. Like Zlata, she must have seen me kissing Dmitriy, but unlike Zlata, she had leaped, assumed. With good reason of course; there is a proper order to things. Unless you choose to abstain from it . . . Zlata confessed, out of earshot of Vitaliy, that she had had sex with Volodya. She liked him enough for now.

Or had Mama and Papa assumed? Had they been telling everyone their daughter was marrying? I should have been furious, but I could see that I had been handed a gift. Jonathan did not look happy about the news. Could he even be jealous?

I shook my head. "Oh, no, I'm not engaged!" I gave him a smile that reached all the way to my eyes. "Grandmothers telling fortunes always say two things."

The dress I had worn to dig Nika's grave, I rescued. I had let the mud set completely, then scraped it away with the edge of a spoon before rubbing in liquid soap and attacking it with a soft-bristled brush. Only when I had checked every inch for stains did I let it dry.

"What do you think, Nika?" I said, putting it on in front of our mirror, arranging my locket neatly in the neckline. "Good as new."

I'd taken Mama's hardly used curling iron and done my hair in waves around my face to make it look glamorous, copying a picture in one of my magazines. I did it to distract from my scar. *It'll heal before your wedding*—that's what I used to say to Nika when she fell and bloodied her knee. *You'll live!* This scar would never heal. It would always be there—a silvery worm of a reminder—but Dmitriy had made me believe I could be beautiful regardless. Perhaps.

The curling iron had smoked with dust as it warmed, and it left a burned smell in my hair. I picked through the apartment in search of perfume but could only find a truly ancient bottle of Red Moscow. Still, I dabbed it around my ears. It was a smell that made me think of Saratov, a place I couldn't remember with any of my other senses.

You are Vasilisa the Beautiful! I imagined Nika saying, lying in her bed of gifts.

"No," I said out loud. "I am the hare that is scared of nothing."

Diana opened the door. This I had not prepared for.

"Look at you!" she cried. "Your mother has done something very unusual to your hair!"

I swallowed my tongue.

"Is the New York journalist at home?" I asked. "I have an important message for him."

"Oh, yes, he's here. But he's very busy." The frown did not mask her enjoyment of her role—obdurate secretary. "He works so hard that it really cannot be good for him. Your message will need to be very urgent. I have been asked not to interrupt him, not even for tea." *Poor Jonathan,* I thought. A chatterbox must be a treasure for a journalist, just as it is for a spy, if only she had something worth listening to.

"I assure you, Diana Petrovna, my message is of the utmost importance."

I was bustled into the living room. Jonathan was sitting just as I'd seen him the day I came asking Aslan for a shovel—in the armchair, hunched over a laptop. The TV had been moved into this room, and his eyes were on the news crawl running beneath the images—people searching through the remains of another disaster, wading through floodwater.

He took in the sight of me in the dress, my hair fixed, and said nothing. He did not need to. We could light a fire, just like Zlata and Vitaliy. We could burn this place to the ground.

"I'll fetch tea!" Diana said, an uncontrollable reflex. She walked backward from the room, as if Jonathan might strike her down should she turn away, and was soon back, fussing with the pot, clattering the cups, telling us exactly who she'd seen that morning while collecting her pension. "Vera Yankova is still not coping well. Such a poor duck! Crying in the post office! But little Syoma Alpakov's neck doesn't look half as awful as you'd expect now the bandage is off, though he won't be growing up to be a handsome *tsarevich*, if you get my meaning. Not that he was going to anyway. Just take a look at his father!"

"Thank you, Diana Petrovna," Jonathan said.

"And Lyubov Kapralova was talking about your father again," Diana continued, a burst dam. "I think that young woman has ideas."

"Lyubov?" I said, peeling my gaze away from Jonathan. "Ideas?"

"Who is she to your family? A relative?"

I had never heard of the woman, and Diana did not wait for my answer.

"She knows far too much of your father's thinkings and likings, if you ask me." She folded her arms beneath her breasts. "Or rather, she does not know to keep them to herself. He visits her most evenings, she says, to help with the grief. His or hers, it isn't clear, but—"

"Thank you, Diana Petrovna," Jonathan said again. "You have been very kind, but you can leave us now." She nodded proudly, taking Jonathan's words as a compliment, and moved off to the kitchen.

He watched my face and everything that must have played across it. I watched his—those compassionate eyes, a willingness to wait.

I had known, of course, but had not let myself think it. Papa was all that remained, though he had been slipping, slipping, gently from my grasp. I saw his forehead fall against that woman's, saw him throw on a coat in the hallway and tell his Anya, his sweet Anechka, that she worries too much. I saw the long, limp hair and blue eye shadow of that skittish woman at our door, asking for Pasha. I had felt sorry for her. She was deluded, I had told myself, if she believed a moment of tenderness at the height of the siege was anything more than kindness.

But it had always been there within me, the understanding, buried deep. The question that had stuck in my throat the evening I had asked Papa what we were supposed to do next: *Tell me, what is her name?*

Lyubov. In English it translates as *love*.

13

AN EXTRA FINGER

He watched me cry, holding my hand, his fingers tanned and soft, the nails so clean. And then I asked him what he wanted from me.

"The whole Megillah," he'd replied. "Tell me everything."

But that was too much.

There once lived a girl named Darya Pavlovna who was not exactly beautiful. Or perhaps she was. Darya simply hadn't had the chance to find out. Her mother did not die when she was very young, though her heart did stop in another way. The girl was left with a doll to care for—a special doll, with special gifts. Love this doll, she was told; feed it and keep it with you at all times, and though you are busy loving and feeding and keeping yourself, this doll will bring you solace. . . .

It was my story, but not my story. I told it to Jonathan as if I were reading to Nika. It was easier that way, to describe a life populated by *tsars* and spirits, fools and wolves, than to explain the one I had lived. Vasilisa outwits her relatives and

Baba Yaga, meets three princes in red, white, and black who serve her well, and finds love.

But Jonathan was well trained at this—finding the story hiding beneath the story.

"So, tell me . . ." is how he started each sentence, every one a gentle nudge, pushing me toward the truth. The truth as I saw it.

So I chose another tale.

There once was a little hare who was scared of everything— the wails of the wind, the coming of the night, the long grass, the short grass and the murmuration of the birds. She had always feared the arrival of the wolf, but had never imagined a wolf as big as this. . . . She would have to jump so high to get away and did not know if her back legs, though they were strong, were up to the task.

He wrote it all down. We kept going until the tea was gone, until he said that we were done. My story was not finished, but we had to leave it somewhere. He picked up his phone to call a photographer he knew who was working in the area.

"Oh, no," I told him. "I'm not being photographed."

"Why ever not, Darya Pavlovna?"

Because then it really would be me, I thought, *telling this story, living this story.*

"You must," he said, "when you are looking so beautiful today."

She was a woman—that was surprising to me. She was tall and masculine but not robust enough to handle Diana's verbal tide when she arrived at the door. Or at least she did not have enough Russian to escape. We went into the hallway to save her.

127

"This is Hope," Jonathan said, and the women held up the palm of her hand as hello. Her face was hard. She had been taking pictures of corpses all month, I presumed. Would I make a pleasant exception, or did she prefer the pliable dead? *"Hope* is like the Russian name *Nadezdha,"* Jonathan explained, and I thought of Vera, crying in the post office, Lyubov, whom my father loved as a dog loves a stick. Vera, Nadezdha, and Lyubov. *Faith, Hope,* and *Love.* The three virtues. What did a name mean, anyway? I was supposed to be regal if *Darya* was ever to be believed, and in those photographs, I was far from that. Hope placed me against the wall of the apartment's concrete lobby, next to crude graffiti and flaking doors.

"It's not pretty here," I said.

"Nope," she replied, like this was something good.

They peered together into the back of the camera because the photos could be seen there, right away—no need for developing. They spoke to each other in English. I pulled out the odd bright stone—*dark, light, more*—but the whole thing did not come to me with any sense.

"Let's walk over to the gym," Jonathan suggested, as lightly as a drive to the mountains. He leaned in to entice me.

I shook my head. No way.

"But we need to tell the story."

"I've told the story," I said. Two stories—what more did he want? I felt that horrible panic again, like the day we'd played Bulldog, my heart beating out of my neck. Hope angled a hip, chewed her cheek, waiting for Jonathan to persuade me.

"We could go onto our balcony," I said, the words spilling from my mouth before I could think them through. I needed to please him. I was close to getting what I wanted. I couldn't spoil things now. "You can see the gym from there."

I let them in, took them through my kitchen, watched them cast their heads this way and that, just as Zlata had done the first time she'd visited. I had a very clear understanding in that moment that our kitchen did not look anything like a New York kitchen and that all the details of it would end up in the article as proof of something. And they were proof of something. I could see it now, framed as though through the lens of a camera. I was no prisoner in this town. I had made a prisoner of myself. Baking bread, stewing beef, feeding a family who would never feed me back. Mopping the floors, kissing the boy chosen to take me away, lists of excuses. All I had ever wanted when Nika was with me was my freedom, but how much easier it was to complain about being trapped than it was to be set free. By staying still, I was running scared. I would only turn into my mother, sick in bed at life's disappointments.

We went outside. I let the sun bleach my thoughts. I had the urge to pick up each one of those jars on the pallets and throw them over the railings, let them explode like bombs.

"Very good," said Hope, "very good," as I stared down her camera. People in other countries believe that having their photograph taken removes a part of their soul. I handed mine over willingly.

"So what happens now?" I asked Jonathan after he had said goodbye to Hope, as I walked him to the front door.

"What do you mean?" he replied.

We were inches from each other, and I could smell him, the muskiness of some scent he was wearing.

"What are we supposed to do now?" I pressed, my voice just breath. My father had not had an answer for this question. I had been asking the wrong person.

"I file my copy," he said. "I go to Moscow on Friday, after the 40th Day vigils."

"Moscow?" The word was like a bullet, a firework, or a spoonful of jam.

He took my hand and squeezed it. He had touched me like this before, but now it was different.

"That's my usual beat," he said. "Kremlin nonsense."

I was gripped by two things at once: the awful dread that he was going—another person leaving, another, another, another, that constant echo. But also the kick, the possibility, a new sky widening. Moscow. Fate was leaving a fresh trail. *Follow me, little girl, into the forest. Be brave.* I thought I would be willing to stay if Jonathan was here, but if he was to leave . . .

I went up onto my toes in the hallway of our apartment, the hallway I had walked across so many mornings, my finger casually linked with Nika's, the place where my father made his excuses to leave us every evening, the route my mother had traced when she was but a ghost, a place where I had both joked with my brothers and fought off their violence, and in that space I made a grasp at love. What must you do for a New York journalist? This. I kissed Jonathan on the mouth, the contact sweet and desperate. I pushed in my tongue and he pushed his back. He grasped at me too, pulling me close, and just when I thought there was no more fascination, no more delight greater than this, he was stumbling backward, shaking his head.

"*No!*" he said in English. It was for him as it is for me — the first language always fires to the surface when there is too much passion or too much pain. "What are you doing?" he asked me. Or maybe he was asking himself. He wiped the kiss from his mouth. His face was white. I am sure my face was red.

"Didn't you do this with Luiza?" I said.

"Of course I didn't!" And I took this answer as a reason to close the gap between us.

"I love you," I told him, carried away with my new strength.

"No, you don't, Dasha. No. You've got that all wrong, and I'm sorry if I —"

"And I want you to take me to Moscow with you."

"No."

"I have given you everything. Everything you asked for . . ."

"No."

"You have to! I need to go! I have nothing here! Nothing!"

He edged away from me toward the door, not turning first. Perhaps I also had the power to strike a person down if they put their back to me, so he didn't dare.

"I do love you," I told him. I went to place my hands on his chest, just the way I had practiced with Dmitriy Vasiliev.

"You can't, Dasha! I have a daughter and —"

"A daughter?" I stopped, hands raised, paddles that might restart a heart. In class, Jonathan had not spoken about a family of his own. This omission now felt like a lie.

"Almost the same age as you. A few years off, but . . ."

"But . . . ?" I didn't understand. "You have a wife?"

He shook his head. "We were both young and —"

"Where is she? Your daughter."

"New York."

Of course she was, I thought. Why would she ever be here?

Jonathan took advantage of that pause, my moment of doubt. He opened the door and left.

At our English lesson that evening, we talked about age. If it had not been the next chapter in the book, I would have thought Jonathan had planned it, to prove a point—to me, and to himself. He did not expect me to be there. He thought I would run scared. But that wasn't what I did anymore. I had nothing to lose. Absolutely nothing. It was not possible to break something that was already in pieces. I came back to be ground to dust.

"I am eighteen," I learned to say. *"On my next birthday, in July, I will be nineteen."*

The book asked us to arrange ourselves in a line according to age and then talk about where we were positioned.

Olga started: *"I am the eldest."*

Then Marina: *"I am the second eldest."*

Then Luiza: *"I am the second youngest."*

My turn: *"I am the youngest."*

I did not feel it. I had seen enough to age me ten years, twenty, thirty.

"Where do you stand?" I asked Jonathan, but he was avoiding my gaze now, pretending not to hear whenever I spoke. What was the point of being brave if those around you wouldn't join in? I stormed from that room at the end of the class, not giving him the satisfaction of seeing me loiter. I strode through the dusk, wishing the distance home was longer so that I might build up a sweat. In the night came a voice as I passed the guts of the school.

"Dasha! Dasha!"

I made a sharp left at the garages where I'd seen Papa and Lyubov standing, foreheads touching. It was Dmitriy who was on my tail, but I wouldn't slow down for him, dying light or no. He'd be sorry if he caught up with me.

"Dasha! Wait up!" His voice was spun sugar. "What have you got there, my *zaychik*?"

"Don't call me that!" I spat it at him. I kept walking. "Shouldn't you be at the factory?"

"I've had the whole day off. I'm working the weekend."

"Good for you!"

He jogged to catch up and took hold of the book in my hand.

"I'll carry that. It looks heavy."

I let go of it, like a relay baton, not pausing, not altering my speed. We continued this way, walking fast, side by side, breathing hard all the way to the apartments. A race of some kind; a desire to win.

"Hey, Dasha. What's going on?" said Dmitriy as we neared the doors. His voice was all borrowed soap. It didn't suit him, acting smooth. "Let's slow down. Let's talk."

I called him on it, stopped dead, stared cold into his sad dog eyes.

"Go on, then. Talk."

He searched my face for a glimmer of warmth. *Anything? Anything?* I put my hands on my hips. "Go on," I said. "I'm busy right now, Dmitriy Dmitrievich. What is it that you want?"

"Well," he said, gentle, confused, the charm falling from his shoulders like a suit he couldn't make fit. "I want you, Darya Pavlovna. You know that."

I had asked to see his hand, and he was holding aces. The boy was nice. He liked me. He wasn't showing interest to please Papa, or if that was how his interest had started, he now believed in it. And maybe he would make a lovely husband. There was an evenness to his skin, a dewiness. That lump on his nose, it made him vulnerable; I could have grown used to it, grown to love it. Perhaps I already had.

But no. I would not. Could not. I refused to be just another bottle on my father's conveyor belt. I would destroy everything he put in my path.

I took hold of Dmitriy's hand just as I had the day my brothers left. I dragged him toward Aslan's shed, but farther this time, into the recess behind — a passage of maybe just a meter wide. I yanked the book from Dmitriy's hand and tossed it into the weeds. Then I edged backward into the alley, Dmitriy in tow.

Into the muck we went, into the filth, my hair collecting dried leaves and spiders' webs. He kept on asking questions. "What are you doing, my Dashen'ka? Where are we going? Are you feeling crazy?"

So I pushed my face into his to make him be quiet. He smelled clean, powdery, male. He kissed me back with his hands on my waist, so I grabbed his bony wrists and forced them upward toward my chest. This gave him new force. He squeezed. He licked my face. We stumbled backward over concrete blocks and broken broom handles until my backside was against a brick ledge. He pulled at the buttons of my dress.

He made a weird noise—not really a grunt, not quite a moan. The starlings were screeching in the trees above, getting ready to curl into the sky like smoke, sending their warning signals that no one ever heeded.

I felt strong, violent. I had made Dmitriy go this far and now he would not be able to stop. I put my hand between his legs, reached for the hardness I knew would be there. He pulled his lips away, closed his eyes, readjusted something in his mind, as if he wanted to step back. So I undid his belt buckle, popped the fastenings of his jeans to bring him forward. He lifted me up onto the brick ledge, got himself a better purchase. He shoved up my skirt and ripped at my underpants and entered me. The pain was indescribable, unrecognizable. I cried out, but I did not wrench away.

"Go on," I growled. "Go on, then."

"I don't want to hurt you," he whimpered, feeble, useless.

"Go on," I said. So he went at me harder, and I pulled his hair and bit down on his shoulder and thought about how sorry I felt for him and how I might love him so hard if I did not hate him, truly hate him, for making me feel the way I did. He gasped and pulled free of me, firing a hot, horrible stickiness down my legs. I looked down and saw that there was blood, my blood. I slipped down from the brick ledge before he could kiss me again, wiped myself clean with my skirt. I pushed past Dmitriy, his trousers around his ankles, and I collected my poor book from the weeds.

"Don't you tell anyone about this," I hissed, pointing a finger. "Don't you ever dare." And even in the face of that, Dmitriy was smiling; a loyal dog no matter how hard you kicked.

I ran back to the front of the apartment building, crying and crying. The book in my hands was smeared with mud, no longer any different from all the others I'd been given. Ruined. I held it over the garbage can by the front path. I wouldn't go back to Jonathan's lessons anymore. There was nothing for me there. What was the point of learning a third language in a town like this? It was a stupid luxury. An extra finger. And I would have dropped that book into the can if an unfamiliar vehicle had not pulled up — shiny and new, like the ones in magazine ads. It was an odd shape: half car, half van. The face in the front passenger seat — Yelena. She had been gone for weeks. And there she was again, with a new short haircut all the way from Germany. I moved closer and watched the car come to a stop with its hazard lights flashing. Yelena and the driver got out and went straight to the back doors, where the driver flipped down a ramp and started a motor that was noisy in the night.

Something heavy needed to be lifted from the vehicle, and as I clutched my dirty book to my chest, tears still running down my cheeks, I knew exactly what it would be. It was a wheelchair. And inside it was Polin'ka, missing one of her legs. I could not see her eyes, because her head was lolling. *She's just asleep*, I told myself kindly, hopefully. *She'll wake up in a minute. She's only asleep.*

14

THIS SINKING SHIP

On the 40th Day, we chased our ghosts from the church to the school to their graves and home again. Nika would leave me today. Again. For good.

Not everyone agreed when to observe the vigil. Do you count forty days from when the gym was lost, or from when your loved one was found and you knew for sure? Our family went with the first date. A consensus. In volatile times, there is safety in numbers.

In the days before, tents went up on every spare patch of land so family members from out of town could join us for the last farewell. Dyadya Misha and his wife, Valentina, took over my brothers' camp beds in the living room, choosing to leave their own three boys back in Balakovo with Valentina's mother. Safety, for them, also came in numbers—small numbers, divided numbers.

We led the best of our livestock into town for slaughter— a final gift—and once the animals were butchered, the meat was boiled. Some of this stew was held back for the mourners, but the rest was carried to the cemetery as a last meal for the dead. That thick scent of beef, the ripe grassiness of lamb, it filled the air as the choir and congregation moved from one wooden marker to the next, singing a Panikhida.

Memory eternal, memory eternal, memory eternal . . .

The day pulled the very last drops of grief from our bones.

I made my own way back to the school later, prepared now to retrace my and Nika's steps. The classroom first, its walls pockmarked by bullets, stained with blood, graffitied with pleas for the lost to come back, please come back. I imaged Nika leading me — *This way, Dasha, this way, remember!* — her finger casually linked with mine. Clutching at the locket that contained a small piece of her, I walked down the steps where my little sister made her entrance for the Ceremony of the First Bell. I tried closing my eyes slowly like she had, to feel what she felt, that last passing breeze, happiness flying fast. I looked out across the railroad track to where the men and women had come running, then up to where Nika's balloon had flown away. Where was that balloon now? *Gone, Dasha.* The thought came to me in my little sister's voice. *It's gone.*

I walked across the yard and stood for a moment by the boiler house, my hand against the brick. It had happened just a month and a half ago, yet I felt as though I was revisiting the scene in an old photograph, curling at the edges. I closed my eyes to hear the songs that we had sung before the bangs and shrieks — that last moment when all was intact. I spooled through the images I could salvage: Nika climbing the mound of sand, turning, looking for me, not finding me.

It was time to walk her route.

Inside the gym, a thousand colors, toys, and photographs overpowered the shadow pictures left by the flames. Not a piece of floor was spared a flower. People stepped between the stems, lingered, muttered to the God that looked down from above the basketball hoops. *Why them? Why us? Why not me?*

I placed a bottle of water with the other hundreds of drinks for our thirsty ghosts. I opened my cigarette packet and left smokes for the men who were the first to be shot. I stood as if to make a speech, but my mouth stayed empty.

In the evening, as the light faded and the rain came, the bonfires that had been used to boil the meat were kept burning to grill food for the living. Papa and Dyadya Mischa stood in command of one fire, water sluicing from a slope of corrugated iron above their heads. I sheltered beneath the apartment building's back porch and watched everyone move about the yard, each trapped in his or her own individual limbo. After tonight, would life begin again? No one seemed to be making any promises. When the tents came down on the edges of town, what would change? Would we face a torture of a different kind? A stronger will for revenge?

I carried fresh skewers of *shashlik* from our fridge upstairs down to the grills whenever they were needed. Mama was in the kitchen in quiet celebration with Valentina and some of the other mothers. Every time I entered to collect more food,

I felt like an intruder, a prisoner returning to a cell. When I delivered the meat to Papa, I did not speak to him. He could blame it on grief, but I know he saw the change in me. Feared it, even.

I played waitress, pouring vodka into the glasses of the men who sat at the long tables not caring about getting wet. I took away their empty bottles, placing them on the floor against the wall so they would not stand on the table as bad omens. Alana helped. Her mother had forced her into a dress for the mourning, and she wore it like a coating of tar dripping from her arms, threatening to stick forever.

"Tell me what to do, Dasha," she said, giving a small salute. "I like being told what to do." So I let her fetch and carry the fresh meat so I didn't have to face my parents. The women in our kitchen would coo over her, I was sure. Alana did not realize it, and she would not have welcomed my saying it, but she was adorable with her face and hair washed, the dress pinching her at the waist, best shoes, white socks.

I took a bottle of drink to Yelena, who was sitting with Polin'ka, her wheelchair pushed close to a table. There was an oilskin canopy above them keeping away the worst of the rain. I held the bottle over her glass, but Yelena shook her head. "I need to be able to carry her back upstairs."

I had carried Polin'ka up those four floors the night they had returned.

"Where is the elevator?" the driver had asked, pushing the wheelchair into our lobby, while Yelena and I bore the weight of the bags.

"There isn't one."

140

"But how . . . ?" His hands fell to his sides.

"Ah, Grishka!" said Yelena, leapfrogging the man's despair. "Take Polin'ka's bag, will you?" Grigoriy had dashed, so eager, down the stairs to greet his returning mother and sister but was now rigid at the sight of this girl in the wheelchair, this girl who wasn't asleep. Had Yelena not told him what had happened in her phone calls home? Was this what it meant to be kind?

She weighed so little—a baby in my arms—but still I took the stairs slowly, as if performing a ritual, keeping pace with a psalm.

"It is so good to be back," Yelena had said, moving aside all the gifts piled onto Polin'ka's bed. "The food in Germany is very bad." I thought of Nika's bed, where the gifts would always be spread across the duvet. I laid Polin'ka on the sheets, looking into her eyes to see if she recognized me, if she understood where she was. The idea came, of course it did: Would it have been better if she had gone with Nika, hand in hand, over the horizon? I started crying again—for Polin'ka, for Nika, for me, for the darkness in my heart to have considered such a thing.

"So, how have you been?" Yelena asked, pulling a quilt around Polin'ka's neck, pushing away my sadness. "Because you look like shit, if you don't mind my saying."

I had told her I would help whenever I could. I said it the night they came back, and I said it again as I tried to pour her some spirit. I think Yelena understood that I needed to be needed.

"We can't stay," she told me, hand over her glass. She meant that evening, but also forever. Though the food was bad in

Germany, the care was better suited to Polin'ka's condition. They were looking at ways to go back.

They were all leaving me, one by one, along with the ghosts. Rats fleeing this sinking ship. And that included Zlata. She came that night, not wearing her yellow anorak; she was dressed as herself, representing no one. The bounce in her voice was gone. Without responsibility, she was somehow naked.

We found a bench to sit on, and I poured a drink for both of us, lit a cigarette. We said a toast, not touching glasses.

"Tell me what she was like, your sister," Zlata asked, sipping at her drink. I tipped mine down my throat, poured another.

"Funny," I said. "Cheeky. A pain in the ass."

Zlata smiled and sloshed vodka onto the floor, desperate to be rid of it, passing it off as an accident.

"It came from Papa's factory," I told her. "It is safe to drink, I swear."

We both looked over to my father—Zlata's opponent in the battle to get the boys to Moscow, my opponent in ways not so easy to explain. He was turning the coals, prodding the spitting meat, slicking sweat from his forehead with a hairy arm. Papa was the only one hot and bothered on this wet October night. Was he worried about crossing paths with Lyubov with my eyes so meanly on him? What would I do if I saw them?

"I'm leaving." Zlata finally said it.

"Thought you might be." I poured another glass. I had never drunk before, no more than a can of beer. Nadya and Olya had stolen drink from their parents and drunk it out by the river; they had boasted about it at school. But I couldn't see what their excitement was about. There was no swooping arc of pleasure with vodka, just medicinal pain, the misplaced belief that life would come to good.

"There are other charities lining up to be here and do their thing," Zlata said. "We need to step aside." I pictured this line—all those well-meaning hearts, such clumsy hands.

"Where will you go?"

She swallowed hard before she spoke, creased her face in apology. "To Moscow."

I laughed a horrible laugh. I was crying and I didn't care.

"Sorry, Dasha," she said, hugging me very tight. "But it's a lonely city, you know, Moscow. It's cold, whatever you think about the weather. You are lucky that you can stay here."

She let me weep into her shoulder for a while before I handed out some advice of my own: "You should tell Vitaliy that you love him. Before you go."

"And you," she said, "should tell Dmitriy that you don't. Think of that poor boy's heart."

He was standing just a few meters away—Dmitriy—drinking with the other boys from the factory. He looked more gangly than usual in his smart shirt and black trousers. Every time he made a move toward me, I fired him a silent warning shot and he edged away.

I was waiting for the final rat. My battery commander. The New York journalist.

He came after midnight, the 40th Day over. The men at the tables had broken into song—sorrowful at first, growing rougher as the ghosts ascended. Jonathan had followed us around all day, he said, though I had looked for him in the gathering journalists and not seen him once.

"Very emotional," he told me, no real emotion in his voice. Though I doubt there was any feeling left in mine either.

We leaned against the wall by the pile of empty vodka bottles, and he told me he had spent the past few hours at Aslan and Diana's apartment, writing his copy, packing his bags.

"I wanted to bring you this."

His eyes were animal-bright once again as he handed it over, wanting me to be delighted. It was an American newspaper turned to a large photograph of me. I stared at myself—wild and messy. I did not look beautiful at all. The picture seemed to suggest that I was responsible for the black shell of a school behind me. I was the dark-haired animal that had chewed through a wire. I tried to sound aloud the headline but the alphabet tripped me up.

"What does it say?"

"'The Last Lost Hare,'" he said in English before offering me the translation. He was nervous about this, I could tell.

"But she isn't lost," I told him. "We found her."

He shifted his boots in the mud.

"It isn't talking about Nika."

I handed the paper back.

"It's yours to keep, Darya Pavlovna. I want you to have it."

I shook my head. "What use is it to me?" I looked away, along the long line of the tables, my eyes searching for more rogue bottles, an excuse to walk away. It was too painful standing beside him, being drenched in his pity. I wanted his hand to take mine again, pull me in, as he had in the hallway, let his heart win, tell his mind to be quiet.

"I'm sorry," he said deeply, meaning it. "I didn't come here to . . . I didn't want just stories. I wanted to get involved, so that is perhaps why I . . ."

Dmitriy caught my eye, a glance that asked hopefully, *Can I rescue you?* I pinched my brow, shook my head. *Stupid boy! Of course not! Stay away!*

"I wanted to do small things," Jonathan went on. "Like the lessons. He who saves one man saves humanity. I do believe that."

"But not one woman."

"Well, this is it, Darya Pavlovna . . ." He turned to me with new passion. I saw him move to take my hands, then think better of it. "You are a woman now. So if you want to go to Moscow, you can just go. You are a smart and capable girl and—"

"Woman."

"Yes, woman!"

I wasn't his daughter. I wasn't a little girl.

"You don't need me to save you," he said. "You don't need me to take you there."

I laughed bitterly. Jonathan thought the world was flat too. None of them understood. We turned to listen to the men as they started a new song with new vigor.

In the darklands of the forest where the aspen leaves tremble . . .

"What is it they're singing?" Jonathan asked.

"A song about hares," I said. They really were. Fate was playing with pattern again, sewing up its hems.

*We don't care, we don't care, we're not afraid of a wolf
or an owl.*

They were singing about hares, but at the same time they weren't.

"How would I ever afford a ticket?" I said quietly, once the men had hit their last table-slapping swell. It was my turn to talk deeply and to mean it. "Where would I stay when I got there? What would I do?"

That good blouse, the glass pot filled with its sharpened pencils, my worldly new friends—the image of them was evaporating along with the ghosts. I was a factory girl who would never leave town. It was time that I accepted it. Fighting only led to heartache.

"You would find something," Jonathan crooned. Then he said it again, like a spell: "You are a smart and capable woman."

"What a shame that I will never get to find out."

I untied my apron. I'd had enough of farewells. I wanted my bed.

"See you later," I said in English, because I did want him to see that he had helped me. One of his small things had borne fruit. *"See you later,"* I said. *"Alligator."*

15

NOTHING TO DO BUT
MOVE FORWARD

I fetched a cardboard box, and I began packing away a life. In went her soft toys and colored pencils, a snowstorm and a china girl. I broke open one of the bags of chocolate shapes from the pile on the bed and bit into a heart with a red strawberry center. It tasted bad if only because it was wrong to eat gifts that were never meant for you. I spat it out.

There would be a space when I was done, and I would fill it with a bookcase, or a dressing table, perhaps; maybe a desk. Olga or Marina would know someone who had one of those things to spare. Diana certainly would, if I could face the gossip my asking would trigger. *Anna Mikhailovna's daughter is trying to swap a child's bed for a bookcase. Oh, doesn't it make your heart break!*

The night before, I had dreamed I was carrying a doll around the streets of the town and it came alive in my arms; it became heavy like a human. It laughed when I tickled its belly. The sun was shining, everything soaked in the yellow of a happy memory. But as soon as I took the doll inside, it became lifeless. The baby died. I ran to Mama with its floppy body, begging her to revive it, but she was not moved. *There's nothing you can do*, she told me—a fact that everyone else around me seemed able to understand—and she carried on with her busyness.

I took the box of toys and chocolates from our room, my room, and placed them on the kitchen table in front of Mama. Nika's bed I was willing to take care of, but this collection of well-worn things . . . What was the best place for them? Was there any place for them? Mama could scatter them on Nika's grave for the weather to turn them brown or sell them to make funds for her meetings and rallies. I didn't care.

She took off her glasses to examine the box. She had been writing a letter. This was how Mama filled the empty hours now, letter after letter in her blocky cursive, even though she rarely got one back in reply.

"Wait," she said as I walked away. "Don't you want to keep anything?"

"They're toys," I said. "What use are they to me?"

"To remember," she replied, her hand going tentatively to the fluff of an orange chick, its head poking from the top of the box.

"It's OK," I told her. "I won't forget."

The doorbell saved us. Those quiet conversations often swelled into arguments. *Why do you refuse to grieve exactly like me?* was the message lying beneath everything Mama threw my way. *Why do you feel you have the right to grieve at all?* was the message of everything that I threw back.

148

Alana was at the door. Again. My tying of her hair and making her a waitress had convinced her we were friends. I had led her on. Jonathan had taught me other things aside from English. Now I could also be cruel.

Since he had left, I lived off the memory of that moment in the hallway, his mouth on mine, the way he grasped at me. I went to bed with it and woke up with it.

Each time Alana knocked, she asked if I could come out to play. I feigned distraction, told her I was busy, said, *not now, another time, go away.* That day, because I had not unleashed my anger on Mama, I let Alana have it instead.

"What do you mean 'come out to play'?" I spat.

She danced nervously at the threshold, her dirty cheeks turning pink. "I dunno, just . . . play."

"Yes, but what does that mean?"

She was searching my face for warmth, the way Dmitriy had that awful night. *Anything? Anything?*

"Are you asking me what playing is, Dasha?" she asked slowly.

Silence.

The shame of it. Yes, that was, beneath it all, what I was asking. Like the English words for *window* and *ceiling*, I had learned once what it meant to play, but I had not used the knowledge enough, so it had faded away. Alana had found me out.

"Well?" she said. "Are you gonna come?" Her persistence dismantled me—that willingness to ask, the willingness to get a "no."

"Oh, for goodness' sake!" I made a great fuss of putting on my coat and hat. "I will come and play with you, Lenochka"—

I pointed a finger at her—"but just this once, if only to stop you from sticking to me like a bath leaf."

She cheered, jumping and clipping her sneakered heels together. She made for the stairwell right away, so I had to run to catch up.

Out on the scrubland, Alana insisted on more running.

"Let's do races," she said. Every stretch of the way, she picked a point ahead as our finishing line, and we dashed toward it.

"So what 'playing' are we going to do, then?" I asked, out of breath after beating her yet again.

"We're already doing it," she said. "This is it! Now, can you do a handstand without a wall? I can."

We were nearing the make-believe house and the grave I had dug, the black mountains growing large in front of us. It would be a lie to say that I had forgotten about the day I had buried my sister, but just as Zaychik was deep in the ground, that afternoon was submerged in my memory. I did not run so fast in our next contest.

"What do you want to be when you grow up?" Alana asked as we arrived at the house. She pulled me into the living room and we sat among the rubbish on the ground, our backs against the wall. I lit a cigarette, and Alana begged for one herself. "You're too young," I told her. She grabbed a stick instead and stripped it of its bark.

"I want to sit at a desk in a good blouse with a nice skirt," I said, too preoccupied with the thought of the grave to think up a decent tall tale to keep Alana amused. "I'll learn to type, and I'll have this glass jar with sharpened pencils in it. I'll go on dinner dates."

"Oh." She looked sad for me. "Well, I want to be a gymnast."

At that, she was up and out the door, throwing herself into a crooked cartwheel, twitching her wrists and sticking out her bottom like Anna Pavlova on the balance beam. I felt sad for her right back until she yelled out suddenly, "Come and look at this, Dasha!"

I had made a marker for the grave, an oval arrangement of stones, just as we had for the baby hare. There were two lollipop sticks bound with grass as a cross. Did I really do this? I could not remember. Alana and I stood on either side of the small memorial, our hands clasped in front of us, our heads bowed.

"It's nicer than my brother's grave," she said at last. Then: "I won't ever be a gymnast, will I, Dasha?"

I shook my head. They say it's good to know the truth, but better to be happy—but I'm not sure I believe that.

Alana nodded. "Will you ever be a secretary?"

I shrugged. The knowledge of something had been sitting heavy on me as I cleared that bedroom of all traces of Nika, preparing it supposedly for my new life in the town. I could not talk to Zlata about it, because she had gone. I could not bother Yelena when her problems were so much greater, as she jumped through hoops to get a visa to Germany. Dmitriy hated me now, and Mama and Papa would not listen, would offer no good advice. Perhaps Alana and I were friends after all, because it seemed right to tell her and hear what she had to say.

"I have been given money to go to Moscow."

I sighed at the weight of it. It was too much to carry. Now that I had said it out loud, I would have to go. Or at least make the decision not to. I was crouched on the floor of that boiler house again, wondering whether to burst free or to stay still. Should I take the path that claimed to lead to riches or the path that offered certain death? Devils played tricks.

The day Jonathan had gone, an envelope was pushed under our apartment door, my name handwritten on the front. I can only imagine what would have happened if Mama had seen it first, if she had felt justified in opening it.

"He who saves one WOMAN saves humanity."

He had written these words on the sheet of paper inside.

So here is money for the train or the plane, should you decide to go. I have an ongoing "relationship" with Hotel Alexander near Kuznetsky Most Metro station. There is a room booked in my name. I won't need it until New Year's. It's yours.

There was another quote:

"They have nothing to do but move forward, for the sea will not stand in their way."

Then:

You are a smart and capable woman. See you later, alligator.

I had dreamed of domes and spires, store windows and curtained restaurants, fur hats and thick snow. That all melted, instantly, now that the offer was real.

"Wow!" said Alana, her face a mixture of awe and terror. I was about to become one of her echoes, another person leaving. "Are you going to go?" she said, before quickly correcting herself: "Of course you are! You must!"

I nodded. Good advice from a good person.

"Well, I'd take you with me if I could," I said, which wasn't exactly the truth, but neither was it a lie.

So I booked an evening train a week from then, telling no one but Alana. I wanted space on the day of departure to say my goodbyes. I wanted a whole day to change my mind. A plane was too much of a leap; a train had stations where you could get off, turn back. Nothing was set in stone. Maybe I wouldn't even do it.

The morning came, and I packed a black duffel bag from the charity, the same one given to each of the boys who went to the Moscow school. It was my consolation prize from Zlata for not being given a ticket. I put in all my clothes—the bag was big, my wardrobe was small—leaving behind only the solemn dress I'd worn to Nika's funeral. In went my stubby eye and lip pencils, my powdery blocks of makeup, my alarm clock (for getting up early for a new job), Papa's camera (which he rarely used), my muddied English workbook, Jonathan's letter slotted inside, and the play I'd been reading over and over since the siege. Inside that, I slipped a photo of Nika.

She was six years old in the picture, posing for the camera, but moments earlier I'd watched her from the doorway of the living room dancing wildly to a music video, not knowing I was there. I remember thinking how perfect it must be to be her—funny and silly, yet focused and true. I envied her innocence and her future, all of it still to work out. You can see in the picture that she had been dancing, even though she is wearing her serious photograph face, with her back upright, ready for the camera click.

I packed a shopping bag of food for the trip—slices of *kolbasa* and boiled eggs, a couple of *bublik* and a bottle of liquor from Papa's factory. I hoped there would be a restaurant car that was cheap and clean for the next day's travel. I trusted that strangers would be kind in exchange for good vodka.

At lunchtime, I went to find Papa. I gave him that last chance to make me stay.

I walked up the ramp that led to the factory's flat gray offices, and in the main room, with its fluorescent strip lights and wall calendars, with its brown veneered desks and unhappy potted plants, was Lyubov. I had looked and looked for her in the face of every woman since Diana had joined the dots and made me see. I'd searched for her long, limp hair and tried to sniff out her distinctive perfume. I could not understand how Papa had come to find this young woman in the first place. Here was my answer. Papa had gone to no trouble at all. She was in the office he passed every day.

She shifted awkwardly in her chair when I entered, pretending to be occupied with her handful of yellow papers. What did I want with her now that I had found her? Absolutely nothing.

An older woman swooped—"Galina Feodorovna; can I help you?" She had orange lipstick and gold hoops that stretched the holes in her lobes.

"Darya Pavlovna," I said. "I've come to see my father."

Galina was friendly then, toady. Lyubov shrank further into her shoulders. We left the office and made for the buildings that housed the production lines, Galina's heels clip-clipping on the stone floors in the caged walkways. Inside the factory, bottles sang their complaints as they jostled from a bundle into a line, forced to line up for their destination. Dmitriy was there, in a hard hat and earmuffs, but he did not run to greet me. He held his post at the conveyor belt, monitoring the obedience of the bottles. He watched me as I walked past, and I watched him, neither of us giving anything away.

Papa's office was behind wire-meshed glass that did little to keep back the noise. He was shoveling into his mouth the remaining lumps of a *solyanka* that Mama had made the night before. Galina gave a nod to show her task was done, then clip-clipped back toward the offices.

"My Dashen'ka!"

Papa looked scared. I had never visited him at work before. I had not seen his office, the white sparseness of it, the piles of paper with oily fingerprints, the *Playboy* calendar on the wall. Papa stood and moved to the front of his desk, his arms outstretched to catch the terrible news I had surely brought.

"What are you doing here?" A glob of something from the soup hung from the end of his mustache, which somehow made it easier to say what I must.

"I'm leaving town, Papa. I'm going to Moscow."

He stared at me for a moment, trying to grasp whether I was serious. The chiming protest of the bottles filled the gap. His soft look of surprise changed into something stern.

"No, you are not, my girl."

"It's too late for this, Papa. It's all booked. I go tonight."

"You're not going."

"I'm eighteen, Papa. There's nothing here for me anymore."

"But there is Dima! We shall start planning your wedding. That's what you want, isn't it? That's what this is all about. I have the money saved up."

"I don't love him, Papa."

"Of course you don't! Love is what comes later, after you are married, when . . ." He trailed off. Who was he to be giving this sort of advice? He took a new tack. "But what about me, hey? You're just going to leave your papa? Leave me hungry?" He grabbed a handful of his belly through his overalls, gave it a squeeze. "Don't tell your mama, but your cooking scores a five!"

I looked away. I wouldn't be charmed. "And what about Lyubov's cooking, Papa?"

His mouth fell open. I had fooled myself that I did not know, and he had fooled himself that I had not guessed. He smacked both hands down on his once-white desktop three times — *bam, bam, bam* — making me jump with fright.

"Do you still love Mama?" I asked as he collected his breath.

"Yes," he said.

"Sometimes," I told him, "I would like to rip her eyes out."

"You take that back, Darya Pavlovna!" He lunged toward me, as if to hit me, but kept his fists pinned to his sides. I thought of the way Jonathan wanted to take my hands on the 40th Day and had stopped himself. All this passion never delivered. I would give Papa the truth.

"Sometimes," I said, "I wish that Mama would —"

He would not let me finish. "You do not speak about your mother like that! After all she has been through!"

And that was what did it — his defending her over me, that woman who might as well have been dead for seven whole years. Now that she had woken up, he had forgotten the pain she had caused, chosen not to see what I had done to fill her shoes. Instead, he had packed the gap in his affections with that cowering woman in his office. My mind was made up.

"I only came here for money," I told Papa, my hand held out for the cash, "as you have so much saved up."

I expected Mama not to care, to behave as if she was pleased to be rid of me. But I'd also allowed myself to hope for something else. Like with Papa, I gave her an opportunity to make me stay. Perhaps my leaving would push her to say sorry. We could both admit that we had failed. What I did not expect was her rage.

I waited in my room for her to come home. I listened as she took off her coat and placed it on the hook before moving through to the kitchen, rustling plastic bags as she went. Then I followed her path. I held on to the door frame.

"I'm leaving, Mama. I'm going to Moscow."

She said nothing at first, carried on emptying her shopping onto the table — cans and packages, meat wrapped in paper. She had bought supplies for dinner — but just two cuts of flesh. Nothing for me. Papa must have gotten to her first. All afternoon she had been brewing this anger.

"Oh, that's just wonderful!" she hissed. "That's it! You take your sad story to Moscow, where you'll no doubt dine out on it for months!"

"What do you mean?"

She edged away from me until her back was up against the stove. A cornered snake.

"Oh, don't think I didn't see you hanging around with that *Amerikanski* journalist, all soft for him. I know what you did, for shame!"

I covered my face with my hands.

"You're not so special here, are you? Everyone's got a story like yours."

"I'm not special," I said from behind my fingers.

"Oh, no, no, you go." I listened to her smash pans onto the stove. "You left my Nikousya, and now you're leaving us. Go on, run away! It'll be easier for the horse with one less on the cart!"

I peeled my hands from my face. Mama was crying. She had crumpled into a seat at the table. Her shoulders shook. My throat clenched tight. She was right. I had left Nika. Neither of us was there for her at the end. And I thought that is what I would say when I opened my mouth, but the words that came out were "You never loved her." Quietly at first, then I was shouting it. "You never loved her. I did! I did!"

Mama looked up. She mopped the tears from her cheeks with the backs of her hands.

"Have you finished?" she asked.

I nodded. I had told Papa that I wanted to rip out her eyes, but what he had not let me voice was my stronger desire—for her to hold me. I wanted to wrap myself around her and be told that everything would be all right. *You did your best, my Dashen'ka.* I had often wondered what that would feel like, to be a grown woman and to be held tightly in the arms of your mother.

"I won't come back, Mama," I said—a final poke to see if she would bite.

She levered herself to standing, her knuckles braced against the tabletop. Then she went back to the stove and started making dinner. I shrank back to my room and listened to the noises coming from the kitchen. This was how Mama had received the news from Papa: resigned herself to it, gone to the shops, and, with bad grace, crossed me off her shopping list, no thought of persuading me to stay. Just as she had taken to her bed all those years ago, she had given up. If only she had said, *We're not so very different, you and I. I have wanted to run away my whole life.* Perhaps then I would never have left.

16

THROW AWAY
THE KEY

I'd not given the mountains much thought — the furniture of home, that cardboard backdrop — yet I found myself hoping Moscow would have mountains too. If it didn't, at least I would be homesick for one big thing in my weightless future. My shapeless future. Even on the platform, when the *provodnik* was asking for my ticket, I thought I might not go. Jonathan's words were in my bones: *They have nothing to do but move forward, for the sea will not stand in their way.* But so was Zlata's caution — that Moscow is cold and lonely. There could be nowhere more desolate than our apartment with its view of the remains. Such a place, I believed, did not exist.

I met Alana at the playground for our final goodbye.

"Make sure you go to school," I said. "Don't waste your chance." And I watched her brow become heavy, irritated by my grown-up's voice.

"Push me on the swing," she said to snap me out of it, making me think painfully of Nika.

"No, you show me a handstand without a wall."

So she did. And as I walked away, watching her dust gravel from her palms, the pride in her acrobatics still glowing from her face, I said, "And learn to comb your own hair, Lana. It's a valuable life skill."

The last thing I did before I left: I said goodbye to Yelena, stopping to knock on her door with my bag in my hand. I felt like a cheat, giving up on the town without a reason as real as hers, as real as Polin'ka.

"Oh, it will be good for you, Dasha, to have some fresh air." She held my shoulders and nodded her assurances. "You will come back brand-new!" She winced a little at her choice of words. That was what we had believed for Polin'ka, that she would return from Germany all fixed up.

"I'm not coming back," I told her.

"Whatever you say, Dasha. Now, did they do the sitting down with you?"

I shook my head.

"Then, we'll do it here."

"That won't work."

She folded her arms as an end to it. "It'll work just as well as not doing it at all."

She marched me inside to the living room, where Polin'ka sat in her chair in the shaft of sunlight coming through the window, as if it might help her grow, as it did Yelena's shelves of orchid cacti, dill, and chives. Grigoriy was told he must join us on the sofa as well, and he wriggled at my side, reminding me of Igor and a younger Boris from years ago.

"Good luck," Yelena said as I stood to go. "I wish you neither fur nor feather."

I had a bottom bunk with a wipe-clean mattress in a cream-painted carriage with tens of other tomblike beds. In the bunk above me, a large man was already on his back, his arms folded across his chest, resigned to the thirty-seven hours of travel that lay ahead. The smell that drifted down: stale drink. I would see little of him on my trip but hear plenty. His snores made the bed fixtures rattle.

I sat on my bunk with my black duffel and bag of food beside me, not stowed away. The train juddered into life; we were moving, but still I had not committed to the journey.

"You want tea?" It was the same *provodnik* who had taken my ticket, a hefty boy with a constellation of moles on his neck. He gave me a hot, thick black drink that tasted of courage.

I paid for my sealed bag of sheets, pillowcase, and towel, and so did the man above me, reluctantly, stuffing it behind his head. I was mentally deducting the cost from the change from my ticket, plus the money Papa had given me, borrowed with an IOU from petty cash at the factory. He promised to wire me more when I arrived, but I doubted the wedding fund existed. Papa must have been supporting Lyubov. What else was she in it for, sleeping with a fat old man with no intention of leaving his family? What if Papa and Lyubov had a child that he was supporting too? Was that why Papa was comforting her the night of the siege? Did they have a child together who was held hostage? Did that child survive and not Nika? Would that be fair?

Though my mind was stuck at home, we moved forward. Through the window came a continuous story of overhead wires, graffiti, and rectangle factories. Later, a change—chopped trees, horses, rundown farms. I watched until the sun became a red spark on the horizon. A family game of cards started up in the bunks next to me—a mother, father, and a blond boy and girl who could have been twins. Opposite, a stout woman who introduced herself as Valeria had changed into traveling clothes—a loose, flowered T-shirt draped over generous breasts, pink sweatpants, and matching slippers. She had gotten herself some pickled cucumbers from a seller at the station before we left and was working through them with satisfied crunches, reading *Caravan of Stories* magazine. She offered me a pickle from the Styrofoam carton, and I took one not to be rude. The heaters pumped out stifling air that stole my appetite.

I followed Valeria's lead and pulled out my untouched copy of *Elle Girl*. I'd bought the November issue from the kiosk before we left. Beyoncé was on the front, wearing a tight dress and an illegible smile. At the corner, a picture of Hello Kitty. Usually this would be a treat—the first read of a magazine, the smell of fresh ink. I would be eager for the makeup lessons, tips on how to know if a boy truly loves you. But I could not bring myself to open it. *Elle Girl.* That was how Jonathan had seen me, as a girl, like his little daughter. But I was a woman now, smart and capable. What was I doing buying this?

I watched the sky turn black instead, the same arrangement of stars that I would see at home — a view that soothed me and frustrated me. I didn't want the same sky. I wanted to get away. I wanted to go back.

I did not sleep. That first night, I listened to the snores of the marinated man above, the whispering catch of Valeria inhaling, pausing, exhaling. The carriage smelled of stale breath and other people's food. The grinding pulse of the wheels on the track did not lull me. The rhythm kept my mind turning. *I am moving away from Nika. She is trapped in the school. I am moving away from Nika. She is trapped in the school.* I climbed out of my bunk.

Smoking was allowed in the vestibule near the samovar by the bathrooms. I liked to go right outside, in the space between the cars, a foot on either side of the exposed couplings. The air was cooler there. I could watch the ground blur beneath me as I dropped ash between the gaps. If the train jolted, I risked dropping too. And if I did let myself slip, would I get to see Nika again? Is that what happens when you die? My beliefs had been there, solid, from when I was very small, but now that they were being tested, they felt paper thin. Were they just fairy tales to help you sleep?

Valeria changed out of her flowery traveling clothes and got off at Rostov-on-Don — to be replaced by a slim, well-dressed woman named Lidiya. Lidiya was continuing her journey all the way through to Moscow to visit her sister, Inna. As the train replenished its supplies, Lidiya ran through an inventory of Inna's health concerns so I understood exactly why she was traveling to the city. I watched the sellers on the tracks offering balloons, cheeses, fruit, rainbow-colored teddy bears as I listened sympathetically to Lidiya's stories. I also listened selfishly. Lidiya had brought a large basket of food that I was praying she would share. All of my supplies had gone. The restaurant car did not look clean. I could not trust it.

When we were moving again, Lidiya's basket was opened up: chicken pieces, salad Olivier, black bread, and hard-boiled eggs. The salty smell sent saliva running in my mouth. I tried not to stare as she searched out a cloth to spread across the small ledge table between our bunks, as she removed the lids from the containers, but the ceremony of it took so long. I could not help myself. Lidiya understood that I was hungry. She filled a plate for me too.

"Stop," she told me as I thanked her over and over. I wiped away a tear before Lidiya could see. I was very tired.

"So where are you from, my sweetheart?" She tore flesh from the chicken wing with her fingers, stopping every now and then to clean herself on a paper napkin. "Where did you get on?"

I told her.

Her face fell.

"Oh," she said. "Oh."

She shook her head, put her napkin over her mouth as if she might be sick. I looked around the train to see who else was listening. Had they seen our conversation turn? A group of young boys, a sports team in matching green T-shirts, were throwing a tennis ball to one another across the compartment as they sat in their bunks, cheering the catches and groaning the drops.

"Are you OK?" I asked Lidiya.

"Oh. It's awful," she said. "It's terrible what happened there. All those children!"

It hadn't occurred to me that saying the name of my town would now be more powerful than a spell, more potent than a curse. All those journalists and photographers and TV crews had been there, but I hadn't considered that the world outside had seen as much as I had. That they might have seen more. Hearing this stranger talk, watching her cry, was bewildering. Horrifying. The strength of one word.

"Yes, terrible," I said. "Yes, it was."

"Did you lose someone?" she asked. "Were you there?"

She had forgotten the food, hungry for something else. She twisted her napkin into a tight spiral, her gaze focused on something above my left eye — my scar. *Such a very pretty girl, what a shame.* I put a protective hand over the locket at my neck. I tried to keep eating.

"No," I said. "No. I was lucky. I escaped it all." I thought that she would stop then, but this only gave her permission to go on.

"Blowing up children!" She almost shrieked it.

I put down my forkful of salad.

"The bastards! The bastards!"

I looked around the train again, to see if anyone else had heard her swear.

"The bastards," she muttered darkly. She looked at me, expectant. I was supposed to join in. I wondered what my face looked like. I felt blank, made of stone.

"Here," Lidiya said. "Have some more." And she gave me another chicken wing, another egg, another large scoopful of salad. There was something defiant in the way she piled up my plate. Feeding me was an act of revenge. Of course I thought of Mama. *You take your sad story to Moscow, where you'll no doubt dine out on it for months.* I'm sure that I offended Lidiya, but I could not finish what she gave me. I could not come close to clearing my plate.

That evening I asked the *provodnik* if I could walk through to one of the *kupe* cars, where they had showers. He shrugged as if I hadn't needed to ask at all and went back to chewing a matchstick and reading his paper. The train was due to arrive in Moscow just before 7 a.m., and I wanted to arrive clean. My skin did not smell like my own.

In the play I was reading, one of the characters describes her heart as a locked grand piano with a missing key. I liked that—the idea that you could shut a small part of yourself away so you did not have to feel it anymore, hear it, or show it to anyone else.

I threw away my key.

I put my head under the water, soaking my hair, repeating the name of home quietly into the flow. Water poured into my mouth and out again, taking the word with it, spilling it down my chin, sluicing it down my body. As the train raced through the last stretch of countryside toward Moscow, the name of my town fell onto the gravel of the tracks. I left it behind, somewhere in the dark.

MOSCOW

17

WHO'S YOUR
LITTLE FRIEND?

This was how it was going to be. The train would steady itself
into the station, and they would be waiting. Someone, just
someone. I'd step off, be given no chance to speak, before I
was snatched into an embrace. I was a bird of passage — yet one
they had suspected might arrive all along. Music would play — a
street musician with an accordion, giving his soul to "O Fields,
My Fields," making me feel sad for what I'd left behind but so
happy to be in the arms of Moscow, ready for life to begin again.

No such story could survive the harsh blue light of Kazansky
station. My fantasies, like my breath, turned to vapor as I
stepped from the humid fug of the carriage into the sharp,
crunchy air of the city. I let the other passengers overtake
me — the vodka-soaked man, a hat pulled down over his ears;
Lidiya, clucking instructions into a cell phone. All around
me, people yawned away the uncomfortable night and picked

up their pace along the platform. There was no music, just the rising *bing-bing-bing* of the station loudspeaker, the *clip-clip-clip* of footsteps echoing beneath the ironwork roof. I pulled my jacket from my bag, knowing at once that it wasn't going to be enough, and put it on over my dress—the one I had worn to dig Nika's grave, to impress Jonathan, and now to escape. I took a head scarf and tied it over my damp hair and ears.

"Where are you going, huh? Where are you going?"

These were not words in my head but a voice speaking them out loud. A short man with a very big mustache was in front of me all of a sudden, far too close. His leather jacket was zipped right up to his chin.

"You need a taxi? I have a taxi. Nice car. I'll take you. Where are you going, huh?"

Overwhelmed, I could not answer—this tiny man speaking my giant fears.

"Where are you going, huh?"

"Um, I don't know. I can't remember."

"OK. Well, I'll just hang here until you do." He took on the deliberate, wide-footed stance of somebody waiting. I searched for the English workbook in my bag. Jonathan's letter was tucked inside with the name of the hotel and its location. But I stopped myself just in time, realizing how green I was being. I did not know this man at all.

"No," I told the stranger. "I'm fine, thanks."

I swerved past him and made for the crowds and the pink lights of the kiosks. I would eat—my stomach was gassy and empty—and then I would find the hotel. By myself.

The little man followed.

"Yes, that's right, this way, my car is this way, I'll give you a good price."

I walked faster, past the green-sports-team boys who'd been brought to a halt at the end of the platform for a head count, onto the main concourse, where times and numbers and cities droned from the loudspeaker. Still I was followed by that difficult spirit, dressed in a leather flight jacket. *You shall not pass, little girl. You shall not pass!* I broke into a jog. Ahead of me a woman ran in towering black heels toward the open arms of a man. A father steered his daughter from my lumbering path. I dodged a worker with a trash cart, who took in the sight of my head scarf and sneered. People were pushing through a bank of wooden doors ahead. I would do that too.

"Give me your bag—I'll carry it." The taxi man jogged beside me and got a hand on the strap of my duffel.

"Get off!"

A woman in a red beret and animal-print boots saw us tussle, then quickly pretended she hadn't. A nearby baggage-cart attendant chuckled, saying something about lovers and their quarrels. The wooden doors were close now. I didn't fancy the little man's chances in a race. Alana had trained me well. I made the last dash, the baggage attendant yelling in my wake, "Give the man a break!"

There was no fresh air, no sky, beyond those wooden doors, only green walls and chandeliers, another huge waiting hall, this one looking more like an opera house than the last. I kept on running, past the arcade games and *bomzhi* sleeping on the benches. Still he was behind me: "That's right, through the doors ahead of you, my car is waiting. Nice BMW."

I wove in and out of chiseled women walking purposefully toward the Metro, past a pair of stray dogs fighting over a thrown-away sandwich. On the wall above me, an enormous painting of a mighty figure in a red cloak loomed, its arms aloft, invincible. I burst through the doors into the outside air at last. People with wheeled suitcases sliced across my path. Beyond them: a jigsaw of parked cars, traffic cops arguing about the law. The roads on the square were roaring—lanes and lanes of traffic, headlights like furious eyes. In the middle of it all was a bronze statue directing the traffic, appealing for calm.

I would head for one of the fat, grand buildings on the edge of the square, I decided. One of them must house a clean place to eat. I cut through the pedestrians, edged between the parked cars, pausing for a moment to understand the flow of the traffic. I stepped over a barrier, put a foot into the road, and the taxi man's hand was on me.

"No, no, no!" he bellowed over the boom of cars and buses. "You can't cross here. You'll get killed. Or arrested. You'll get killed *and* arrested." He kept his grip, not so hard now. Fatherly, almost. The tail of my head scarf beat against my neck. He had saved me, I suppose. *He who saves one woman . . .* I was steered toward a once-white wreck of a BMW, both front corners staved in. He let go and stood proud, regarding the car, and I was supposed to do the same. I wished that I could be that red-cloaked figure on the station wall and tell this man to go away, leave me alone, but my voice had disappeared.

"You are a lovely girl," he said, his salesman's slickness gone now. "This is a big, bad city." Caring words, and I was no warrior.

"I'll look after you," he went on, and my heart sang at the

idea of it. "You have a husband?" he asked. He was no longer regarding the car, but me, up and down. I shook my head. "Well, I'll be your husband, then."

He made a move for my arm again, but I was quick. I jumped free, made the journey three sides around a rusting Volga, and smacked shoulders with a traffic cop who was heading his way. The taxi man did not follow me to the sidewalk. Could not. He was holding up his palms to the cop. I ran away, down the side of the railroad building, my bag bumping against my hip.

I summoned the ghost of my sister as I walked the streets that silver-skied morning. I imagined her as a bright flicker in the gray puddles. *Come on, Dasha! Come and see this!*

While I smoked, she painted the city vivid colors. She had always made the everyday or the frightening transform into something wonderful if I only took a moment to see it through her eyes. The peach glow of the Leningradskaya Hotel. The candy-pink walls of the *Petra i Pavla* church. The golden arches at Krasnye Vorota.

We stood together and looked up at the fierce, flat forehead of Mikhail Lermontov, high on his column, his coat carved to look like it was blowing in the wind. The inscription:

Oh, Moscow, Moscow, I love you, like a son.
Like a Russian — tenderly, ardently, strong.

Could you come to love a city in the same way that you loved a child? I hoped so. I needed to find something, someone. And I did — in a neon-lit corner café on a boarded-up street.

175

We had walked in a circle, my imaginary sister and I, finding ourselves on a muddy bank, lined with the wooden backs of the billboards that shouted out across Komsomolskaya Square. I don't know why I climbed the cement steps and opened that plastic sprung door. The signs for Coca-Cola and grilled cheese glared like a warning, not a welcome. Maybe it was the sugary smell of warm bread. Maybe I could walk no farther.

There was a small triangular seating area, with stools at the window. A macramé pot holder dangled empty from the ceiling. On the back wall, a bug zapper crackled above glass-doored fridges and a coffee machine. Behind the counter stood a girl, her hair cut sharply to her jawbone. Her nose was pierced, and her incisors seemed as large as a dog's.

"Hey, village girl," she said, "who's your little friend?"

I thought she was talking about Nika, that I had channeled my sister so successfully that others could see her too.

"I don't want no funny business," the girl went on, pulling herself up tall. Her apron was grubby, but her top beneath was fancy, black, and gauzy. When she stepped out from behind the counter I saw her skin-tight jeans, and the spikes of her stilettos.

"Don't even think about it." She pointed a finger at me and then the door. "Because I've clocked it. He's backup, right? Your getaway guy?"

My ghost sister disappeared in the sallow light.

"And I reckon I can take on a midget." The girl laughed. "Just try me."

I followed her gaze. Standing outside the café at the bottom of the steps was the little taxi man, shifting expectantly from foot to foot. I skittered toward the girl.

"I don't know him," I blurted out. "He's following me. He wants to marry me. And he wants to give me a ride."

"I bet he does."

She snorted and, without decision, grabbed a broom, pushing past me to get to the door. She yanked it open, letting in the rumbling sound of traffic. She tottered down the steps, yelling, "Hey, fuck off, midget!"

The door snapped shut and I was left with the buzz of the bug zapper and the chug of the fridge. The rest of their exchange was muffled. I went to the window to watch as she swung the broom through the air. The taxi man threw up an arm to protect his face and jerked backward just in time. I flinched too. This girl was the red-cloaked figure from the wall of Kazansky station. She had warrior blood in her veins. The taxi man made his stumbling retreat, realizing his scythe had hit a stone, and the girl barked out some final insults before stomping back up the steps and in through the café door.

"Now, what can I get you to eat?" she asked, as if the whole thing hadn't happened at all.

I sat at the window and tore at that first sandwich with a desperation that ignored the limpness of the bread and the strange orangeness of the cheese. It made not a dent in my hunger, so I went back to the counter and ordered another, pulling out my embroidered purse and the roll of rubles from Papa. I gobbled that sandwich just as quickly as the first, my English workbook in front of me so I could pull out Jonathan's letter and read it again.

Hotel Alexander near Kuznetsky Most Metro station.

I would need a map.

People drifted in and out as I ate—workmen whose coats looked too heavy for their backs; a small, sinewy teenager who carried his bike all the way up the stairs and inside. A foul-smelling *bomzh* staggered in at one point, announcing that he'd "come for the celebrations!" and was swiftly evicted without need of the broom. I was ready to move on, find the hotel, but that was when the girl threw a "Hey" in my direction. I watched her hips roll toward me. She sat down, hooking her heels like claws over the footrest of the stool. She was an owl. I was but a baby hare.

"Appetite comes with eating, huh?"

I pushed my empty paper plate away and wiped my greasy face. I thought of those stray mutts in Kazansky station slobbering over a sandwich.

"I'm Viktoria."

"Darya. Pleased to meet you."

This made her grin. She showed me her teeth.

"And where are you from, village girl?"

I paused. "Saratov." I arranged my hands neatly on the counter, saw how odd they looked, then pressed them down hard between my thighs.

"Saratov! No!"

"Yes."

"No!"

I nodded, thinking if I said "yes" again, we might go on and on forever.

"I had you down as a little girl from the provinces," she said.

She put an exaggerated singsong into her voice and scraped at the phlegm at the back of her throat.

"I don't talk like that," I snapped back. She didn't speak so elegantly herself, all lazy and mis-stressed.

"Yes, you do!" Viktoria cackled, the sound coming from her belly. I reached for my coffee cup and sipped, though I knew there was nothing left but the dregs.

"Cool scar," she said, returning to her owl-like study of me.

I pulled my head scarf farther down my forehead, but Viktoria leaned toward me, placed her fingertips to my skull, and slid the fabric back across my hair, making the scar more visible. I was so shocked that she had touched me that I let her straighten the collar of my dress too and pat it flat, finger the locket at my neck while I sat rigid, praying she did not open it.

"You can call me Vitya," she said. A boy's name. She offered me her hand to shake. I thought of Jonathan offering his hand the first time we had met, saw his face again as he apologized, when it was I who had missed the beat. I grasped Viktoria's hand and shook it. It seemed such an odd thing to do, but if Jonathan had wanted it, and now this Moscow girl, I presumed it was sophisticated. I looked down at her long nails painted a dark purple.

"You got somewhere to stay, Miss Saratov?"

I nodded.

"A job?"

"No."

"No?"

"No."

We were off again, into one of her teasing loops. She sucked air through her teeth.

"But I'll be OK."

"'Course you will. Because I can get you a job."

"I'm OK, thanks."

"Swanky restaurant, not like this shit pit. Lots of Western men. I'll speak to my boss."

She unhooked her claws from the stool and snip-snapped on her heels back to the counter. The seam of her jeans twitched between the cheeks of her backside as if trying to escape. I didn't move, unsure if I had permission to go. The homeless man from earlier was limping along the sidewalk, flapping his arms at a damp pigeon. Slowly I found my courage. I reached down for the handle of my bag. But it wasn't there. My clothes, makeup, clock, camera, the play, Nika's photograph, my everything—gone.

18

NOT MY HORSE

I went down on my hands and knees on the greasy floor and searched between the legs of the stools. I wrenched open the café door, expecting to see my bag on the steps like a late apology. I dashed a hand along a dusty shelf on the wall, though my eyes told me it was empty. Viktoria stayed behind the counter and watched — a scientist observing a strange astral phenomenon that must fly its course and burn out.

"It's gone, Dasha. Just accept it."

I sat at one of the low tables and cried great heaving sobs. Viktoria pulled up a chair.

"You're better off without your stuff," she said gently. "If what you're wearing is anything to go by."

Then she said: "You're a size 42, right?"

I was wrapped back up in my inadequate coat, zip fastened, turned by the shoulders, and walked toward the door. I stuffed my hands in my pockets and clutched at all the things I owned:

a packet of cigarettes, a lighter, a purse with a significant but finite supply of money, a letter from an *Americanski* journalist. It was the lost photo of Nika that hurt the most — my last artifact of a past age. I thought of Mama in the kitchen, asking me that day if I wanted something physical to help me remember Nika. She had been right. Without that photo in my hands, might I forget her face, the way she moved? I understood Mama's desperate fury now as she had searched the house for Zaychik. In my mind, I raced across the scrubland, found that mound of stones, and dug Zaychik up so I had something real to press against my chest.

Viktoria freed herself of her apron and said curt goodbyes to a fat man in a stained white T-shirt who had arrived to work his shift.

"Don't forget this," she said, grabbing the English workbook from the counter where I'd eaten my sandwiches — a meal that now bubbled, oily, in my stomach. I hugged the book to my chest in lieu of a hare and we left. Outside, on the curb, two boys in hoodies waited with scooters. We nodded our hellos, and Viktoria clamped a heel on the outside edge of one of the machines, swinging a taut thigh over, wrapping herself around the driver. She had told me that friends of hers would give us a lift. I thought she had meant in a car. I considered running again, like I had from the taxi man, but this was kindness, from a warrior. She could have chased me from her café with a broom. I mimicked Viktoria, with much less elegance, and clambered aboard the other bike. I shoved the loose fabric of my dress between my legs, tucked the book down inside my coat. The heat of the boy's body warmed my thighs.

"OK?" he said, handing me a helmet, and we pulled away with a jolt that almost threw me to the sidewalk.

I squealed with terror the whole way, pulling myself closer and closer to the boy, no matter that he was a stranger, pressing the front of my visor hard into his back, leaving a dent in the fleece of his hoodie, and probably in his flesh. We wove in and out of stationary traffic — fast, so fast — mounting curbs with neck-wrenching bumps. The boys punched the air and whooped if a pedestrian was sent scurrying. When we pulled up, Viktoria was as calm as the moment we'd left. I was quivering, too shaken to speak, but euphoric at the same time. I had survived. She offered the boys no thank-yous — the scooter rides were hers to claim, that was clear. The transaction completed, the boys zipped away, two hornets chasing each other's tails.

"You're still here," I said.

She bared her bulldog teeth. "You betcha, Miss Saratov."

The building stood proud, each of its angles lit up, the name Hotel Alexander spelled out in illuminated letters above a revolving door that sucked in good-suited businessmen and spat out wealthy tourists. I took Jonathan's letter from my coat pocket and read it again.

"There must be another Hotel Alexander," I said.

"Not near Kuznetsky Most, there isn't."

Viktoria's arm was through mine before I could sound any more doubts. She pulled me inside, into the kaleidoscope glass of the revolving doors, onto a sea of pink marble, striped furniture, patterned rugs. A piano gleamed white in the corner. We passed pillars coated in soft maroon fabric that Viktoria stroked like obliging cats. The place was a symphony of whispers until:

"Erm, no! No! No, thank you!"

A man in a ribbon-edged suit and a silly flat hat slipped out from behind a leather-topped desk. He took hold of Viktoria's other arm and pulled her in the opposite direction, as if we were about to swap partners in a folk dance.

"No, you don't," he kept saying. "Oh, no, you don't."

"Excuse me!" Viktoria yelled, her voice bouncing off marble. She wrested free of both of us and claimed her own space on the polished floor. "Who do you think you are to touch me?" Her voiced had changed, gone up an octave. All the stresses were in the right places now.

"You are not allowed in here." The man lowered his voice in a way that asked her to do the same. "You know that. You need to leave." Every head was turned in our direction. The whispers gone, we could hear a dribble of piano music, not coming from the piano itself.

"You have mistaken me for someone else!" said Viktoria, stamping out every word. Then louder: "This ain't me and this ain't my horse! I shall be expecting an apology from your superior."

The man shook his head and laughed. "No, it's you, all right! It's your horse. You're the bloody driver!" And suddenly, there were reinforcements, two men in white shirts and bow ties. Both took hold of Viktoria, her new partners in this unfathomable dance, and started dragging her toward the revolving doors. She lost a stiletto, and I scuttled over to pick it up. I wasn't sure what else to do except play the prince, clutching a glass slipper.

"OK! OK!" Viktoria cried, shaking them free. "I am capable of walking! Take your hands off me!" She kicked away her other

184

stiletto, making a great show of flicking it, skidding it, across the reception area. "Let me go, or you will regret it! You will be sorry!" Through the revolving doors she went, barefoot, chin high, more willing to risk frostbite and an infection than damage her pride.

We watched her go along the cobbles, the ribbon-suited man and I, and when the dust had fallen, he said: "You too. Hop to it."

"Oh, no," I said. I picked up Viktoria's other discarded shoe, feeling absolutely that I had a claim to it. "I am supposed to be here. I think." Though after the scene I had witnessed, I wasn't absolutely sure. I looked down at myself—my zipped-up coat with the bulk of my English workbook stuffed down the front, the tired flower print of my dress, my battered lace-up shoes and dirty socks. Viktoria had been right: it was a blessing that my other clothes were gone, because these were my best and still I did not belong here.

"I'm a guest of Jonathan Bruck," I told the man, more of a question than a statement. I slipped the scarf from my head and stuffed it into a pocket, a magician with no knack for sleight of hand.

"Ah!" the man cried, his face transformed—delighted! "You are Darya Pavlovna! And I have been expecting you!"

My room was on the fifth floor; a plastic card was my key. Inside, the carpet was so new that it smelled of its factory, the bed so big a whole family could have shared it and not bothered one another with an elbow. There was a caramel bedspread, a desk and a mirror, beautiful lamps. Two velvet chairs shared a coffee table (looking nothing like the chipped rectangle of glass in our living room back home). In the bathroom: a wall of mirrors, a bath completely separate from the shower. The shower had its own door. The counter had two sinks. There were eight towels. Multiplications of multiplications. So much of everything.

"There's a safe for your valuables," said the ribbon-suited man opening a cabinet. He shrugged. "If you have any." The name on his badge said *Pavel*, like my father. Nothing like my father. He opened another cabinet. "And in here's the fridge." I thought of ours—the only thing back home that could claim to be bigger or fancier. Was it keeping Mama warm, now that we were all gone? I pictured her holding the great white beast in an embrace and felt a prick of sorrow for her, so I shunted my attention back to Pavel, who was demonstrating the TV, mounted high on the wall as if it were art. "All the channels!" he said, poking the remote control at the screen. He tuned it to a music station—the song that Zlata had sung on a loop in that church back-room office, the one about finding a prince in the provinces. I thought of her apology on the 40th Day as we'd hugged goodbye in the rain. *It's a lonely city, Moscow. It's cold, whatever you think about the weather.* It had been a white lie. She had said it so I would not feel so bad about her going.

Pavel made to turn the TV off, his demonstration over.

"No," I said. "Don't. This is my favorite song."

The hotel's restaurant was a green-carpeted ballroom—an immense, moody sea. Afloat on it were enough white-napkined boats to seat two hundred people.

"Dinner is after seven p.m.," Pavel had told me.

"And where will I find the kitchen?"

He'd laughed, thinking this was a joke. "I'll be at my desk," he'd said, leaving me to my room alone. "I'll point the way."

The man guarding the restaurant door wore a ribbon-edged suit of a different style, a different status. He took me to a table far from any of the other diners—women in plain sheath dresses and chic belted trousers, earlobes swinging with stones; men in jackets and open-necked shirts, lace-up shoes that caught the light with their shine. We were being spread around, as if the room would tip and slide should more diners sit on one side than the other. If this was an effort to make the place look busier, it did not succeed. But my position allowed me to stare. In addition to shaking hands, what other new mysterious codes of Moscow behavior would I learn if I watched?

On the menu, there were lists of salads, and fish prepared in all kinds of ways. I searched for something that would fill me up. I'd never eaten in a restaurant before, and though I understood the principle, I did not know the rules. Mama used to be a waitress in a restaurant in Saratov, before I was born. It came to me then. That was how she had met Papa. She had tipped a plate of food accidentally into his lap. She used to pretend to do it again at the family table. I'd forgotten all about it—Mama and Papa's comedy routine. "Look out!" she'd cry. "Dinner's about to land!"

A girl with a head of pixie blond hair was serving a group of men in the center of the room. I listened to their order so I could see how this would work.

"*I want it rare*," one of the men was saying, speaking in English. I could understand that he was expressing a desire, just not the thing he wanted. I pieced that together later.

"Excuse me?" the pixie girl replied in Russian, then in timid English: "*I am sorry?*"

"*RARE.*" The man raised his voice so that the word might penetrate her brain. "*BLOODY. NOT COOKED MUCH.*"

He shared a look with the other men, who snorted and piled on their own comments, each one tripping a switch that set them laughing louder and louder. The pixie girl nodded, wrote something down, but I'd seen how her mouth had trembled. She didn't have a clue.

When she came to me, I said. "*Borsch*, please." It would not fill me up, but it seemed safe. Start small. "Thank you."

"That's it?" She looked up, taking in the sight of me. Without a comb, my hair was a mess; without any makeup, my skin felt oily and dull. The dress was limp and stained from traveling, and my white socks were gray. I could tell from her expression that I wasn't doing this right, so I sank back into my menu. I would try again. The price next to everything seemed impossible.

"Burger's good," she said, moving me along. "The stroganoff . . ." She looked behind her to the man guarding the door, making sure he wasn't paying attention, before she turned back with a wobbly hand and a puckered face, ". . . not so good."

"OK," I said.

"OK, you'll have the burger?"

"OK, I'll have the burger."

"The *borsch* as well?"

"No!" The price of the two together would have fed us at home for a week.

She gave me a polite smile, which I returned as thanks. I read her name badge: *Ekaterina*.

"He wants his steak cooked rare," I said, as she leaned in to take my menu.

"Huh?"

"The English guy. He wants a bloody steak."

"Oh, thank you." A real smile this time.

The burger, when it arrived, looked too handsome to eat. It was a huge slab of beef in a sesame bun, lettuce spilling from it. There were wedges of potato, fried crunchy and brown. Good plates. A gold rim. When Ekaterina came to clear the table, I pulled my purse from my dress pocket and started counting.

"Wait," I said when she made to leave. "I need to pay."

"You are a resident? At the hotel?"

I nodded.

"Well, then, you pay for everything at the end," she said.

The end. The idea felt ominous. There would be an end to this, of course, but I had no clue what would come after.

19

ONCE UPON A TIME

The farther you walked from the center of the hotel, the less you could hear its heartbeat—the sound of silverware on china, glasses clinking, laughter exploding. In the evenings, that hotel had a clamoring heart. Walk the soft, dark corridors, away from the bars and restaurants, down the hotel's veins to its fingertips, and the main soundtrack was your own shoes on the carpet.

I felt protected in those corridors, my first week in the city. Not scared. Never spooked. I was alone, but never alone. Behind every bedroom door was a babbling TV, a conversation tamped down. There were people. Sometimes I would hear two voices climbing together, and I tried to imagine the configuration of their bodies. I tried to imagine doing that with someone that I loved, doing it for pleasure. Had Jonathan thought of me like that before he told himself to stop?

I didn't leave the hotel at all those first few days. Outside, the temperature was sliding. I needed a hat, better boots, that's what I told myself. I needed a chance to adjust. Inside, of course, it was a constant climate—not one difficult thing. The shrieks and sirens beyond the glass could not touch me. The hotel became my oak tree to climb inside until I had made a plan.

I washed out my dress and underwear in the bathroom sink, using the small wrapped bars of soap that appeared as fast as I used them. I hung my clothes to dry on the room's heater—a heater completely at my control, not warm only at the whim of Aslan (or, as I always suspected, Diana). While they dried, I wore the bathrobe that I found in the wardrobe the morning I'd arrived. Left by the last person who used the room before me, I had thought, until I saw the words *Hotel Alexander* embroidered across one breast. Sometimes I would put on Viktoria's shoes, stuff the toes with toilet paper, and practice. All the women whom I watched through the window from the hotel's lobby wore heels as tall and thin as the legs of herons, and they wore them like it was nothing. I spent hours among the velvet cushions and green exotic leaves of the lounge, peering out at this new wildlife that surrounded me. I thought of Papa and me watching those loris navigate vines and branches on nature programs on TV. Someone in a ribbon-edged suit would always come along and ask, "Would you like tea?" and I would always say, "Yes, please, with milk and sugar," trying to be sophisticated, thinking of how Zlata took it, though they always brought the tray with everything. I did think I might spot my loris as I watched the crowds on their way to Red Square and the Bolshoi. *Look at me, Zlata!* I'd say, banging on the window. *I've made it.* Or maybe she would see me first. People stared in as they walked past, just as much as we stared out. Perhaps we — the residents — were wildlife to them.

Up in my room, on the expanse of the bed, I worked through the undiscovered pages of my English book. I used the pencils provided by the hotel, branded with its name like everything else and positioned on the desk and bedside tables at an angle across custom-printed notepads. I started hiding these pencils because, like the soaps, they were replenished with each room clean, and at the end of day three, once I had enough, I placed a handful in a glass that I'd taken from beside the minibar. Seeing that display of pencils made me believe, each time I glanced at it, that I had made definite steps toward achieving my ambition.

One exercise in my book asked me to write out these dreams for myself. *Create your own fairy tale*, it said. Parts of the sentences were already written. *Once upon a time there was a* . . . My task was to fill in the gaps using the list of characters, scenes, objects, and actions. *And they lived in a* . . . It was up to me. Did I want my story to be about a beautiful *prinsessa* or an evil spirit? A fool or a fox? *And the thing they wanted most in the world was* . . . The book said that this was a useful exercise in learning to talk about the past, but to me it was about the future. The plot, the cast, the setting — I got to decide. Good could triumph over evil; all I had to do was say so. The rest of my life was only a matter of choices.

I took long baths that week, the water running hot forever — again, not metered out by Aslan or Diana. I'd sink down, bubbles up to my chin, and lie there smoking until the water turned cool. I used the little bottles of shampoo and cream that, like the never-ending flow of soap and pencils, just kept coming and coming. *If you require any further toiletries,* said a small folded and laminated card, *do not hesitate to speak to a member of the staff.* So after three days of rubbing at my teeth with a washcloth and chewing the mints that sat in cut-glass bowls on the reception desk, I asked Pavel for a toothbrush and toothpaste.

"And a comb if you have one."

"Why don't you ask the girls in the spa for some samples too?" he said, handing me the things I'd asked for, packaged in lovely gray cardboard boxes that seemed such a shame to throw away, so I didn't.

The spa was in the basement belly, where the temperature was even warmer. The lights were dim, and the air was thick with herbs and menthol. The girls that Pavel had directed me to see were dressed like nurses but had the painted faces of performers. I did not know what he meant by *samples* but asked anyway. Everyone had been so nice since I'd walked through the doors of the hotel, since Viktoria had walked out, that it had made me open and trusting. It was a feeling so alien that I can accurately describe it only now: I felt cared for, so I felt free.

As I waited for the *samples*, I was handed a menu of all the things the nurses could do for you: paint your nails, improve your complexion, remove the stress from your back. For a price. Though the cost was beyond my reach, it did not seem such a ridiculous thing to do, to hand over money for the kind physical touch of someone else.

"Have you swum in the pool yet?" asked the girl who had remained at the counter. Her hair was so tightly pulled back into her ponytail that her head shone like the marble floors. It made my efforts with Alana's hair seem pathetic.

"Pool?"

She pushed open the double doors with their portholes, and the air became warmer yet. There it was, long and thin, the surface as still as a lake at night, the spotlights making a new constellation of stars on the surface. Around the edges were shelves of rolled towels and wooden slatted beds padded with cushions. I put a hand to my mouth, and the nurse with the polished hair giggled when I gasped. That lesson with Jonathan where we had drawn our homes—here was my swimming pool. Fate was playing games again, giving me gifts—that's what I believed; it was rewarding me for leaping.

I headed back to my room with a small, stiff, glossy bag filled with packets and vials, the smell of the *banya* on my dress. An unnumbered door on my corridor opened a crack.

"Hey, village girl!"

I stopped, but the voice said, "No, keep moving, there are cameras."

I did as I was told—trusting and open—looking up to see the red winking dot of the CCTV.

"Open your door and leave it open," hissed the voice. "I'll make a run for it."

"Vitya?"

"Shhh!"

I did as she said, swiping my card and stopping the heavy door with my foot. And in she burst, carrying some stiff, glossy bags of her own — larger and battered. Viktoria. Dressed all in black again, wearing a fresh pair of heels.

"Nice going, Miss Saratov," she said, kicking off the new shoes and placing them next to her other pair under the desk. She saw the toes stuffed with paper and gave me a look — a teacher's glare, but there was something congratulatory in it. She did a tour of the bathroom, palming body lotions and boxed shower caps, shoving them into the pocket of her jacket. She opened up drawers in the main room, considered the weight of a crystal ashtray, then dropped it into her shoulder bag. She tut-tutted that the hair dryer was attached to the wall.

"You eating here? I haven't seen you leave."

She wrapped a hand around the pencils I'd placed in the glass and took them all except one. I winced to see them go but didn't dare protest. After all, I wanted streetwise friends too to fix up this dream, and wasn't Viktoria exactly that?

"I eat in the restaurant," I told her.

"Well, get room service," she said. "That way you can keep the knives and forks. The saltshaker too."

"Why?"

The teacher's glare again, but this time cold and simple. I would need to try harder if Viktoria was going to score me a five.

"So . . ." she said, taking in the view beyond the curtains. Downward was the neat hotel courtyard; across, another building, more hotel rooms. She waved sweetly, but menacingly, at a woman opposite, who backed away from her window rather than return the gesture. "What's the story, Miss Saratov?"

"Story?"

There once was a hare who was scared of everything . . .

There once lived a beautiful girl whose mother died when she was very young . . .

"Yeah, how does a little village girl like you end up in a place like this?"

"It's . . . from a friend," I said. "I've come here to work."

She nodded, but her face said, *Don't believe you*. And I could see that she was right. I was taking baths and drinking tea, reading books and putting pencils in a glass. I did not have a job. Jonathan might come and find me, I realized. The idea filled me with excitement but also with dread. If I was not working when he got here, like the smart and capable woman I was supposed to be, he would never think of me as a grown-up. He would never let himself love me. Then there would be no *happily ever after*, as my English book called it, as Zlata had called it back home.

Viktoria came close, so I could smell the meatiness of her breath. She was ugly, but so striking at the same time, all sharp edges and dark lines. There was something hypnotic about being in her presence. She stroked a thumb over the silver line of my scar, and I flinched, not expecting it. If she called it beautiful, as Dmitriy had, would I believe her? What flaws of her own would she pull up as a comparison? I think Viktoria believed herself to be perfect.

"Well, aren't you going to open them?" she said.

"Huh?" I thought she meant my scar, that the story of me might be sealed within.

She nodded at the bags on the bed. "Open them up. They're my present to you."

I was scared to, but I did what she said—found no pig's head, no bomb. I pulled out pairs of pressed jeans, a red stretch dress, a diamond-buttoned sweater, a pink cardigan with a halo of fluff, sleeveless tops, two pairs of boots, a coat, a hat, lacy underwear, and, last, folded on its hanger and sealed in plastic, a good blouse. Silk. Viktoria watched my reactions like a proud parent. Fate gave a belly laugh.

"For me?"

"I'll take two pieces for all of it," she said.

"Oh, I see." Not a present. I pulled my purse from my pocket, and Viktoria watched me count.

"Actually," she said, "make it three and a half."

I did not mind. She was the mouse from the stories, or the beetle or the wolf—the creature that asked, *Give me coins and someday I will be at your service.* This was an investment in my future. I had my worldly friend, my good blouse—something to tell Jonathan. And anyway, the things spread across the bed were worth five times as much, maybe even ten.

"We're going out," she told me. There was no asking with Viktoria—she just laid out her plan. We would leave separately—she through a fire exit, I through reception—and then meet at the front of the building.

"So what's *your* story?" I asked her before she went. She was a hare that was scared of nothing, for certain. I could not imagine that she had ever been anything else. But I wanted to know why Pavel had been so ferocious with her, when he had been so kind to me—the true outsider. He was always eager to tell me where to find things and would sometimes come to sit with me in the lobby. He was generous with his stories, each one invariably beginning with *Now! When I was eighteen years old* . . . Pavel always had a joke too. *A rabbit goes into a bookshop and asks for a carrot* . . . *A man goes to the doctor and complains that he can't sleep* . . .

"It was a stupid argument over a bar bill," Viktoria said. "That schmuck at the front desk likes to hold a grudge." She cocked her head around my door, checking left and right that all was clear, then slipped her hips through the gap and was out into the corridor.

I walked through that lobby as if stepping from the wings onto a stage — dressed for a production, not for my life. Viktoria had helped me choose what to wear — tight jeans, the pink halo cardigan, the heavy wool coat, heeled boots. She had snapped the labels from the tiny, scratchy underwear with her teeth as I'd undressed.

"Take off those silly little-girl underpants," she'd instructed, "and put them straight in the wastebasket."

Pavel looked up from his desk as I made my way past reception and across the marble. He took a breath to speak but stopped. I looked so different. He could not fathom this better-dressed version of me. I willed him to say nothing, because how could I explain? Though he was nothing like my father, he became a parent in that moment, one with the power to send me back to my room.

"Darya Pavlovna!" he announced, with his usual cheer, finding his words.

I stopped by his desk, because I couldn't not. He would know that I had gotten all this from Viktoria. He would think that I was up to something. I thought of Mama, how she had kept her mouth shut when she'd seen me in that pink top and denim skirt, let me go out dressed like that and make the mistake for myself. I was scowling at Pavel now; I could feel it.

Perhaps that is why he said, "A man comes out of surgery and the doctor says, 'Bad news: I'm going to have to operate again. I left a glove inside you.' 'No worries,' says the patient. 'Here's a thousand—go buy yourself a new one.'"

He snickered at his own old joke. I looked down at my new coat, thinking I would be the final punch line.

"I'm having a little gathering for my birthday, Darya Pavlovna," he went on.

I was still waiting for the catch. "Right."

"It's not for a week or so, but you will come, won't you? You will come and celebrate with me?"

"Um, yes."

"They let me do a small something in the staff room for my friends, you see, to thank me for my loyalty. And Jonathan would never forgive me if he knew I'd thrown a party and not invited you." He lowered his voice for the next bit. He leaned in. "I'm only letting you know now so you have time to buy me a present." He gave a wink.

My gaze skittered to the revolving doors, worried that Viktoria, sick of waiting, would come bursting through like the Siberian High and make another scene.

"Thank you," I said.

"No, thank *you!*" And that was that. He clasped his hands and rocked on his heels, as if doing a comedy impression of a concierge, as if he were not really one himself. "Have fun this evening, Darya Pavlovna! You look absolutely wonderful!"

We went for drinks, Viktoria and I, a short walk through the sleet that I had been watching thicken as I drank tea in the lobby those past few days. The skies were turning to steel with the weight, and I was about to get the Moscow snow I had dreamed of.

Inside, the bar was all leather booths and dark wood. It looked like a saloon you see in an American film. The music matched up too—happy and angry with lots of guitars. Viktoria seemed to know everyone. "Greetings, eagles!" she cried as we came through the doors, and many heads turned. I trailed her, feeling invisible but happy to be so in this instance. If this was a stage, that night was a rehearsal, and I still needed to learn my lines.

I was introduced to person after person, no chance of remembering names. "Pleased to meet you," I'd say, and they'd grin at Viktoria, as if I were her new puppy demonstrating a trick that she had taught me. A tall bearded man named Alexei was Viktoria's favorite. His shirt was crisp, though half-untucked in an affected way. Her body shifted in his presence. She tried to be bold and impressive with him, but this only made her seem soft—as soft as Viktoria could ever be.

"Alexei manages a chain of dry cleaners," she told me proudly. "Oligarchs' wives get their maids to drop off all their expensive things." She put on a voice. "Clothes so rich they would dissolve if they came into contact with water!"

"Except they wouldn't," said Alexei with a laugh, "but don't tell them that." The two exchanged information about mutual friends in a businesslike way. This was no report of who they'd seen crying or boasting in the post office; there was no washing of anyone else's bones. There was currency in what they had to say to each other. When Alexei gave his goodbyes and shouldered his way back to the bar, he stroked my arm, long and deliberately. "Nice cardigan, Dasha," he said. "Rinse it in cold water and you'll be fine."

Viktoria and I drank bottled beer like boys that night — free beers, of course. They were part of some unspoken agreement with Anna, a small girl with spidery blond hair who was serving behind the bar. I tried to glug my beer the way Viktoria did, her throat like an undulating snake, but it was harder than it looked. She talked about the job again, the one she could get me at a fancy restaurant. I didn't have the courage to tell her that this wasn't the image I had brought with me on the train. I had the blouse and the pencils; I just needed the desk. But Viktoria painted bright, exciting pictures with her words, and her ambitions for me began to paper over mine. The tips in this restaurant were unbelievable, she said: one girl had bought a fur coat in her first week.

"It'll take a bit of setting up, Miss Saratov," she warned, scanning the room as she spoke, looking for more friends, perhaps, someone more exciting than me. "So in the meantime, if you need anything, you just ask."

"Actually," I said, "there is something."

"Oh, yeah?"

"A bathing suit."

"A bathing suit? You are just fucking perfect!"

Our conversation halted there. We were ambushed by two

boys in matching V-neck sweaters. They slid into our horseshoe booth in a pincer movement.

"So, tell us your names, lovely ladies."

I opened my mouth to answer, but Viktoria got in first.

"I am Lyubov," she announced, the name sending a little stab to my throat, "and this is Natasha." She drew out the syllables of my "name," dancing it with her eyebrows. The boys grinned and nodded their understanding. I had not understood. I looked to Viktoria for an explanation, but her eyes were not on me.

"So, are you 'lovely boys' going to buy us dinner?" She narrowed her gaze, showed them her teeth. "And a nice big bottle of something to share?" The moment switched, just like that. This was how she was. It was terrifying when she did it to you but exhilarating to be with her on the ride. She reached out and grabbed whatever she wanted, as easy as swiping the complimentary soap from a hotel bathroom. I watched her take those boys gently by the hand, then flip them onto their backs. They never saw it coming. They had not ambushed us. The fools had wandered into a trap.

20

QUIET POOLS

Viktoria steered us to a restaurant with red armchairs and exposed-brick walls. The boys slowed down as we approached the entrance.

"Is there a problem, guys?" She fluttered her long, glued-on lashes. "Not to your taste? Not to your wallet?"

They could have walked away, but pride would not let them. They bluffed and blustered, saying they ate at places like this all the time.

Inside, Viktoria ordered for us both, poking her finger at the most expensive wines on the list.

"Natasha can eat as much as she likes," she explained, loud enough for the whole restaurant to hear. Thick-necked men in shiny suits glanced our way; tall girls with big hair and tiny dresses twinkled to get their partners' attention back. "Three plates of *cassata* and she still wouldn't put on an ounce!" The boys gulped, chose small plates for themselves.

The arms of the chairs kept us distanced from our hosts, yet when the desserts came, I felt the hand on my knee that I knew was coming. I may not have understood the transactions with the scooter drivers, with Alexei, or with Anna behind the bar, but this one was obvious. I gave Viktoria desperate looks that asked, *Will we have to pay, at the end?* Ekaterina's words in the hotel restaurant developed a new meaning. Viktoria offered no reassurances, but the situation was never not in her control. I watched it like a master class. The last spoonful of *cassata* passed our lips, and she was up, her thank-yous dripping with syrup, clicking her fingers at a waitress.

"Girl! Our coats!"

"Where are you going?" asked one boy, rising to half standing, his napkin falling from his lap.

"Home," she said in a way that branded him an idiot and would stand no response.

As we swayed back to the hotel, our stomachs full and our heads fizzy, Viktoria mimicked the boys' shock. She repeated their boasts about fishing and cars, belly-laughing at the detail. I tried to join in, but I was shaking a little from the lucky escape.

"I thought we were going to have to—"

"God, no!" she cackled. "They were in town just for the weekend, didn't you hear? Not worth the effort."

I felt guilty, as if I had stolen something. But then I thought of Dmitriy Vasiliev, how I had handed myself to him with no expensive meal in return, and still he had been shortchanged. I had used it as a weapon. I missed Dmitriy suddenly, painfully. Why had I not gone to him to say a proper goodbye?

I got a kiss from Viktoria, on the mouth, before she left me. The hotel's revolving doors would not spin for her. I really was Vasilisa the Beautiful—the only one who could stand before Baba Yaga's hut and be let in. *Little house, little house, stand the way your mother set you, your back to the forest and your front to me!*

"I've decided that I'm going to show you where I live, Miss Saratov," Viktoria said proudly, strutting off into the darkness, refusing to be cowed.

"When?" I called after her.

"Soon," she said. "Soon."

I could not wait. But she made me.

That night, from nowhere, Nika came.

I had been sleeping so well in that bed big enough for a whole family, no crying into the dark now that I was away from our old bedroom. The warm hum of the hotel going about its twenty-four-hour business was as comforting as an extra blanket. But that night, I woke with the immediate sensation that someone was in my room. And it was her—dressed in her uniform for the first day of school. I had wondered where her ghost had gone since the 40th Day. I had never imagined that the answer could be Moscow.

She spoke to me—*Come on, Dasha! Get up!*—and she pulled away the sheets. It was no dream. She was a vivid outline, flesh and three dimensional. *Come on, Dasha! Come and find me!* Her voice was playful as she took hold of my hand. I could feel her skin, not cold, but pulsing, alive, her fingers gripping me tight. *You thought they'd gotten me, didn't you?* she said. *They didn't get me!* She was talking about a game of cat and mice, nothing more, and I believed her. I sank into the fantasy. I went to swing my legs from the bed — my limbs of sludge not answering my brain's command at first, and then — *khlop!* I hit the carpet on the floor by my bed — cold, sweaty, awake, alone.

I stayed up late at the hotel bar the evening after that, drinking tea and smoking, not wanting to go upstairs and turn off the light. I listened to piano music trickle through the air while the white grand piano itself stood untouched. All around me, people drank vodka in tall glasses, the American way, sucking olives off sticks. And Ekaterina was serving.

"I thought you worked in the restaurant," I said.

"Restaurant, bar . . . I've done some housekeeping shifts too," she said. "I'd be up on those platforms with the pulleys cleaning windows if they'd let me."

The moment with the rare steak had bought me her kindness. She was stiff and formal with the other guests, mouth a flat line, placing the custom-printed paper doilies on the table first, then the drinks, then the check to sign, doing it all with a bob at the knees, her nose high, keeping her distance. She dropped all of that with me, leaning right over as she left fresh tea and removed the empty pots, so she could talk quietly, more casually. She had a locket around her neck, I noticed, similar to mine. It swung forward as she worked and knocked against her chin.

"I'm saving up," she confided.

"What for?" It couldn't be travel, because she was in Moscow already. Did she need a fur coat?

"I want to go to Venice," she said, the idea of it lighting her up. My face must have been blank, because she felt the need to add. "It's in Italy. The place with all the gondolas."

"I know Venice," I said. It was in one of the books Yelena had given me — a weird story about a man who was convinced he must go there but spends all of his time in a hotel, then dies of cholera. I gulped a little at the parallels.

"What's it like?" Ekaterina cooed. "Did you love it?"

"Oh, no, I haven't been," I said, though I liked the idea that she might mistake me for someone so worldly. "I've only read about it."

"My brother is working there," she said. "I miss him like crazy, you know?"

I nodded. Because I did know. Here I was, in the same city as Boris and Igor, with no address for them, no number. I think I expected them to wander into the hotel one day, sensing that I was near, or I would spot them in the street, just as I had thought I would see Zlata. Three people among millions.

"Can I get you anything else?" she asked, straightening up.

"I'd really like some more hotel pencils," I said, thinking of the ones Viktoria had stolen.

"OK!" Ekaterina laughed, heading off. "Pencils, it is!"

I pulled the paper coaster from beneath my cup and saucer, fingering its scalloped edges. I wanted to call Ekaterina back and ask for more of these too. They reminded me of home. They made me think of the warm, oily heads of Papa and my brothers, leaving their marks on the sofa, proof that they had always been there.

* * *

A whole three days later, she came for me. Three days of tea and the English workbook, music videos on television, and smoking in the bath. Three days of trying out various combinations of the clothing that now hung in my wardrobe. Three days of daring myself to wander the city alone. Three days of finding excuses not to.

We traveled there on the Metro, buying a single ticket and squeezing through the barriers as one. Viktoria negotiated those globe-lit escalators and white stone archways like water flowing downhill, never pausing to get her bearings. I tried to be brisk and carefree like her, but I wonder if you have to be born that way. I was transfixed by the NO EXIT signs. *There is no way out*, they reminded you at every turn. *There is no way out*.

In the lime-green light of the Metro car, I examined the other women there — the girl holding on to the railing, with perfect spirals of red-brown hair, pitching an amber scent of spices into the atmosphere. This was the smell of accomplishment, I thought, a smell that could be bought with your first week's wages, along with a mythical fur coat. The woman opposite was reading a folded copy of *Kommersant*, her knee poking out between the opening of her thick wool coat, not one snag or pull in her fine nylon stockings. These were the women I'd seen walking past the hotel as if they were gliding inches above the ground, and whom I would see negotiating the snow when it came, as if it was a beast they'd tamed long ago. These were the women whose army I would join.

Viktoria lived in a large gray building, a many-legged hunk of towering concrete, in one of the outer ring roads of the city. We passed the *babushka* chewing her cheeks at the front desk, a transistor bouncing old songs from the paneled walls. Viktoria nodded a hello, but the woman did not nod back. Her eyes followed me as we took the pebbled stairs scuffed loose of their gleam. On the first floor, Viktoria attacked the locks of a steel-reinforced door with a serious bunch of keys. There was a puddle of old vomit in one corner, and Viktoria saw me see it and make my judgment. She'd led me to think she lived in a palace, a magical kingdom that would beat the Hotel Alexander for splendor hands down.

"There's a dog that gets in," Viktoria said. I thought she was blaming the animal for the mess, but no. "That's its favorite thing, puke. It will be all licked clean by tomorrow."

Beyond the steel door was another concrete foyer lit by two tiny squares of window. The smell of freshly made soup mingled with an underbelly stench of garbage. It made me nostalgic for our concrete landing back home, with its graffiti and peeling paint, its lack of an elevator and its guttering lights. It was a better place than this.

"These are the communal areas," Viktoria said—a tour guide voice, oddly pompous and pleased with the squalor. On our right was a living room with yellowing mismatched furniture. A dubbed soap opera on the TV played out to no one, I thought, until we moved into the room and saw the dark-skinned man buried deep in the sofa, shoveling stew into his mouth from a bowl held close to his chin. He did not acknowledge us. Viktoria ignored him.

"Who was that?"

"How should I know?"

The kitchen was a vast room with a wall of windows that

overlooked the glass-and-cement face of the neighboring apartment building, the area divided into separate stations, each with its own greasy stash of bottles and cans. So many cooking appliances—gas stoves, plug-in hot plates, assorted antique microwaves. Viktoria's space was in one corner, a health-hazard oven topped with blackened burners.

"We never come in here," she said. "There's a fridge, a kettle, and a toaster in our space. What more do we need?"

"I could cook you something," I told her. I had not been in a kitchen for almost two weeks. I felt the unexpected pleasure of being in familiar territory. "I'm a good cook."

She looked at me sideways. "You're a quiet pool, Miss Saratov. Please tell me there's a devil in there somewhere."

My tour visited the bathroom, a large echoing room with hospital tiles, tough steel fittings, and the feral tang of piss. Everything had that yellow tinge of age, exactly like the furniture in the living room.

"We have our own toilet seats," Viktoria qualified.

I laughed.

"No, really," she said. "If you need to go, you can borrow mine."

I did not understand why she was showing me all this, pointing out every fault. Viktoria was not one for sympathy, or one to fear the evil eye. She liked to impress. We crossed the concrete foyer.

"Now this is *my* part of the flat," she said, deep voice, shoulders back. "We keep it locked."

And that was what the whole tour had been leading up to—*I will show you the rest, then show you the best.* We kicked off our shoes in the doorway of Viktoria's autonomous region and stepped onto the parquet floor of a living room. There was the smell of detergent and it looked like it was laundry day. Sheets were strung from the ceiling—but they weren't there to dry. These were the walls. Jonathan's floor plan on the whiteboard came to mind. What did this home look like from above? Viktoria had divided one enormous space into a living room and several bedrooms via a maze of suspended bedsheets. It felt like being a child again, making a den, playing house.

We moved past the neat velvet sofa and portable TV, beyond a pink stretched sheet that took us into Viktoria's sleeping area. There was a rack of clothes, a monster of a chest of drawers, and a desk stacked with cut-up magazines. A pair of scissors sat alongside a tube of glue and a collection of scrapbooks. More stuff of childhood.

"I used to love doing this!" I cried before realizing how that sounded—that I was far too grown up for it now.

"Stay away from those!" Viktoria hissed, and I shrank back, as if from a door that was there to stop all the world's evil from tumbling out.

"They are just books of things I want," she said, casual now, realizing how she'd sounded—weak. "Shopping lists, basically. Shoes, holidays . . ."

I don't believe you, I thought, but this made us even. I was allowed to keep my story a secret if she could too.

We shed our coats on the mattress on the floor and moved through a yellow sheet to find a tiny girl asleep, her mouth gaping. It was Anna from behind the bar the night we had gone out.

"She works late," Viktoria whispered. "Doesn't get home until seven a.m."

I watched Anna breathing while Viktoria swiped through the clothes on Anna's rack. She stopped at a green knitted jacket, pulled it free, and slipped it on. I saw Anna open one eye but shut it quickly and carry on feigning sleep.

"This way."

We pushed through a blue sheet next into a jumble of bags, boxes, and clothes. A set of bunk beds was pushed up against a wall. The smell made me think of our living room in the mornings after the boys had just woken up. I understood now why Mama wanted a spray to take it away.

"The boys' room. Misha and Danya." Viktoria's lips were tight, the mess of the place spoiling her display. She stepped across a scattering of socks to rescue an empty food wrapper, balling it up. "Cockroaches don't need any encouragement," she told me, making it clear that she wasn't a girl who would usually tidy up after a boy.

We settled into Viktoria's space. She put on a CD of deep, grinding music, no thought for Anna sleeping beyond the fabric wall. Viktoria danced and sang the riffs, encouraging me to do the same. But this was no Lezginka. It had nothing to do with your wrists and feet. You had to dance from your groin, and I couldn't match the liquid motion of Viktoria's hips. She painted my face after that, dipping into a full shoebox of eye shadows, lipsticks, brushes, and sponges. She combed my hair for me, and I enjoyed the touch. I tried to think of it as a childhood game — playing hairdressers, dress-up. I tried not to think of Nika, sitting at the mirror as I put flowers in her hair.

Goodbye to play and summer days,
We welcome in our future bright and new.

I tried not to think of the Nika that was waiting for me back in my hotel room, preparing her next nighttime visit.

"I'm going to give you bangs," Viktoria announced, and I shrieked back a "No!" I put a hand over my scar and the curtain of hair that covered it. The other hand went to my locket.

"But it's sexy, your scar," she said. "Where did you get it, anyway?"

I saw it in a magazine and I just had to have it. The words came into my head, but I dared not say them out loud, unsure how the joke would land. Or rather, I was sure it would land badly.

"I fell," I said. "I hit it."

"How?"

Our eyes locked in the mirror.

"Just tripped. There's no story."

She twisted the back of my hair into heated rollers, pulling hard in acknowledgment of the lie. Then, with the concentration of a surgeon, she sliced away the front of my hair regardless.

"You've drawn attention to it," I said.

"I know. And men will fucking love it."

When Viktoria wasn't looking, I picked up some of my hair from the wooden floor and pushed it into the pocket of my jeans. I'd place it in the locket with Nika's hair later.

The game wasn't over. She sharpened my nails to a point and painted them red, then thrust clothes at me from her rack, instructing me to change, change, and change again. She chose soft, animal-like fabrics that slipped against my body, clung and draped. I did not know where the material ended and my skin began. I moved differently when I was dressed like that.

"Perfect," she said eventually.

The skirt was white and violet, tight as a bandage, my thighs pinned together. On top I had a sheer blouse — a good blouse, or was it a bad one? — the black of my bra showing through.

"I need a slip under this," I protested, but Viktoria wasn't interested in my thoughts.

"Stand there, put your hand on your waist, let the other arm hang."

I did as I was told, and there came a flash I wasn't expecting. A Polaroid photograph slipped from the mouth of a camera. Another piece of my soul. We sat on the mattress together, waiting for the image to appear.

"You next?" I said, as the image went from white to brown, smoky shapes. I imagined doing this with Alana when I got home, when she came to our door again, asking me to play. Then I remembered that I wasn't going home, and that Papa's camera was gone, stolen with the bag.

"Nah, I'm just a jeans-and-heels kind of girl," Viktoria said, as if she was quoting someone else — a phrase cut out of a magazine and pasted into a scrapbook. "But look at you, Miss Saratov." We watched my figure emerge — not the dark-haired animal photographed for the American article. I was Vasilisa the Beautiful, after all, though my eyes were tight shut, startled by the flash.

Viktoria kept the picture. She needed to show it to her boss — the boss she was meeting later that evening, the one who could find me work in the fancy restaurant. Viktoria used the word *boss* for several people, or at least that was how it seemed. One man could not be doing so many unrelated things.

In my hand—as a reward, it felt—I was given a piece of fabric as slippery and silver as a fish. A bathing suit, just like I'd asked. I could wish for anything, and Viktoria would make it appear. That's what I believed. I thought of asking her to find my brothers, imagined her summoning them up as easily as clicking her fingers at a waitress and demanding to be brought her coat. But that would have meant giving her a little of my story in return, so I held back.

I left Viktoria's apartment in a taxi that she hailed for me outside her building, arm aloft, issuing a sound that was not quite a shout and not quite a whistle. The fare she paid in advance.

That night, the hotel caught fire. The bedroom, the bathroom, the corridors—all ablaze. I ran through the smoke, downstairs, past Pavel's desk, the leaves of the exotic plants curling, the velvet pillars inching black. I could have escaped there and then, out the front door, but I didn't. I went down to the basement instead, to the spa, panting and coughing. I wasn't sure what I expected to find—the staff had gone. I skidded across the corridor to the double doors with their round portholes and pushed through to the other side. The fire had reached this far. If the building collapsed, this would be the worst place to be. The towels on their shelves were alight, the cushions on the slatted beds too. And she was in the pool, treading water. I knew that she would be. I couldn't see her legs, only how the pumping motion of them was playing out in the rest of her body. The flowers in her hair were wet and wilting, but she was vital, breathing hard. I could almost smell her below the sharpness of chlorine. Every so often, her chin dipped beneath the surface and she had to work harder to stay afloat, but still she spoke, and confidently.

Come on, Dasha! she said. *Come on in!*

No. I stood on the sandstone tiles and shook my head.

What's wrong, Dasha? she asked. She was angry with me, or disappointed. *What's wrong with you? Don't you want to be rescued?*

And I choked awake, my upper body hanging over one edge of the enormous bed.

It was 6 a.m. I had promised myself the night before that I would put on my new bathing suit first thing and dive into the pool. My pool. I was looking forward to it. But now the task seemed cursed. Still, I got up, went to the bathroom, and put the suit on. It looked ridiculous. I was dressed as someone else again — an ice dancer missing her skirt — and I wondered how many times you have to make the same mistake before you learn your lesson. I pulled my old dress from home over the top, to appease my mama, even though she wasn't there, and I headed downstairs. I signed myself in with the woman at the desk and pushed through the double doors toward the water.

"There is a changing room if you need it," she called after me, but I only had to lift my dress over my head. I did not need a changing room for that.

I had the place to myself. I laid my dress on one of the lounges. The water was as still and flat as the first day I had discovered it. I stood with my toes at the grille of the filter, trying to fathom the depth, but I couldn't. The tiles beneath

216

were black, which made it seem bottomless. Below me was a great inky chasm, and suddenly I was very scared, not of the water, but of something. And because there was nothing else to place it on, I decided it must be the water after all. I put my dress on and left.

Upstairs, I climbed back into bed, still wearing the swimsuit. I sensed that fate was giving me another chance to jump, just as I had stepped from that platform onto the train, but I could not make the leap. I had become stuck inside the hotel, when it was supposed to be my one big chance, my life's opportunity. I did not know what I was jumping off, or where I should be jumping to.

21

TA-DA!

We played the dress-up game again. This time at the hotel.

I'd put up the DO NOT DISTURB sign after returning from the pool. I didn't want housekeeping to knock. I needed to sleep. I would make my own bed today, wipe down my own sink. But still a knock came.

"Room service!" called a voice, though I hadn't ordered anything. I got up to find Viktoria there on the other side of the door, smirking at her own joke, being bold with the CCTV.

"Look at you, little fish!" she said, taking in the sight of me in bathrobe and bathing suit, pushing me back into the room. "It's time to celebrate. My boss wants to see you."

We called for room service for real—Viktoria's idea. The day had crept past lunchtime without my noticing. She raked back the curtains, the sunlight like knives, and there was my Moscow snow, falling fast and fat, the courtyard painted white. Viktoria said we must have champagne with the food, and though I said no, she ordered it anyway, telling the person on the end of the phone to "make it snappy."

"What do you care?" she said, hanging up. "You're not paying."

"I am," I told her. "I pay for all of my food." I would not dine out on my misery. I would find a way to pay, at the end. I would prove Mama wrong, make her proud.

Viktoria sat me in front of the mirror and got to work, brushing my hair, putting in curlers, painting on a new face. That done, she said, "Time to sort out the hair below." She pulled a small plastic slow cooker from her bag, plugged it in, and threw in cubes that looked like *pastila*.

"You mean . . ."

She nodded gravely, the messenger of bad news; she could not be blamed.

"But no one is going to see that at my interview!"

She didn't respond. She turned to the pot and stirred with a thick wooden stick.

"Vitya?"

She sighed. "You're not a little girl anymore. Get that bathrobe off and lie on the bed."

The true call of "Room service!" saved me. I leaped up to answer. Ekaterina was there, one hand on the cart.

"Hello!" I cried, with too much enthusiasm. She only stared at me in my makeup and curlers.

"Oh! It's you!" she said, recognition landing. "You look so different. You look . . . older."

"Do I?"

"Oh, I didn't mean it bad!"

"Of course not!" I was pleased that she'd said it. *You have woken up bigger, Dasha,* I thought, and then, *If only Jonathan could see me now . . .*

Ekaterina pushed the cart into the room, the wheels giggling. When she saw Viktoria—sprawled now on the bed, a pet signaling that its stomach must be rubbed—she stopped. Her face went gray. I looked from one girl to the other, wondering what Ekaterina was supposing. Was she frightened by Viktoria's startling appearance? Was she envious that I had another friend? Had Viktoria's reputation traveled farther than the front desk?

Ekaterina fell back on ceremony, transforming into that girl who served all the other people in the bar—stiff and formal, nose high. She stood beside the cart, a rehearsed moment, then removed the silver cloches from the club sandwiches with a flourish.

"Ta-da!" cried Viktoria, like a joke, but a key too flat.

Ekaterina's face twitched just as it had when the English men had shouted their demands for bloody meat, but she continued the ritual, carrying the plates to the coffee table one by one, then the silverware, then the salt and pepper. Viktoria watched the back and forth with amusement—a cat with a feather. Tension was climbing, but I did not know what to say.

Her last trip was with the two glasses of champagne. She slid the tray onto her arm, navigated the end of the bed, and as she went to place it down, Viktoria stretched out her foot and nudged Ekaterina's elbow. The glasses toppled—a great flood across the armchairs.

"Fucking hell!" Viktoria erupted. She was up on her feet now.

"Leave it, Katya," I said. "It doesn't matter."

"No!" Viktoria breathed fire in my direction. "She needs to clean this up."

"I will," Ekaterina sputtered, righting the empty glasses. "I will."

"I'll help," I said, moving to the bathroom for towels.

"You stay where you are!"

I did as I was told, frozen in the bathroom doorway. I stared at Viktoria as she put on this show of ferociousness, for it was a show, just as she had pretended affection for those boys at the bar. Any moment now, she would flip Ekaterina onto her back.

"Ekaterina has fucked up," Viktoria said, enunciating each syllable as if they were bullets, "so, Ekaterina will unfuck it. That is, if she doesn't want us to tell her employer how incompetent she is."

I watched Ekaterina shake her head, close to tears, as she blotted at the puddles on the chairs with her serving cloth. Viktoria loomed.

"I'll bring you fresh glasses, a bottle, to say sorry," Ekaterina mumbled. "I can ask housekeeping to swap the chairs."

"Of course you will." Viktoria took a breath—here was the pause for emphasis. "And then you'll rip up the whole check. We will not be paying for a thing."

"No," Ekaterina muttered. "I'll make sure of that."

When she was gone, our champagne replaced, we finished our sandwiches without talking, the music channel filling the space. Viktoria ate voraciously, gulped down several glasses. I picked; I sipped.

"She might lose her job," I said eventually, but Viktoria only shrugged.

"You didn't need to do that," I went on. "She's actually really nice."

"No one is *really* nice, little fish," said Viktoria, wiping grease and her dark lipstick on the napkin. "Learn that lesson straight off."

No one is really nice, except, it seemed, Oleg Konstantinovich. As we walked to the restaurant, Viktoria calmed my nerves by saying, "He's really very nice, old Oleg. There's no need to be scared." It had been Viktoria who had ramped up the anticipation in the first place. *I could get you a job, maybe not. The fur coat is yours, maybe not.* She was playing my emotions, her bow on the strings. But it was attention all the same, so I drank it up. I slid my arm through hers. She was skilled at using her heels like picks on the slippery pavement; mine would not grip. The bandage skirt reduced me to a waddle. When I had imagined my snowbound Moscow life, I was striding along the flow of the *Moskva-reka* in *valenki* boots and a hareskin coat. I may as well have been Miss Russia now, shivering in bikini and sash. What made me feel truly naked was not wearing my locket. Viktoria had instructed me to take it off and put on a necklace of hers, gold and heavy, like an Egyptian queen's. I had shoved the locket into my bra because I did not want Viktoria seeing me go to the trouble of putting it in the room safe. I did not want her to know it meant anything.

We reached a pink awning and Viktoria said her goodbyes on the sidewalk.

"You're not coming in with me?"

She shook her head and grinned. I was a child overreacting at the dentist. She kissed me on the lips, as she always did, and patted the snow from my hair.

"Will you wait for me?" I asked.

"I've got things to do."

I was still angry with her for humiliating Ekaterina, yet I didn't want her to leave. I didn't want that. She was already heading off.

"Party at my place," she told me, not looking back. "On the 21st."

I think I did love her then, just as strongly as I'd loved Jonathan. If that had been love. How do you know? Does it grip you like a visc or pin you down, then leave you, as if waking from a dream? The 21st was too far away. I couldn't wait until then and didn't understand how she could either.

"I'm done with 2004 already," Viktoria called, slipping away, into the crowd. "I'm starting New Year's in November."

I was also done with 2004. I looked up at that pink awning and thought, *I could go to Kazansky station. I could get on a train and this would all be over.* I was shocked at myself . . . Wasn't this what I wanted? To be in Moscow. Would I only ever be a timid hare, one that always ran away?

I opened the restaurant door and pushed past the curtain.

The sharp, blond girl at the front desk barked at me, "We're not open. You need to go away." But when I gave her my name, her face reluctantly softened. She took my coat. I sat on a chair, three cushions deep, under the reddish glow of a huge curving lamp. The restaurant had a poured white floor with spaceship lighting. The bar was leather-bound and buttoned.

"Darya Pavlovna?"

Oleg Konstantinovich was tall and thin, his black hair gelled close to his scalp. He strode over and gave a small bow before taking the second seat angled beneath that alien lamp. I had an unexpected memory of early chicks being kept warm in a sawdust box, Mama telling me that the electric lanterns would replace the heat of their mothers. I was small and started to cry, thinking the lanterns weren't enough. And Mama squeezed me. She squeezed me very tight.

"Vitya says that you have waitressed before."

"Um." I straightened my blouse, my skirt, my hair, looked around for the blond girl, but she seemed to have gone. "Yes," I said. "Yes, that's right."

I waited for a question on serving that I wouldn't be able to answer.

"And she also says you would be willing to do a little extra . . ."

"Extra?" I thought of Ekaterina, balancing on a window cleaner's scaffold, ten floors up.

"Like . . . learn a little English."

"Oh, I can speak a little English."

"Vitya never said." He sat back, a face of disbelief. "Go ahead, then."

I cleared my throat. The first thing that came into my head was "*Once upon a time there was a young girl . . .*"

"Go on."

That's all I had memorized, so I went back, flipping through the chapters in my mind, the things written up on that whiteboard at the Palace of Culture. "*I had a sister,*" I said, kicking myself for using the past tense, so to cover up, I blurted out, *"I have a swimming pool."*

Oleg Konstantinovich clapped his hands and bellowed out a laugh. "Marvelous! Marvelous! They will just adore you."

"Thank you!" I said, realizing it might be possible for other people, apart from Jonathan, to find me delightful. *I have got myself a job in Moscow*, I would write in my first conciliatory postcard home to my parents. *I got a job because I am able to speak a foreign language.*

Oleg Konstantinovich grinned. "So there is no need to button your blouse so high."

"Huh?"

He had said it so quietly, so casually, I was sure I had misheard.

"You can undo a button or two." His expression was serious, businesslike, perhaps even bored.

There had been no time for Viktoria's waxing. Ekaterina's embarrassment had saved me mine. Now would I regret it? Would I get my dose of shame regardless? My fingers fumbled at the top of my blouse. It was already unbuttoned low at Viktoria's suggestion. Somehow I was able to give him some English, but a simple refusal in my own language felt impossible. I undid one button.

"And another."

My chest was rising and falling beneath my fingers, the gold fan of the necklace conducting heat, the buried locket pressing into my flesh. I undid the second button, the black of my bra completely on display now, my skin goosing in the air, even though the restaurant was warm. I could see Ekaterina's proud face as she lifted those cloches, then the humiliation that followed. Perhaps I thought of her so I did not feel so bad for myself. Oleg Konstantinovich surveyed my work.

"Excellent," he said. "Excellent." Then: "Welcome to the team."

The signal to my arm took a moment to arrive. He wanted to shake hands. Was it really such a sophisticated thing to do? I wasn't sure anymore. He gripped my sweaty palm in his cool, dry fingers. The blond girl reappeared, cradling my coat, not surprised to see me hurriedly buttoning my blouse. I did it so fast that I got it wrong, the front crooked and snagged. I was shown out via the back entrance, now that I was staff. A cluster of busboys stood smoking by the trash bins, stamping their feet against the cold and shooing away dogs. I cut down an alley to return to the main street. In my fingers was a piece of paper, listing the hours that I would work the coming week. The dogs, they slalomed past me.

22

HEARTS WITHIN HEARTS

Had I known there was a back entrance to the hotel, I would have used it, said Baba Yaga's spell in reverse: *Little house, little house, don't stand the way your mother set you, put your front to the forest and your back to me!*

I walked through reception in a cloud of my own cigarette fumes to hide the black mascara that was rolling down my face. They say it's easier to bear shame than smoke in the eye—I disagree. I'd shown off my English tongue too proudly. I'd called the evil eye upon myself. Mama could have warned me. Viktoria certainly hadn't. Though she did not know what Oleg was planning; she couldn't have. Viktoria loved me. I was a village girl with a broken face, yet she'd chosen me as her friend. She was my big sister in this hostile city. I was willing to admit it now: Zlata had been telling the truth. Moscow was cold and lonely.

I passed Pavel's desk, and he called out, but I didn't stop. I caught a just-leaving elevator and turned away from the family of tourists who rode to the fifth floor with me.

Housekeeping had visited while I was gone, fixing the bed, sweeping away the cotton buds and tissues that Viktoria had shed about the place as she'd made me pretty. The armchairs were a different color, green ones swapped for gold. On the table sat a basket of fruit in cellophane tied with ribbon as an apology. I would take it back to Ekaterina and say it wasn't necessary. Or would that only make things worse? I did not want Pavel, or anyone else at the hotel — a place that had been kind to me — thinking I wanted trouble.

Housekeeping had also taken away the small cardboard boxes I'd saved and stacked on the desk, the ones that had held the toothbrush and comb. I felt a stupid sadness for them. The things I'd lost . . . I could make a list. At the very top I would have to write *me*.

I threw my coat onto the bed and turned on the faucet for a bath. My plan was to make the journey to Viktoria's place, or walk into that bar of eagles to find her. When she heard what Oleg Konstantinovich had done, she would fetch her broom and swing it at his head. I walked the carpet in my heels as I waited for the bath to fill, practicing my ice grip, wondering if I should take myself into my own hands, get my own broom.

There was a knock at the door, and joy spiked. Vitya! My Vitya! She was too excited to wait until her party on the 21st. She needed to know how the interview had gone. I wrenched open that door, all black-eyed and big-haired, in my bandage skirt and see-through blouse, and there stood Jonathan. I threw my arms around his neck before he had a chance to protest, before I had the chance to question the action.

"Oh, no, Dasha," he said, not *hello*. He pushed me away from him so he might look me up and down. "Oh, good God!" he cried. "What have I done!"

He waited downstairs with the tea and the big-leafed plants while I washed the interview from my skin and changed my clothes. I stood at the wardrobe wondering what I should look like when I stepped out of that elevator and into the lobby. He had come back for me! Now what did he want? I needed to seem older, but not that girl in the bandage skirt who had upset him when I opened the door. It's just dress-up, only a game—that's what I had wanted to say—but I wasn't sure he'd understand. He hadn't wanted the last lost hare in flowers and a head scarf either, so I decided on the red stretchy dress that I had gotten from Viktoria. I would be the warrior from the wall of Kazansky station. I put on my shoes from home. I put the locket around my neck again.

We went out for dinner across the buried cobblestones, slush from the earlier snow seeping through my shoes. He was calmer, his earlier reaction forgotten now that I was transformed again. He took my arm as we passed splendid buildings and gleaming billboards, lit-up trees and brass-band street musicians. Moscow was not cold and lonely—I had been too rash. It was beautiful—if you were there with the right person.

I expected another glamorous dining room hidden behind a curtain, men in shiny suits and twinkling women. Instead he walked us to a modern castle of glass, glowing orange and green in the night. We went through a wrought-iron gate decorated with the Star of David.

"You know this is a Jewish place, right?" I whispered.

"You know that I'm Jewish, right?"

We climbed the stairs to a light canteen on the top floor. The other diners were dressed soft and beige, checked and some horizontally striped, not shiny at all. They did not stop eating to watch us take our table by the window. Their own conversations kept them happy.

He ordered gelfite fish, *chrein* relish, and a basket of bialy bread for both of us. He'd asked me what I wanted, but I'd said I didn't care. He was back! I ate up the sight of him instead. He wore a good sweater, navy and smooth. His animal-bright eyes were in front of me again, the skin creasing at the edges, though as soon as the waiter left, the frown returned.

"Pavel says you've gotten mixed up with the wrong kind of people."

"What?" Pavel was on my side. I didn't understand.

"Come on, I saw what they'd done to you."

"Done to me?"

"You are only a child, Dasha. I should never have —"

"Oh, why are you even here?" I tore at the bread. I was furious. I was not a child. Why couldn't he see? I'd noticed the way Jonathan tapped the back of the waiter before we were sat at one of the best tables in the room, how he did the same to Pavel before we left the hotel. He got his scooter rides just the same as Viktoria, just the same as anyone else. What made her the wrong kind of the person and him in a position to judge? The hotel room I was using was not "free" to him — how could it be? It certainly wasn't to me. This was my price.

His face crumpled at the blow of my anger, and this was my

only consolation. If he was upset, he must love me, because no one is adored with indifference.

"I'm back to report on the bodies," he said.

I put down the bread. I thought he meant the ones from home, that they were somehow here. Mama had talked about how she would come to Moscow eventually, she and the other mothers, to make their case. I had thought about that every day since I arrived. I wanted to stand at a distance and watch her protest in the street and think, *That defiant woman is my mother*, and think it proudly, not with any disappointment.

"What bodies?" I asked tentatively, imagining that terrible carriage on the tracks where we had found Nika, coupled to the train that had brought me to Moscow.

"The ones in the river," Jonathan said. "They found another girl this morning."

"Oh." I nodded as if I knew. I had questions, of course—like *Did you come back because you were worried that I could be one of them?*—but he did not give me the opportunity to speak.

"Oh, Dasha!" he cried, suddenly loud. He dropped his head almost to the table. Was he crying? "I wanted to help. I only wanted to help. But I've done the opposite. Dropping you into this place, thinking you'd be OK."

"I am OK," I shot back. I wanted him to be proud of me, impressed. I was a smart and capable woman. "I even have a job. At a fancy restaurant. It was my grasp of English that swung it." I could not help thinking of brooms.

Jonathan lifted his head. "Which restaurant?"

I would be brave, I decided, because that was what smart and capable women did. I reached forward and placed a hand

231

on top of one of his. He looked at what I'd done, tenderly, I think. I told him the name of the place with the pink awning, and his hand flew from mine, as if he'd been bitten or spiked with a current. He braced his hands behind his head, preparing for a crash.

"That's not a restaurant, Dasha!"

"Yes, it is. I was there only this afternoon."

"Did you see any food?"

"Yes," I lied.

"Well, that's only a front." His head dipped toward the table again. My stomach fell. Did Viktoria know? Had she known all along?

"What am I going to do with you?" Jonathan groaned.

"Nothing," I replied, gathering up all the pride that was left for me to have. "Because I'm not yours to do anything with."

I still thought we would share a bed. Not because I believed that we would do what I had done with Dmitriy, what I could hear going on between couples in the rooms along the corridors, but because I couldn't see how Jonathan's "relationship" with Hotel Alexander would extend to two rooms. We would share like friends, if he wanted, like family members; the bed was big enough. Just because you are angry with someone, it does not mean you don't want them close.

But Jonathan said his good nights in the lobby. He let himself kiss me on the cheek, which seemed more distant than not kissing me at all.

"Tomorrow we'll be tourists," he said. "I'll see you at breakfast."

I lay on my back, lights out, but I left the curtains open, allowing Moscow's night glow to come through and pick out shapes. The fruit basket in cellophane, the glass of pencils restocked. My heeled boots and flat shoes pointed toward the wall—like invisible students reacting to a teacher's scolding. Viktoria's discarded heels faced forward, as if ready to go.

I must have drifted into sleep, because Nika came. She lay on her back beside me, making her own smaller dent in the mattress. She was not as frantic as before, but still she wanted action.

"Shall we go visiting, Dasha?" she said, as if she were Vinni Pukh and I were Piglet. "And get ourselves a little snack?"

I shook my head.

"We could go to the pool."

"No."

"Well, then, we might as well go home, Dasha," she whined, so sadly.

"No," I said. "No." And I woke up shouting the word.

As Jonathan drank black tea with nothing else, he opened a folding map across the table. I searched the seasick ballroom for Ekaterina. I could not see her. Had she lost her job because of Viktoria? Because of me?

"Some people see the rings of a tree," Jonathan said, "felled and sliced down the middle." I studied the map with him and washed my guilt away with coffee. "But I see a heart," he said. "Veins and arteries." I had likened the hotel to a heart. So then it was a heart within a heart.

"You've seen Red Square, of course . . ." Jonathan remarked.

I flushed hot and said nothing. He looked up, incredulous. "You've been here over two weeks!"

I shrugged.

"You do know it's just around the corner?"

But then there was Ekaterina, refilling baskets of bread at the buffet.

"I have to get more eggs," I said, jumping up, avoiding all excuses.

I stood right next to her, and across the displays of fruit I muttered, "I'm sorry." I glanced at the man at the door of the restaurant, just as she had that first evening when she warned me off the beef stroganoff. I didn't want to get her into any more trouble, wasting her time chatting with guests.

"Sorry for what?" said Ekaterina, keeping her eyes on the arrangement of apples, straightening forks and positioning tongs.

"About the champagne."

"Oh." She nodded. "Well, let's forget about the past." She moved to the other side of me, started combining two half-empty smoked salmon-platters into one.

"Are you . . . ?" Ekaterina stopped to choose her words. "Are you working for Vitya now?"

"What?"

It made no sense. How could I be working for Viktoria, a girl who did shifts in a sandwich café in a dirty part of town? A girl who lived in a playhouse where dogs licked clean the lobby? But of course, as I stood with my mouth open, choosing how to answer, staring at croissants and cottage-cheese dumplings, I understood that Viktoria was not those things. Jonathan's words from last night: *Well, that's only a front.* I turned to see if he was watching, and Ekaterina's head went too. He was — craning his neck, his journalist reflex as sharp as if he'd been struck on the knee. Or perhaps it was because he cared. Perhaps I was being unkind.

"How do you know her name?" I asked — such a particular sweetening of Viktoria, hardly a sweetening at all.

"Everyone knows Vitya," said Ekaterina as she left my side, called to her station to clear a table. "Everyone knows to stay out of her way."

In the wide expanse of snow that had fallen on Red Square, just a few streets from the hotel, I felt exposed — in a rifle's sights. Who it was holding the rifle, I didn't know. I had kept myself so boxed up in the city, moving from my room to the lobby and back again, stepping out only in the company of Viktoria. She had shown me dark basement bars and curtained-off restaurants, an apartment boxed up in ways all of its own. Nowhere like this. If I went back to the black mountains and the wide, flat scrubland, to the long roads stretching into nothing, would I cower? *You are scared of the long grass and the short grass and the murmurations of the birds.* No. I wouldn't be scared anymore.

I stared up at the dizzying frontage of the GUM shopping mall and the sweetshop turrets of Saint Basil's Cathedral, wishing I had Papa's camera so I could take pictures. Pictures to take home — that was what I was thinking. But I chased the thought from my head.

"Ivan the Terrible had the architect of the cathedral blinded," said Jonathan, playing storyteller, "so he wouldn't build another like it." I drifted out of myself, looked down on us, standing there in the deepening snow, a Russian girl being taught about the Motherland in the tongue of an American. I'd let myself be angry with Jonathan, and now I let myself think he was a little ridiculous. He could tell these stories, but he didn't understand them. They got lost in translation.

Next we visited the mighty Tsar Cannon on the grounds of the Kremlin, and Jonathan took my photograph—another fragment of my soul. I wondered where this picture would end up—where that Polaroid was that Viktoria had taken for her "boss." Did she hand it over, or did she keep it? Did she look at it sometimes and feel guilty? She wouldn't just give up on me, I believed that, even if she had sent me knowingly into Oleg Konstantinovich's trap. I was Miss Saratov, her little fish. All that time and effort put into being my friend. It couldn't all have been a front.

"Smile!" said Jonathan, a strange request, but one you could hear every other tourist calling out as we went from monument to monument.

"This cannon fired the unpopular ashes of the ruler Dmitriy back to Poland," Jonathan told me. *Climb in, Dasha!* The command came to me in Nika's voice. *Let's point it south and be home in time for supper!* It was Nika's voice but not her voice.

We finished up at the kiosks, picking through souvenirs. Birchbark pots and Soviet medals, amber necklaces and lacquered boxes. Jonathan told me about his baba Sabina from Minsk who had moved to America to escape the Nazis. She always spoke in Russian to his mother, and to Jonathan, right from when he was a baby, ensuring there would always be someone close by who could listen to the contents of her heart in exactly the right language. Jonathan's daughter—the one who was almost the same age as me—could speak it too.

"Baba Sabina watched the SS shoot her father," Jonathan said as I pulled apart a set of painted *matryoshka* dolls. More hearts within hearts. These dolls were painted as animals—a bear, a deer, a fox, a hare, an owl—which was absurd, as these things did not come within one another. "Everyone stood back and let it happen," Jonathan went on. "Baba Sabina took her fury to her grave."

He was drawing us equal by telling me this, a piece of his story in exchange for mine. Tragedy always repeats itself, and his family had had their share. I wondered what would happen now if I turned, went up on my toes, and tried to kiss him.

I knew the answer. I would be rejected. How many times do we have to make the same mistake until we begin to learn?

"Would you like to get those?" Jonathan asked. I considered the deer and the hare in my hands. Nika had not come from me, yet I had been her mother. I set them down and shook my head. Jonathan had called me a child the day before, and these were toys. I did not want him to think that I needed them. But more than that, I wanted to believe it for myself.

23

OH, DARK EYES

You had to walk down a carpeted corridor beyond the reception desk, then through a pair of white swinging doors marked STAFF ONLY. Pavel had given me directions.

In my hand, I had pieces of chocolate cake, wrapped in a napkin taken from the restaurant, to give as a gift. I had made a kitchen of my hotel room. Ekaterina had put her hands on the two bowls and a tray I needed, borrowed from the main hotel kitchen. In the smaller bowl, I broke up a bar of chocolate and set it into the bigger bowl, filled with boiling water from the room kettle. I used the hair dryer to move things along. Into that, I crumbled cookies, raisins, and nuts.

Since our trip to Red Square, I had begun to venture out on my own while Jonathan worked. Alexander Garden, the Cathedral of the Assumption, the state library that houses more than seventeen million books. And a kiosk to buy supplies for Pavel's present.

I poured the mixture into a tray and set it in the minibar. I could have just given him the bar of chocolate, but it wouldn't have been the same. Cooking was how I showed my love. I was angry with Pavel for snitching to Jonathan, but that did not mean I wanted to push him away. I was learning.

Beyond the white swinging doors, grand illusions ended. There was no marble, no velvet, no shiny piano. It was all a front. Here were chipped tiled floors and once-white walls bearing scars. The air smelled of hanging meat. I was watching a magician from a different angle and seeing that there had never been any magic. But I wasn't disappointed; it was reassuring to know the staff did not exist forever in a world of quiet whispers and polite nods.

I passed the kitchens, where the bang and scrape of stainless steel mixed with bellowed instructions and swear words among friends. I followed two chattering waitresses who were removing bow ties as they walked and letting their long hair out of yanked-tight buns, past walls papered with staff rosters, charity sign-ups, and posters advising the best way to wash your hands. I went through a door into their staff canteen—the afternoon party was in full swing.

On a table sat a young boy strumming tremulous chords on a guitar while Pavel conducted and warbled along:

Oh, dark eyes,
Oh, passionate eyes . . .

When he saw me arrive, I became the focus of his operatics. I played the maiden.

How I love you! How I fear you!

There was applause, more songs. The cake was taken grate-
fully from my hands and replaced with a loaded plate of food.
The atmosphere was festive, so much warmer than what was
on offer at the front of the hotel. It felt like visiting friends.
It felt like a family.

Ekaterina arrived not long after me, removing her bartender
apron and seeking out a piece of the chocolate cake, eager to
know what her borrowing of bowls and a tray had produced.

"I wish we had a piano," she told me, squeezing onto my
bench, making me scrunch up close to one of the night porters,
who was sloshing drink into any nearby glass that dared to be
still. "If we did, I'd be joining in."

"You play?"

"I'd serenade the residents in the evenings if they'd give
me the key for that thing in reception. But it's only there for
show."

We talked about Venice and all the other European cities
that might be in your grasp once you got that far. We talked
about our brothers—me being careful about what I gave out to
Ekaterina. Yes, they were in a school in Moscow, but no, there
was no special reason for that. She asked me when I planned to
meet up with them, and I confessed I had no contact details.

"Well, isn't Jonathan a journalist?" she said. "He could find
out for you in a heartbeat."

"Of course!" I said. "Of course!" And our conversation turned
to him. Again, I kept things imprecise. Yes, he was helping me
get set up in the city, but no, there was no special reason for

that. I tried to find out what favors he did in return for the room, but Ekaterina shrugged. She knew him only by name, nothing more, because he was often around for work, using the hotel as a base.

"He's really good-looking, though," she said. "Don't you think?"

This didn't feel like a test, her trying to fish for information, who he was to me, yet I still found myself saying, "He's old, though." And I think I did mean it. The battery commander was old, no matter how he seemed. "And did you know," I said, loose-lipped from the vodka, "he has a teenage daughter?"

As people started filtering away to start evening shifts or head home, Ekaterina asked me, "So, when I head off to Venice, what about you?"

I looked at her, confused. This reminded me of that exchange with Alana, how I had asked when the playing would start and she had replied that we were doing it right now.

"This," I replied. "I'm doing this."

Ekaterina stuffed a *trubochka* into her mouth, catching the escaping cream with a hand. "What, living in a hotel?"

"No!"

We laughed together as cream slid down her chin. She waited for me to explain. So I grasped at a story, the only one I had that would fit.

"I have a job," I told her. "We just need to iron out a few wrinkles first."

" 'We'?"

I remembered her face at the buffet as she had said, "Everyone knows Vitya."

"I mean, I have some boxes to check off."

"Or you could go back," Ekaterina said. She focused on the boy playing the guitar—something delicate and folky—so she did not have to look in my eyes. She said the name of my town. "You could go back there."

It was as surprising as a wasp sting. My hand flew to my scar, to my locket, as if they had suddenly reappeared, giving away exactly who I was. I had created pillars of velvet and floors of marble, but Ekaterina had always known. It was a front.

"Because after everything that has happened to you," she went on, "why on earth would you want to be here?"

"But how do you . . . ?"

"Pavel told me. And Jonathan told him."

I couldn't breathe. I felt small, reduced, sliced through. I hated Jonathan now, truly hated him. That was my story, not his. In Moscow, I was going to be someone different, and he had stripped that all away. This was how it would always be. This was how love treated you, at the end. You were left with only the desire to tear out eyes, to ruin or destroy.

Ekaterina's hands were on my arm. She pushed her cheek against mine. "We've been looking out for you, stupid," she said. "Because we wanted you to be OK."

The room broke into the birthday song then—that crocodile promising free movies and five hundred ice-cream cones.

And I'll play on my accordion, in sight of all passing near.
How unlucky that a birthday only comes once a year!

I could not bear it. Love would always be like this, like knocking on your mama's bedroom door and getting no reply.

"Where are you going?" Ekaterina called after me.

"For a swim!"

And that's what I intended. But I put on my bathing suit and I went to bed, the one big enough for a whole family but that held only me.

Jonathan knocked, but I did not answer. It was my turn to mete out the love I wished to give. I was Mama's daughter, for sure, because I knew how to do this: take to my bed for days and days. Ekaterina came whispering words of persuasion; Pavel brought his jokes. *A baby worm says to Mama worm . . . A woman goes into a food store and asks for some meat . . .* I thought housekeeping would insist, that Pavel might break down the door, but they let me be. I ate the complimentary cookies that I had hidden, like the pencils, so that they would leave me more. I worked through the overpriced snacks in the fridge. Things I might never pay for at the end, because I could see no end. How would this end?

"Just give me a word to know you are all right," Jonathan appealed through the wood of the door.

"Here's two," I yelled back from beneath the duvet. "Go away!"

He did — went back to his bodies, those *rusalki* calling from the deep. And I slept. I dreamed of Nika racing me frustratingly from one end of Red Square to the other — *Can't catch me, Dasha!* she cried. She had that gymnast's ribbon in her hand, a flash of happiness that could be mine if I could only get hold of it. *You'll never catch me!*

I went back to my English workbook. One exercise asked me to join pieces of sentences to create a route across the page.

These are present perfect, the book said. *They use the past to talk about the now. For example: It has snowed.*

You have spent nearly all of your money, I thought. *You have not found a job. Your friend has let you down. The commander has decided you are a child. I have used up all my patience.*

On the 21st, I left my room and slipped through the palms and fronds of the lobby, making sure I was not seen.

On that first day in Moscow, I had run scared from a taxi driver. Now I went in search of one. I threw an arm into the city traffic and made the noise I'd heard Viktoria use to hail a car. It wasn't a legal taxi, but the driver looked sober. He was tall and dark-skinned, the way people were back home. I felt safe. I told him my destination and my price.

Beside me were bags of ingredients, enough for a huge *zakuski* table. I'd spent the last of my money, but no matter. I would give Viktoria one last chance, like I had Papa and Mama. My Vitya was made of a tougher substance. She would take this chance and use it to her advantage. If she could find me one job interview, she could find me another. A position that suited me. I'd get that fur coat, after all. But not before I had proved myself to her. Tonight she would see what I was capable of. We would eat eggplant caviar, pickled herring, stuffed eggs, and a towering Napoleon cake. Oh, how we would celebrate this early New Year that we both so desperately needed.

The old lady *dezhurnaya* at the reception desk watched me accusingly as I took the pebbled stairs, but when I knocked on the main door of the communal flat, a man I did not know let me in without a question. I made straight for the kitchen, emptied my bags on the counter. This was my territory. Here I was in control. Blue light streamed in from the wall of windows as I cleaned down the surfaces and fired up the oven, turning the handle on the gas and lighting a match. The tenants in the building opposite moved around their kitchen, frying eggs and stirring pots. I sifted flour, broke butter. As the sun began to set, music started in Viktoria's part of the flat, not deep and grinding like before, but twanging guitars, lisping drums, a seductive beat. I spread crumbs across the top of the Napoleon. It was my final task.

I held the cake in front of my face as I knocked. I had heard others arriving, singing out their greetings. The cake would speak for me. I waited for her squeal of delight.

"What are you doing here?" Viktoria said.

I lowered my offering. I was Alana at the door of our old apartment. *Do you want to come out to play, Vitya?*

"Isn't there a party?" I said. I could see that there was. People moved around the sheeted rooms, and Viktoria was in her usual black but dressed special, her hair slicked to look wet on purpose. Her lips were a menacing violet.

"Well remembered, Miss Saratov." She gave a tight smile and stepped aside, a gesture that said *Come in* but also *On your head will fall the consequences.* I had nothing to do but move forward. This plan was all I had. So Viktoria watched, sort of appalled, as I threw a paper cloth across the table in Anna's empty section of the flat, shifting a hairbrush, some books, and medicine bottles to the bed. I made trips back and forth from the communal kitchen for the other dishes, losing more and more confidence with each journey, just waiting for Viktoria to nudge my elbow. But her interest in me quickly fell to nothing.

She slipped behind the sheet into her room, where laughter rose in waves above the music.

The table finished, I stood back to admire my work. Alone. Food was my currency. But it held no value here. The platters were gaudy and ridiculous. I should have left then, hailed a cab, gone back to bed, but I wouldn't give in. I needed my answer. Whatever it was. *Do you love me?*

In Moscow, I was going to be someone different. In Moscow, I would learn how to fight. So I imagined Nika's voice to comfort me, asking when we could start, because she was hungry, so hungry. If she had been there, she would have been licking her lips and eyeing the Napoleon's cherry. I would have smacked her fingers when she tried to pinch a loose flake of pastry. No, that's not right. I would have told her, with all I knew now, to go right ahead, take all she wanted, have her fill, before it was too late. That was what I was going to do too.

"Hey." A boy came through from the other bedroom, an unlit cigarette hanging from his lip. He was searching for something and not expecting to find me.

"Danya," he said, raising his cup.

"Dasha." I nodded. My hands empty.

"Are you the new Anna?"

I shook my head. "Why?" I asked. "Where is the old one?"

"Oh, she left. About a week ago."

"But . . ." All about us were her things, the rack still full of her clothes. That was her hairbrush I'd moved, matted with blond strands, her book, her pills.

He shrugged, mimed a disappearing puff of smoke. "Hungry, huh?" he said.

We both stared down at the food, and I shook my head. "Absolutely not."

"Then let's go up to the roof." He took my hand. "We're gonna set off fireworks."

The caretaker's ladder took us dangerously high, to a view that stole your lungs. Orange-lit roads snaking with blue, office blocks glowing hot and fluorescent. Beneath us sat apartment buildings with a thousand warm windows. I thought of the view from the balcony at home, how I preferred it because it wasn't showing off. Because I knew it, good and bad. Because it was mine.

I sat on a ledge and wrapped myself tight in Anna's white duvet. Danya had taken it from the bed and put it across my shoulders, spilling her book, brush, and pills onto the floor without a glance. He was giggling drunk, I realized, now that he was reunited with his friends, pretending to slip on the ice and fall from the edge of the building, arms windmilling. I watched him recount the story of a man he'd seen that afternoon struck down by a giant icicle falling from a high window ledge. He did the actions—*hack-shlyop*—the icicle coming down, then a crack of the neck and a tongue loll: dead. The gang exploded into laughter, but I couldn't see the joke. This was no Pavel one-liner. I had the urge to stand and punch Danya in the nose, kick him in the shins, just as I had done to my brothers that day on the landing. But Viktoria's dry-cleaner friend Alexei arrived then, drawing focus, dressed halfheartedly, prematurely, as Ded Moroz in *valenki* boots and a red cape over a designer shirt and jeans. If this was to be a New Year's of our own making, then I could be his Snegurochka, the snow maiden wrapped in white, craving the love of mere humans, suspecting that if I got it, a warm heart would be the death of me, as I was made of snow.

A fake beard slipped around Alexei's neck as he held a flashlight in his mouth and picked through bright papered rolls lying in a wooden box—the evening's entertainment. And then Viktoria made her arrival on the roof. She wore a beautiful fur coat across her shoulders, and Alexei stroked it as she passed, possessively, making her growl and snap her teeth at his fingers. She drank from the neck of a bottle of Soviet Champagne, proving this really was New Year's. She was in command of the calendar and had flipped it forward at will. And, oh, how I needed her to! I wanted to rip away those pages, tear them to tiny pieces. Danya handed me my own bottle of champagne to slug from, and I did, swigging hard to keep back the cold. He and another boy, Misha perhaps, set up a portable CD player, and soon there was music.

"Are we ready?" Alexei cried, positioning beer bottles as launch pads.

Everyone on the roof yelled, "Yes!" Except me. I wanted to go. I should come back in daylight, when both of us were more sober, talk to Viktoria in private, make a plan when the dust had settled. Parties did not suit me. But then she was sitting beside me, her perfume curling into the air. The first firework was hitting the sky.

"You never turned up for work, for Oleg," she said. "After all I did for you."

BA-BAKH!

My body jerked its animal response. Gunfire cracked, sparks

sprayed. I saw a glimpse again of that sea of dark heads and dancing flowers. I grabbed Viktoria's hand. I needed her to be with me now, just as I had needed Mama and Papa to tell me not to go, as strongly as I had needed Jonathan to kiss me in our hallway.

"What is wrong with you?" she said. "Why are you crying?"

"He made me undo all my buttons."

The boys whooped at the sky. It was all boys, I saw then — everyone at this party, except for Viktoria, except for me. And she didn't count. She called herself Vitya for a reason.

"And?" Viktoria said. "So? What did you expect?"

It was a good question.

That my little sister would grow up.

That I might get a second chance at being a child.

"Nothing." I gulped. "I expected nothing." I gripped her hand tighter, my heart racing faster with every detonation. Viktoria cried out at the pinch.

"Let go of me!" She gripped my wrist with her free hand, trying to pull herself away. The panic was hiccuping out of me now.

"Where is she?" I said.

"Where is who?"

Nika.

Me.

Our eyes met, ferocious, but she would not lock horns, wouldn't give me that satisfaction. I was battling for something that could never be fought for, only handed over freely.

"Anna," I said, swallowing air spiked with ice. "Where is Anna?"

Tighter, I gripped her. I dug in my nails, not caring if I drew blood. I would squeeze the love from her flesh, wring it; I deserved it, just a drop.

"How should I fucking know?" she said, finally wrenching herself free. She stood swaying, gold rain dying in the sky behind her. "Where does anyone go?" she said. "She's just gone."

You pay for everything in the end. And this is how it ended: I found the strength to leave. I asked for money for the taxi, though it brought me shame, and I stumbled back through Anna's empty room, finding the cherry missing from the Napoleon cake. *That was mine!* The thought fired hot through my flesh. *That was mine, you bastards! Give it back!* But I knew that it could not be returned.

Other things can be, though.

You don't need to board a train, ride through the night, go to foreign lands, dig down into them. Whether you take the path that leads to riches or the path that leads to death, they always go with you — your things. The ones you can touch and the ones you can't.

I saw it then — though it had probably been there all along. Now was the time to open my eyes. A bag, a black one, decorated with the familiar logo of a charity, stuffed onto a shelf in Anna's room. Inside was a life, rifled through and considered not important. A book, a camera, a clock, a story, time, lost. I pulled out her picture, and there she was, there she always was — my dark eyes. A little piece of my soul.

24

INSIDE A BEAR

We took the Metro east, away from the city's heart, getting off at Partizanskaya. We walked through the park, an expanse of white, past the children's fairground rides, toward the muddled arches of the flea market, familiar to us from the pages of Jonathan's Moscow guide. The pictures in the book had been taken in the bright sunshine of summer. That day, the vivid minarets wore their winter caps of snow.

We waited by the entrance at a stall selling colorful head scarves.

"Try them on! You must try them on!" The stallholder was quickly by our side—smelling that Jonathan had money. She had one of her own head scarves tied over a woolen cowl so she could keep warm and demonstrate her wares. The combination was comical and no advertisement at all.

"This one is beautiful," she clucked, holding up different fabrics to my face. "So beautiful, just right for you." She thrust a mirror in front of me, giving me no choice. I pulled down my hood and took off my hat, placed a red flowered scarf over my hair, tucking away Viktoria's choppy bangs. I tipped my head forward to knot the scarf at the back of my neck. I looked up. There I was.

"You'll take it?" the woman asked, and Jonathan paid. I looped the scarf to the handle of my shoulder bag, as if to remind me of something important I must do later.

Once Boris and Igor had arrived, after we had hugged each other tight and I had held them at arms' length for a brief inspection, after we had lit cigarettes and fallen back into our comfortable nonchalance with one another, we wandered the gray slushy paths between the stalls. The boys tried on Soviet boots and jackets, pinned medals on each other's chest. Igor was growing into his ears, I noticed. Boris was wearing his bulk with a little more ease. Jonathan toyed with the idea of shipping a huge, ornate samovar back to New York, more in love with the effort it would require, the story he would be able to tell, than the object itself. I let him buy me a set of *matryoshka* dolls like the ones we'd seen in Red Square. An owl inside a hare, inside a fox, inside a deer, inside a bear.

And we saw a real bear. Tourists were paying a fee to take photos of it, safe beyond a fence. We stopped for a moment to watch the animal dance solemnly on the end of its chain. Forward a step, backward two, forward a step, backward two. Did it know anything else? The wild forests? Rivers full of fish? If not, perhaps it could be happy here. When its keeper tossed a piece of bloodied meat into the snow, though, the bear showed no excitement for the reward.

"Maybe we should go and eat something ourselves," Jonathan said, feeling the mood settle, and we walked way, following the smoke of the grills — *shashlik* cooked in the open air. It was a smell that could only make me think me of the 40th Day. The boys had left for Moscow by then, but I was sure they were finding reminders of their own — a stall of cheap tracksuits like the one their classmate was wearing, the boy lying facedown, dead in the grass. A display of Vinni Pukh knapsacks the same as Nika's that she hung on a hook in the hallway, installed low by Papa so she would be able to put away her own things. The stalls selling guns. Jonathan mentioned someone named Veronika whom he had met in the course of his work that week, as we huddled in plastic chairs around a plastic table and waited for our food to be cooked. *Veronika* — Nika's full first name. All three of our Ivanov heads had snapped to attention at once at the mention of it.

"She's an opera singer," Jonathan explained. "Extremely talented." He blushed, and I wondered if he was in love with her. I wondered if she looked anything like me, if he had kissed her, pulled her to him desperately. If I could have used this first life, the one I had lived already, as a rough draft for another, I would have made sure I woke up bigger, started older.

As we tore into our food, inhaled it, the cold making us as hungry as wolves, I asked my brothers about school. Igor looked to Boris, as always, to answer for them both.

"S'OK," he said. Which meant it was good, very good. I understood their language.

I had never wanted to talk about the siege before, not when

I was with people who had been there, and not when I was with people who hadn't. But sitting with my brothers for one precious afternoon before we went our separate ways again, the need came strong and urgent. I was Baba Sabina, wanting to empty her heart to people who would truly comprehend. I waited until Jonathan wandered away to make a phone call.

"Does she speak to you?" I asked them.

We stopped eating for a moment, let the meat and warm flatbread steam into the air. Boris met the skittish eyes of my littlest brother, then turned to me.

"Yeah," he said.

"What does she say?"

"That she's not really dead."

We all nodded together.

"But you know that she is, right?" Boris said, in a voice I'd never heard him use before. A sound so tender.

"Yes," I said. "But I also know that she isn't. Not really."

"What I mean is," he went on, "you can't rescue her, Dasha. You couldn't have rescued her in the first place."

I started to cry, apologizing all the time, because I knew how spooked my brothers were by any kind of weeping.

"I'm not crying because I'm sad," I told them. I wasn't. I started to laugh. I had been forgiven, and I felt as light as air. "I'm crying because I'm happy." That gymnast's ribbon was in my grip; I was ready to run, if only to make it fly.

We shopped a little more, while our fingers and toes could bear it. I lingered at a stall stacked with trays of books, their spines up to the sky. So many editions of the play that had been stolen and returned. How easy it is to replace a thing like that. I chose a collection of short stories by the same writer, Jonathan urging me to. I knew my purchases were more for him and his guilty conscience—for bringing me here, delivering me into the hands of the likes of Viktoria. He could not see that I did not regret any of it. You only learn if your mama lets you leave the house dressed as someone else and you make the mistake for yourself.

I chose a book for Alana too so I did not feel so spoiled—an illustrated book of fairy stories that she would think of as babyish but would devour in secret. I picked a film for her too, bought from a boy with a mouth muffled by a scarf, an open sports bag around his neck, loaded with bootleg DVDs.

"I'm not sure you should buy stuff from those kids," Jonathan said, ready to launch into another of his stories. "The people who organize all that are not very nice."

No one is really nice, little fish, I found myself thinking, but I did not say it, even though it contained some truth.

We walked back to the Metro, cradling paper cups of tea as fuel, the snow laid out in front of us, silent and deep, blown into soft ridges, the shape of sighs.

"How are you going to get your presents to Alana?" asked Igor. "I don't even know her address."

"I'm going to take them myself," I said.

Everyone stopped walking, the snow beneath our boots creaking with the weight.

"But I've found you a job," said Jonathan, breathing clouds.

A friendly dragon. He'd been saving this up for me. I'd spoiled his game. "At the bureau," he went on. "Admin stuff. You'd need to speak English, but you only really learn to speak a language if you submerge yourself and . . ."

He trailed off.

I had known that he was arranging this. Pavel had let it slip, not realizing it was a secret. I should have been thrilled — I would have my own desk! My blouse was hanging in the hotel wardrobe, ready and waiting! I did not want for pencils! — but I was not thrilled at all. I hadn't wanted to be what Viktoria had chosen for me, and I did not want to be what Jonathan had decided either. I was writing this fairy tale. I would decide on the ending.

"I'm sorry," I said as we wandered back to the Metro, me arm in arm with my brothers, making the most of them for now. "But the thing I want most in the world is to go home."

My last morning, I rose early and wrote small notes of thanks to Ekaterina and Pavel on old Soviet cards I'd found at the market. A girl embracing a fleet-footed stag. Ded Moroz and a smiling Snegurochka. As Moscow's strange December light burned through the curtains, I packed the black bag, leaving the clothes I'd bought from Viktoria hanging in the closet, along with the bathrobe, for the next person. I took only the good blouse, still sealed in its plastic, because this was an outfit for the person I wished to be. I grabbed the fistful of pencils and filled every available pocket of my bag with little soaps and shampoos, planning to share them with Olga, Marina, and Luiza, maybe offer some to Nadya and Olya as the start of something new. I made my way downstairs, the silver swimsuit beneath my dress.

From outside the revolving doors came the sound of street workers chipping away packed snow from the sidewalk — the *tuc tuc tuc* of a spade edge, then the bone snap of ice giving way. I found Pavel at his desk and gave him his card, hugging him tight, not caring for whispers and polite nods. His parting gift: "A tailor says to his son, 'You have studied for a degree in Russia, another in England, and another in America. I am so proud! So now it is time to decide: Do you want to be a tailor for men or a tailor for women?' "

I sought out Ekaterina behind the bar, restocking for the day ahead, and hugged her too. We made plans to visit each other at our chosen destinations, and it amused me to think that Venice, so glamorous, and my hometown, so familiar, were one and the same.

Jonathan said his goodbye to me before he left the hotel for work.

"I need to pay," I told him as we stood by that white grand piano in the lobby. "Now that it's the end."

He shook his head. "It's all covered, Dasha. Please don't give it a second thought."

"No, no," I told him. "I can't do that, because . . ." I had to say it, be proud, be brave: "I won't be dining out on my misery."

He stared at me for a moment, so solemn and grim, before the smile started to creep around his eyes — the image of him that always remains with me. He laughed so loud that the strings of the piano vibrated with the sound of it.

"Do you think that is what this has been?" I wanted to be angry with him for not taking me seriously, but the laugh was infectious. "You've got it all wrong!" he cried, pulling me to him, not desperately but so affectionately, and that was enough. "This has been my absolute pleasure, Darya Pavlovna. An absolute delight!"

Beyond the portholed doors in the basement, the air was warm. I stepped out of my clothes and onto stone. The flat blackness of the pool still scared me, but I knew I must get in. You don't learn anything unless you are submerged. I am the hare that is afraid of everything, I thought, and afraid of nothing. I am Vasilisa the Beautiful, Miss Saratov, and a little fish. I am a sister, a daughter, and a mother. You are what you are and all that has gone before.

I broke the spell of the surface with my foot, climbed down the steps. The waters embraced me. I pulled my arms through, kicked my legs, and made slow, unsteady lengths. I had not swum much as a child, but I was still a child in some ways, so there was time to learn.

I wasn't sure if I had been scared that she would be there, or scared that she would not, but she traveled beside me, the tips of her pigtails soaking up water, a little fountain shooting from her mouth. Her movements were those of a small, eager dog; my arms were the wings of a swan. Her breath struck out from her lungs in eager little huffs, and we continued like this for some time, crossing the pool, one end to the other. Sometimes I was certain of her wriggling presence in the water beside me, and sometimes my mind went off, to the future, to what I might do when I got home. Nika did not call out to me, insist that I go with her, or come back from my daydreams, because I was there, I was submerged, and she was with me. And that was how it would always be.

HOME

25

THE CHURCH IS NEAR

At the end of a story comes the beginning. We wake up from the dream, from the nightmare, from life — and if we knew where we were going to fall next, this is when we might lay down some straw.

She was asleep. Lengthwise on the sofa. She would accuse me of something later if I did not wake her, but still I fetched a blanket and threw it over her. She let me tuck it around her neck without stirring. I turned off the television, took away her empty mug. I watered the aloe vera and the orchid cacti that I was sure had made the journey across the hallway from Yelena's apartment. She had gone, then. Later, a postcard would arrive from Germany, saying, *I sent it here because I knew you'd come back.* Other postcards followed from Ekaterina and from Zlata. *I got my prince,* she wrote, *then I realized I totally preferred the frog. Go figure!*

I left my bag on the hallway floor. Our bedroom could wait. I moved around the kitchen, reorienting myself, upset with each small change, irritated by the things that were exactly the same. I turned the latch of the balcony door, took a quick stock check of the jars, then also of the scene below. A smattering of snow was doing its best to cover the rafters and the blackened brick. If it is possible to feel pity for the efforts of nature, then that is what I did. *You may have cut yourself some choppy little bangs, oh, skies*, I thought, *but we all know what's there underneath.*

I tossed tea leaves into the kettle and warmed a separate pot for water. I made a tray with lemon slices, sugar, milk, honey, jam, and found some *pryaniki* in a tin that Mama must have baked. The noise of it woke her. I stood for an instant in the living-room doorway so she could see all of me and know who had returned. I watched her rise to sitting, the blanket falling about her hips, the creases falling from her face.

"How long have I been sleeping?" she asked.

"You'd have slept a whole lot longer," I told her, "if it wasn't for me."

I let her be mother. She made it strong and added a good heap of jam to make it sweet. I said I'd have mine the same, and I sipped the syrupy liquor as if it were healing water, something that could cure the fatal. *What happens after tea? The resurrection of the dead!* Suddenly it all made sense. I bit into the spiciness of a *pryanik* and praised Mama on the crunch. What was the secret?

"You need to leave the batter to rest overnight."

Of course. Even Diana's wisdom had rubbed off on me. The morning is always wiser than the night.

We sipped and ate, saying very little. I went to the bag in the hallway to fetch my present to Mama, and while I was there, I freed the Vinni Pukh knapsack from Nika's low hook.

"She loved this bag," I said, returning to the sofa. Mama looked up from her teacup, a little shocked that I had dared to wake this object from its own particular kind of sleep. Then she looked at me like she was asking permission to join in — to come and sit at the table, perhaps to come out to play. We sat and stroked the bag's shiny plastic front, a moment of communion. I would have to unzip it now, I realized, and spill its secrets, though the thought of this scared me. She was everywhere, ready to leap out and make me cry. So cheeky. Such a pain in the ass. Inside was the doll that she carried with her sometimes, the one whose wails and demands for food she would bemoan with drama. There was a coloring book, half completed, and there were flowers collected in the summer that turned to dust in my fingertips. We wept together; we gave Nika that satisfaction. Well done, cheeky. You win. Now it's my turn. . . .

Mama unwrapped the paper from the animal *matroyshka* dolls with a similar sense of foreboding, though when she saw what it was, she smiled. An owl inside a hare, inside a fox, inside a deer, inside a bear.

"How lovely," she said, twisting at the joint of the bear, opening it up.

Word reached Alana. Perhaps she heard about someone coming to the shop, a girl — a woman, if you like — asking to use the canister of helium.

"We had no heart-shaped balloons left," the woman behind the counter would have said, retelling the event. "Because that was what she wanted. I think the last ones were sold when . . ." And she would have trailed off, leaving everyone to silently add their own end to that sentence.

I took the blue balloon to the gym. A bank of tributes rose up in the center, some snow on top, like icing added to a misshapen cake when there is no time to make another. A dog followed me in to snuffle at the plastic of those offerings, hoping for something more edible than flowers, concerned with death only in terms of its own survival. The part of our brain that imagines our future is the same part that stores our past, I have been told. So this means you can choose how to remember and what to forget. Turning it all into a fairy tale is only a kindness, a way of snuffling for sweetness at the foot of a black mountain. I let the balloon go, watched it bounce, gleefully almost, against a roof beam before finding freedom in the sky.

I was cooking when Alana knocked, the beginnings of French veal, since that was the meat that was good that week.

"Do you want to come out and play?" she said, as if I had never been away.

Mama had wandered into the hallway to see who it was, and said, "Give me your apron," handing me my permission to go. "There is only the Mornay to make," she went on. "I would feel better if you let me do it. That way there will be no lumps."

We walked out across the scrubland—Alana and I—competing in small races until the ice got the better of us, making us skid and slide. She tried harder to beat me than she ever had before. She had something to prove, I think. Look what I achieved while you were away. Or perhaps, look how I did not need you.

"You were in the newspaper," Alana said eventually, puffing clouds. "Is that why you went? Did it make you famous?"

"Sort of," I replied, laughing at her all the same. "Does everyone know what it said?"

She shook her head.

"I don't either," I confessed.

"But it was your story."

"Not really. It was written down. It was translated. It would have changed completely. Stories are best from a person's mouth."

"Tell me one, then."

So as we cleared the dusting of snow from Zaychik's final resting place, I told her about Red Square and Hotel Alexander and market stalls filled with animals and amber. I told her the story of the little brave hare, how she decided one day that she was bigger, all grown up, and must pretend that she was no longer afraid.

So she went across the plains and through the forest, telling anyone who would listen just how brave she was.

"I do not care about the wide-eyed owl! The mouth of a fox holds no fear for me!"

"But what about a bear?" said the hares who danced. "Or a wolf with an empty belly?"

"Show me a wolf and I will show you a fool," cried Little Hare, as she beat her chest with her front paws, and her feet

against the grass — grass that, no matter what its length, scared her no more.

Just then a wolf did pass by, his stomach rattling like a kopek in a can.

Little Hare saw the teeth of this snarling beast, and, no matter what she had told the other bunnies, she was very scared indeed. So scared that she rolled herself into a ball, leaped high in the air with fright, and came crashing down quite by accident on the wolf's head. And in turn, the wolf, not expecting a flying hare, was scared right back. He ran for the shelter of the trees, with his tail between his legs. And Little Hare was a hero after all.

There was no time for any kind of prayer over the grave; the cold was biting hard. I told Alana I had presents for her as means to entice her back to our apartment. I wished then that I had bought her a fur hat. Her jacket was too flimsy, and her teeth were chattering.

"Has your mama not fetched your warm coat from storage?" I asked.

"This is my warm coat," she said. "I think."

She didn't sneer at the collection of stories, as I had thought she would, but her face fell when I handed her the DVD. "You keep it," she said. "I have nothing to play it on."

"Me neither."

We stood looking at the useless object until inspiration came. "Let's go find ourselves a charity. They'll have one to lend."

We carried the machine across town — me bearing the bulk, Alana holding the leads. Children trailed us, wanting to know what we were doing. *What have you got there? Did you steal it?* We were the firebirds now, with our entourage of hunters. We were thieves with no concern for being seen. Mama tutted as we lifted the TV off its perch, searching for a socket that might fit the plug that Alana held aloft — the head of a captured snake.

We sat shoulder to shoulder on the sofa to watch, Alana and I. Mama wanted none of this *Amerikanski* nonsense. The doilies had gone, I realized only then. Perhaps because the boys had gone too. Perhaps for other reasons.

It was a shaky, handheld recording, the film, taking in the tops of the cinema seats. The voices in translation were muffled. *What do you expect,* Jonathan's voice whispered in my ear, satisfied to have called it right, *if you buy from kids who are not very nice?* Still, we managed to follow the story of a man and a woman who have their brains wiped so they do not have to live with the painful memories of their failed relationship.

"Imagine doing that," Alana said. She pointed a finger gun to my ear and made a sucking sound, smacked her lips. All my bad memories — *shooo-lup!* — gone. We both laughed — a little. No, we laughed a lot.

Of course, in the film, the procedure does not work. Fate, as always, likes to have its say.

So, what of love? Can you get this English *happily ever after* without it?

She left the company, the woman named Lyubov. Papa announced her departure, and all that it signified, over dinner one evening. The sight of Mama continuing to lift her fork from

269

plate to mouth in the wake of his news, too proud to stop, almost broke my heart.

"Well, then, I will take over her job," I announced, turning the moment into good fortune, saving Mama from the subtext. This did not mean that I was a factory girl who would never leave town. Because I had left. And I had chosen to come back. I needed an opportunity. Fate had delivered.

In the dying light of the kitchen that evening, Papa snoring in a chair in the living room, Mama told me, "I have forgiven him," the words like bees set free from a jar.

"Oh," I said, realizing I would have to release my resentment of the man too. It would do me little good to hang on to it.

"I let him go," she told me, "just like I let you go. I told him as much. But he has decided he wants to stay."

The present perfect. *He has decided to stay.* I translated it backward and forward, forward and backward. Not perfect at all. But then, what is? I wanted to wrap myself tightly around my mother's neck and have her wrap herself around my waist. A grown woman held tightly in the arms of her mother. But I didn't. I had to have something to look forward to. After you get the thing you wanted most in the world, what then?

Instead I said, "You should drop something hot into his lap."

And she laughed wickedly at the thought and then fondly at the memory.

Papa gave me money for a new skirt. I broke the plastic wrapping on the good blouse from Moscow and thought of new uniforms, of first days at school, of the hope that day had brought, not of what came after.

Goodbye to play and summer days
We welcome in our future bright and new

I took my place at that brown veneered desk and let Galina's orange-lipsticked mouth sigh over me, watched her gold hoops shiver as she shook her head. My typing was not quick enough, my filing neither. Let me chase you across the forecourt with a broom handle, I thought, and then we'll see who is fastest. Instead I bought her favor with sweet things baked after work. I took cuttings from Yelena's orchid cacti and propagated them on the office windowsill, so that when anyone ever visited, they commented on the color they brought into the place, and Galina, as office manager, took the compliment. I had brought in my pencils from Hotel Alexander and placed them in a cleaned-out jam jar on my very own desk. What more could I want?

Company, I suppose.

I read books as I ate my lunch in the factory cafeteria—Pushkin and Lermontov, Tolstoy and, of course, Chekhov. I got through fewer cigarettes and consumed more words. Reading slowly transplanted smoking as the easier pastime. I worked through new chapters of my English book. Past simple, past continuous, past perfect. Then one day I realized I couldn't read alone forever or waste all of my time cultivating a language I would probably never speak. I was lost in other worlds when there was a rich one right in front of me, and I was not yet fully resubmerged. I was behaving like a person who was hard to love.

I placed my tray opposite Dmitriy Vasiliev, and together, in silence, we spooned up beef stroganoff that did not need to be avoided.

Slowly, when he was ready, I fed him pieces of my adventure, doled out morsels as if taming a fox. The trouble was, I sounded like I was trying to be mysterious, wise, and untouchable. He did not stand for much of it.

"Why didn't you marry this *Amerikanksi* journalist of yours, then, if life there was so wonderful?"

"Because it was wonderful in a way that isn't forever," I said, the understanding of it coming entirely with the sounding out. "Wonderful in a way that wasn't wonderful for me."

He nodded.

"And I don't think I love Jonathan anymore. I know that he doesn't love me."

Dmitriy scowled. "And you do not love me either, Darya Pavlovna." We leaned in closer. The ladies from the production line liked to watch us as if we were a lunchtime soap opera. "So why don't you leave me be?"

"Love comes later," I told him. "Sometimes." I spoke with an authority that I did not own. Love comes and it goes, I thought; it gets taken away and it is sometimes reclaimed. But I left it at that. Dmitriy had lifted his sad-dog head and smiled for a moment. I was happy to seem enigmatic. A bright ribbon dancing across a blue sky. I was happy to be home.

We went at midnight. The church is near, but the road is icy. Snow was coming down, not heavy like in Moscow; no showy display. Dmitriy drove, me up front, Alana poking her head between the seats. The men had finished clearing ice from the surface of the water by the time we arrived, and were testing the reliability of the wooden steps. The procession came, the priest chanting. Women sang, wisps of incense embroidering the air.

"Will you do it too?" I asked Alana, expecting her to shake her head when she saw what was involved.

"Yes," she replied, but I could tell she was afraid.

We watched the priest submerge a gold cross in the dark beneath the surface. We listened as he told us of the Lord's voice, how it was calling to us across the waters. Sometimes I would feel her touch as well as hear her voice. A kitchen cabinet might close on my leg, and I would think it was her, come to ask something, or just to lean against me as she sometimes did, making sure I was solid, still there.

"Come, you all," intoned the priest. "Receive the Spirit of wisdom, the Spirit of mind, the Spirit of fear of God!"

Dmitriy started undoing the buttons of his coat, an action that set Alana and me in motion. Convinced. All about us, old, round-bellied men had stripped to their underpants. *Babushki* stood solemn, ready, in gossamer nightgowns, their skin toughened to this by now. Men with tattoos reassured their children, who waited wrapped up and doubtful at the sidelines. Dmitriy was in his boxers, Alana her underwear, and I wore a silver fish swimsuit, a locket around my neck, the hair of two animals mixing within.

The bells chimed. A lone male voice, gravelly and sad, sang "God Save the Tsar!" The priest pitched holy water at the bystanders, splashing the women who crouched by the steps, filling their plastic bottles. A young man in swimming trunks beat at his hairy chest with his fists.

We waited our turn, to have our clean hands and pure hearts returned to us. Our bodies shivered. Alana took my hand, steadying herself against it, and I took Dmitriy's. We listened to the shrieks of the ones who went before.

My turn.

I kissed the cross, kissed the hand of the priest, went down those wooden steps. The icy waters took away my calves, my thighs, my stomach—all numb, all feeling gone. I placed the first three fingers of my right hand on my forehead, my belly, to the right shoulder, to the left, and then I sank under the surface. The water blasted into my ears, pierced my brain. I rose up with a cry, caught my breath, went under again. Three times. *Forgive me, forgive me, forgive me, O Lord.* Epiphany. A baptism. The world turned white behind my closed eyes. All of me, white. A scar bleached away.

Though in truth, we were red as we ran for our towels and our clothes, for the warmth of the fire and the hot wine—as we ran toward this new beginning. We dressed as quickly as we could, fabric dragging against the dampness of skin. I watched a mother roll a sock back onto the delicate foot of her small, brave son. Dmitriy and Alana both hooted into the early morning air, exhilarated by what they had done. We tipped steaming wine down our throats and breathed out the spices.

"I thought my heart would stop," Alana said, hopping from foot to foot, jabbering away the pain.

"Maybe it did," Dmitriy said, and Alana became still and serious at the possibility. "Maybe it did, and maybe it started all over again."

"I've heard of that," I told her, playing along, though I couldn't stop my smile. "I have heard stories."

AN AFTERWORD

You can put the story in a newspaper article and
put it very convincingly. The facts are there, anyone
can do it and I don't denigrate it. But what fiction
does, first for the writer, then the readers, is
make that journey on foot. —Edna O'Brien

There were many moments while writing *Mother Tongue*
when I thought I should stop. I even considered deleting the
manuscript from my hard drive and burning my papers. That
way I could not return to it. *This is not your story to tell* was
the echo in my head. I was trespassing.

I went to see Tim Crouch's excellent play *The Author* in the
middle of my first draft. You, the audience member, are cast as
a character and are made to feel entirely culpable as an onlooker
for every twist in the drama. The play questions the prerogative
of writers (and theatergoers) to pick through the remains of
real-life tragedies in the name of art. Isn't it voyeurism? Aren't
we just celebrating horror? Writers are frequently in denial
about their noble motives, the play suggested. We, with our
words, are just part of the problem.

If something distressing comes on my television screen, I will usually switch it off. I have no desire to watch A&E documentaries, or programs about children with terminal illness. When the news covers a disaster in a faraway land, I pledge what I can and then turn away. Perhaps I'm heartless, but it feels like the opposite. These stories make me desperately sad. They make me feel scared and utterly powerless.

Yet when I saw a documentary in 2009, five years after the Beslan disaster, I couldn't switch it off. I kept looking, and I searched for more.

Perhaps it was the timing. I had just had my own children and was experiencing maternal guilt about dropping them off at daycare two mornings a week. There was no one else to help look after them, but still I was questioning my decision to hand them over to strangers when they were so small. What if something happened while I wasn't there to protect them? Would the universe punish me for wanting time for myself?

I realize this thinking is superstitious and overdramatic—a drop in an ocean of real worries—but I was tired and I was lonely. The documentary made me wonder if the women of Beslan, the mothers, the sisters, asked themselves similar questions the day they took their children to school for the first and last time. It didn't feel like a faraway land at all.

So I submerged myself in all things Russian, and gradually the joy of writing about another culture took over. Whether I'm traveling back to the eighteenth century to devise a radio play about love or using a Greek island to stand for the isolation of loss, writing comes alive for me when I explore new scenery. I want to eat different foods, read unfamiliar fairy tales, speak in an entirely new tongue.

But despite this love affair with all things Russian, the idea that I was trespassing prevailed. If I stuck close to the facts of the siege, it felt like stealing. When I added fictional flourishes, I was not honoring the dead. I saw myself, at times, as a driver who slows down past a car accident to stare at the casualties, then takes great glee later in describing the gore.

I'm not convinced, even now, that I did the right thing by writing this book. But these are the things that persuaded me to go on:

I read a profile of the author Tessa Hadley in the *Guardian* in which she's quoted as saying, "What you're writing should hurt and make you feel slightly anxious, and almost ashamed." I wrote the quote out and pinned it above my desk. I took it as an impetus to send the first few chapters to the historical novelist Maria McCann, a writer who never shies away from dark places. She was my mentor for a year, and during that time she convinced me that within those dark places often lies the truth.

I worked with the poet Polly Clark at the wonderful Cove Park, who made me see that I wasn't really writing a book about someone else's tragedy but through it exploring my own loves and pain, my own fascinations and hope. This is a book about Beslan, but also it is not. To be able to create a hopeful ending is cathartic, if only for me.

I heard the novelist Edna O'Brien talking on BBC Radio about her book *The Little Red Chairs*, which draws on the atrocities in Bosnia under Radovan Karadžić, and the quote at the top of this afterword comes from that interview. The words that resonated most strongly were "make that journey on foot."

I am powerless and scared and ashamed—but I am ashamed, more than anything, of feeling that way. I dislike the idea of calling a writer brave when they only sit at a desk, fighting no real fires at all, but I carried on writing because I wished to be fearless. I wished to understand. As Dasha says in the face of terror, "It's your instinct to go toward the floor, make yourself small." *Am I small,* I wanted to know, *or could I be big?*

This novel was given to two Russian beta readers who picked through my cultural references and use of language to check for errors. One reader, though she had been moved by the book, told me that *Mother Tongue* did not have a Russian soul.

At first I was upset. I had desperately wanted to capture that elusive, mysterious thing called *dusha*, that piercing understanding of what it means to be human, described by great Russian writers like Gogol, Tolstoy, and, of course, Chekhov. But perhaps that was too much to ask. I am not Russian, only walking in Russian shoes.

I was consoled by her clarification though: "I mean," she went on, "the story could happen anywhere in the world."

Things happen in faraway lands, but they happen to us all. That is what it means to be human.

RUSSIAN TERMS

Amerikanski — American

baba — grandma

Baba Yaga — a terrifying witch from Russian fairy tales who lives in a hut in the forest

Babaevsky — a traditional Russian confectioner

babushka/babushki — grandmother/grandmothers

banya — a bathhouse/sauna/spa

bitochki — ground meat made into balls or patties

bomzh/bomzhi — vagrant/vagrants

borsch — beet soup

bublik — a chewy roll with a large hole in the middle, similar to a bagel

Chapayev — a game similar to checkers in which the players flick their pieces to knock their opponent's pieces off the board (named after a celebrated hero of the Russian Civil War)

dacha—a countryside home, often a person's simple second residence for the summer

Ded Moroz—Father Frost, the Russian equivalent of Santa Claus

dezhurnaya—a woman who acts as a receptionist/watchwoman for an apartment building

dyadya—uncle, or a term of endearment for someone who is treated like an uncle

Fabrika—popular Russian girl group formed on a TV talent show

kasha—grains cooked in water or milk to make a kind of porridge

kharcho—a soup made with beef or chicken, with walnuts and rice

Kikimora—a female house spirit from Russian fairy tales and folklore

kolbasa—a sausage that can be boiled and/or smoked

Kommersant—a liberal Russian newspaper

kopek—a coin (one hundred kopeks equal one ruble)

Krasnye Vorota—a Moscow Metro station with a distinctive entranceway made up of four arches

kulebyaka—an oblong meat or fish pie with layered fillings

kupe—a second-class train car with four-person compartments (Darya traveled *platskart*, third class)

Lezginka—traditional dance from the Caucasus regions

matryoshka—wooden nesting dolls

Moskva-reka—the river that runs through Moscow

Panikhida — a Russian Orthodox memorial service for the dead

pastila — pressed fruit-paste sweets, similar to Turkish delight or gumdrops

Petra i Pavla — Peter and Paul

prinsessa — princess

provodnik — train conductor/ticket collector

pryaniki — honey-and-spiced biscuits

rusalki — mermaids/water sirens from Russian folklore

Ruslana — Ukrainian pop star

samovar — a large metal urn used to heat water

shashlik — skewers of meat

Snegurochka — the Snow Maiden, a traditional part of Russia's New Year's celebrations

solyanka — a spicy soup made with pickled cucumbers

sushka/sushki — hard bread ring(s) usually eaten with tea

trubochka — a horn-shaped dessert filled with cream

tsar/tsars — male supreme ruler/rulers

tsarevich — the son of a tsar, like a prince

tsaritsa — female supreme ruler, or the wife of the ruler

valenki — felt boots, or felt linings for boots

Vasilisa the Beautiful — well-known figure in Russian fairy tales

Vera, Nadezdha, Lyubov — Faith, Hope, Love

Vinni Pukh — Winnie-the-Pooh, a Soviet-era animated character with a very different appearance from the illustrations in A. A. Milne's books and from the Disney cartoon

zakuski — a selection of canapés

zaychik — bunny or, more accurately, little hare; can be used as a term of endearment

zavarka — a strong concentrate of tea that can be diluted to taste

zharkoye — beef-and-potato stew

A NOTE ON
RUSSIAN NAMES

Russians have three names: their family surname, a first name, and a patronym, usually given in that order.

Ivanova Darya Pavlovna

There is less experimentation with names in Russia, so it is common to know several people with the same first name.

The patronym is created by taking the father's first name and adding a suffix that means "son of" or "daughter of." For men, the suffix is most commonly *-ovich* or *-evich*, while for women it is *-ovna* or *-evna*.

Ivanova Darya Pavlovna
(Darya Ivanova, daughter of Pavlov)
Ivanov Boris Pavlovich
(Boris Ivanov, son of Pavlov)

The end of a person's family surname also changes according to their sex (*Ivanov/Ivanova*).

And when referring to a family as a plural of their surname (as, for example, the Smiths), it is expressed with a *-y* suffix (*Ivanovy*).

In polite conversation, it is common to address someone by their first name and patronym (*Darya Pavlovna*). When someone is a friend or colleague, you might use a diminutive. This is not just a shortening of the name (such as Jo for Joanna): there are specific diminutives for each Russian name, and they are not always immediately obvious. For example:

> *Darya* becomes *Dasha*
> *Veronika* becomes *Nika*
> *Nikolai* becomes *Kolya*

Close family members and lovers may go a step further and "sweeten" your *diminutive* with a suffix. For example:

> *Dasha* becomes *Dashen'ka*
> *Nika* becomes *Nikushya*

When talking to children, you might "shorten" and "sweeten" their names this way too. For example:

> *Polina* becomes *Polin'ka*

A suffix can also be used to suggest contempt:

> *Dasha* becomes *Dashka*
> *Boris* becomes *Bor'ka*

ACKNOWLEDGMENTS
AND REFERENCES

I was accepted into the Jerwood-Arvon Mentoring Scheme on the strength of a few early chapters of *Mother Tongue*. My year under the tutelage of Nell Lyshon, Dalgit Nagra, and, in particular, Maria McCann was transformative. Thank you, Arvon, and thank you to my fellow mentees for your critique and friendship.

Thank you to Polly Clark and Cove Park for redirecting a ship in a storm.

I'm grateful for early advice from Simon Taylor and Annette Green, and for a Paul Magrs writing workshop at the Ilkley Literature Festival that filled pages and pages of my notebook. London Book Festival, your Russian literature event in 2011 was brilliant — can you do it all over again?

I turned to journalists' accounts when researching the events of 2004 and life in Russia beyond Beslan. Most helpful were articles by Luke Harding, Viv Groskop, and Nick Paton Walsh in the *Guardian*, Tony Halpin in the *Times* (London), and reports from the BBC's Steve Rosenberg and Daniel Sandford. (My apologies for not portraying journalists in this book in the best light in return.)

I also made use of the BBC/HBO documentary *Children of Beslan* and the Channel 4 *Dispatches* film *Beslan*. On wider life in Russia and the former Soviet states, I am grateful to Jonathan Dimbleby's *Russia* TV series (and his accompanying book) and Tomás Sheridan's *Radiostan.*

Other hugely informative books were Timothy Phillips's *Beslan*, Oliver Bullough's *Let Our Fame Be Great*, and the late Anna Politkovskaya's *A Russian Diary.*

When Dasha talks about the battery commander, she is referring to Vershinin in Anton Chekhov's *Three Sisters*, and Dasha's constant desire to go to Moscow is a nod to the play. When she says she wouldn't care about the weather in Moscow, when she forgets the English words for *window* and *ceiling*, and when she decides that learning a third language is like growing a sixth finger, she alludes in each case to Chekhov. Diana's encounter with a weeping woman in the post office is inspired by a speech made by the youngest of the three sisters, Irina. You'll find many other references if you care to search for them.

There are a number of tropes from Russian fairy tales dotted through the text too, and I'm particularly indebted to the following books for helping me with this part of my research: Robert Chandler's *Russian Magic Tales from Pushkin to Platonov*, Gillian Avery's illustrated *Russian Fairy Tales*, Moura Budberg and Amabel Williams-Ellis's *Russian Fairy Tales*, and

Edward Blishen and Nancy Blishen's *The Kingfisher Treasury of Stories for Seven Year Olds*. The story of the brave hare is a traditional Russian folktale retold in my own words with my own embellishments, as are "Vasilisa the Beautiful" and stories featuring Baba Yaga and her rhyme.

Other works that Dasha makes references to are *Death in Venice* by Thomas Mann (the book she thinks of when talking to Ekaterina about Venice) and *The Captain's Daughter* by Alexander Pushkin (the story of "romance, rescue, and hareskin coats"). The DVD she buys for Alana is *Eternal Sunshine of the Spotless Mind*, written by Charlie Kaufman. At Lermontov's statue in Moscow, Dasha reads lines from his poem "Sashka."

The birthday song is "Crocodile Gena's Song" from the Soviet-era cartoon and is sung in Russia in place of our "Happy Birthday." Ruslana's song "Wild Dances" was Ukraine's 2004 Eurovision entry—it won. On the 40th Day, the men at the tables sing "A Song About Hares" from the comedy film *The Diamond Arm*. This is a popular, rambunctious song that Russian readers may think out of place here, but I use it for its resonance to the themes of the book and our English ears. The song that Zlata likes and Darya sees on the music channel in her hotel room is "Ribka" by Fabrika. I would thoroughly recommend looking up Fabrika's songs for a taste of Russian pop music. "Dark Eyes," the song that Pavel sings to Darya at his party, is a well-known nineteenth-century Russian song, with lyrics by Ukrainian poet Yevhen Hrebrinka.

All translations, abridgments, and paraphrasing of song lyrics, stories, poems, and plays are my own.

For sharing their firsthand experiences of Russian life,

culture, and language, and for helping with translations, *spasibo* to Olga Powell, Victoria Kusmina, Alison Reid, Mark Barden, Maria Kozlovskaya, Oksana Romina, Olga Vinogradova, Guy Fforde, Victor Stepanov, and Vladimir Orlov. Thank you to Elena Simonova and Yana Mozyakova for being beta readers and for pulling out cultural errors. Any mistakes or misrepresentations that remain are mine.

For Jonathan's lessons, I had help from Sarah Franklin and Russ Litten, who shared their experiences of teaching English as a foreign language. Thank you to David Hadar, Daniel Needlestone, and Sarra Manning for their knowledge of Jewish proverbs.

Many things were thrown away in the edit, but nevertheless, thank you to Anthony Weeden, Alexander Walker, and Stuart MacRae for taking the time to talk about composing and orchestras in Russia.

Artist Anthony Burrill sent me a bold yellow poster saying DON'T SAY NOTHING, as it featured in a scene (now deleted). Thank you, Anthony — it did not go to waste. I framed it and hung it above my desk as a reminder to myself, and to Dasha to always say something.

The Peterborough Marriott (formerly the Swallow Hotel) gave me my first job, when I was fifteen, and, like Ekaterina, I worked in the bars, restaurants, conference areas, and room service. More recently, the Marriott supported me on a project in my hometown, making me their writer in residence. I hope that the warmth I have for the place comes across in my portrayal of the fictional Hotel Alexander.

Thank you to Thom for all the counseling. The same to Rose Scarborough, Jenny Thorburn, Terry Sadler, and Michael Price.

Thank you, Tilda, Jane, Jenny, and the HKB team, for giving Dasha a good home and to Nicole and Katie at Candlewick for welcoming her across the Atlantic.

Thank you, Louise Lamont, for "honking" all the way.